LUCIA'S RENAISSANCE

A Novel of 16th-Century Italy

C.L.R. PETERSON

Dedicated to:

My parents, Howard and Lois Redmond, who encouraged
me to discover Italy

My history mentors, Fenton Duvall and Lewis Spitz, who ignited my
interest in the Renaissance and Reformation

My friends near and far who encouraged me

My daughters, Kirsten and Gretchen, who grew up admirably despite
their mother's frequent mental presence in Renaissance Italy

My husband, Jim, whose loving support enabled and sustained me in
the adventure of writing historical fiction

Contents

Chapter 1

UNFORGETTABLE SIGHT

Lucia Locatelli

Should I blame everything on Martin Luther, the heretic from over the mountains? From his grave, the rogue monk turned my life upside down.

My troubles began in Verona on a sunny July morning in the year of our Lord 1571. I was only six years old. By the time Mass ended that Saturday, San Zeno's rose window sparkled like a *contessa*'s jewels, and I couldn't look away.

"Such glorious colors." Mamma's voice startled me. "But Lucia, the sooner we leave, the sooner you can read your books."

Papa held Mamma's hand and grinned at me, his warm eyes and silver beard reminding me of Saint Nicholas. Usually I returned Papa's smile, but this time I sighed.

"Sì, Mamma." I followed my parents, but paced my steps with the monks' chants, gazing at the rose window and savoring the incense-spiced coolness all the way down the aisle.

Outside, the piazza swarmed with people, especially soldiers and young men. Something out of the ordinary must have made them linger in the midday heat, but I couldn't see what they were watching, even on my tiptoes.

An old woman in front of me swooned, and I peeked through the gap in the crowd. A barefoot man lay belly-down on the cobblestones, leaning on his elbows and lacing his fingers together. He looked like a monk praying, but wore a strange yellow robe.

"Alessandro!"

As soon as I heard Papa's gasp, I recognized the man on the ground—Papa's favorite student. I couldn't count the times he'd walked home with Papa and joined us for supper. After we ate, Alessandro used to take out a book. He taught me to read, even though Mamma and Papa thought I was too young. How often I had wished he was my older brother. But now he looked like a beggar, his hair straggly, his neck and feet covered with bruises and red marks.

I tugged Papa's sleeve. "Help him, Papa!"

He looked at the ground.

"Papa!" I pulled harder, but he turned away.

A tall priest walked toward Alessandro and surveyed the crowd. Two moles on the *padre's* cheek looked like a second pair of eyes watching me. "People of Verona, hear the tribunal's verdict: Alessandro degli Avogari is guilty of spreading heresies with his tongue and through the writings of heretics." He looked down at Alessandro. "What have you to say for yourself?"

"I beg the Church's forgiveness and mercy." He bowed his head to the ground.

"Will you take Holy Communion?"

Alessandro nodded.

The priest placed a wafer on Alessandro's tongue and looked back at us. "Take this man's fate as a warning. The Holy Office of the Inquisition will burn him at the stake so his heresy will infect no one else. Because he confessed, the executioner will make his death quick."

My throat went dry.

Dipping his finger into a vial of oil, the priest made the sign of the cross on Alessandro's forehead. With a nod to the soldiers, the cleric walked away.

The uniformed men grabbed Alessandro's arms, pulling him to his feet. His mouth hung open; his dark eyes bulged and met mine. I didn't want to watch him die but couldn't turn away.

Papa must rescue him. I looked over my shoulder. Mamma stood behind me, but Papa had vanished. I waited for him to step out of the crowd and save Alessandro, but he didn't. No one came forward.

I dropped to my hands and knees and burrowed to the front of the crowd. My mother's voice called me back, but I ignored it. I opened my mouth to tell the soldiers to stop, but their stern faces convinced me they would slice off my tongue with their swords if I called out.

The bearded soldier pulled off Alessandro's robe, leaving only his breeches. He trembled, but not from cold. The welts and dried blood on his back made me shiver, too.

The other soldier looped a rope around Alessandro's neck and dragged him away from the church. He tripped over his own feet.

If only Papa would come.

The soldiers led Alessandro across the piazza to a tall post in the middle of a pile of sticks and straw as tall as Papa. They tied Alessandro's arms behind his back and bound him to the post. Each soldier yanked on one end of the rope.

The cord tightened around Alessandro's neck. He gurgled, his face turned purple, and blood ran out of his mouth. His head slumped forward.

I clapped my hand over my eyes. Before long I smelled burning wood, and the fire crackled.

Strong fingers clasped mine. Even before I looked up, the scent of orange and rosemary told me Mamma had found me. The solid line of her lips made her look like a stranger. I squeezed my eyes shut to avoid her gaze.

"Come with me, now!" Her whisper turned to a hiss. "This is no sight for a child."

"Sì, Mamma." I turned to follow her but glanced back. Flames shot up, setting alight Alessandro's breeches.

"Lucia!" Mamma's grip tightened, and she marched me away.

I looked across the piazza. At the far corner, still as a statue, Papa stared down at the cobblestones.

I strained toward him, and Mamma let me run across the shadeless square. Panting, I grabbed my father's hands. "Papa, why didn't you save him?"

He gazed at me, his face pale as a marble statue. My Papa, who could answer any question and solve every problem, didn't say a word.

Mamma caught up with us and clasped my hand. "Let's go home."

Down the street, San Procolo church shaded us from the sun's rays, but couldn't shield my memory from what I had witnessed. I didn't understand heresy but have never forgotten how it cost Alessandro his life. I did nothing to stop the soldiers from killing him, and that has haunted me ever since.

The same nightmare tormented me the next night. Back in my own bedchamber, I woke up in a cold sweat with my fists clenched.

During my waking hours, fire brought back the dream and my terror, so I kept my distance from flames and smoke. I thought God must be punishing me and hoped my bad dreams and fears would go away if I confessed to Padre Giovanni.

When daylight finally brightened my oilcloth window on Saturday morning, I washed my face and ran into my parents' bedchamber. "Mamma, Papa, get up so we can go to Confession."

Papa squinted at me. "*Pazienza*, Lucia, it's still early."

Mamma yawned. "Sì, Padre Giovanni is probably sleeping."

I stamped my foot and ran back to my room. If only Mamma and Papa would let me go to church by myself.

Hours later, we stood in line outside the confessional, waiting our turns. At last I closed the door behind me and stared at the black curtain separating me from the priest.

"Padre, I need to confess so many things—the seven deadly sins, disobeying my mother and father so many times, thinking bad thoughts about people."

He coughed. "Such a long list, *signorina*. Let's begin with the seven deadly sins. Did you commit all of them?"

"Not all, Padre, but I thought about it. Isn't that just as bad?"

"God loves you. If you confess your sinful thoughts, he won't condemn you." I heard his sigh through the curtain.

"Padre, what about my other sins?" I had so much more to confess.

"Don't worry. As long as you confess them to God, he will forgive those, too." He paused. "Say the *Ave Maria* and go in peace."

I opened the door and whispered, Hail Mary, full of grace... I said it all. Then I saw Alessandro's face in my mind's eye, and a cold blanket of guilt settled back over me. I had been too frightened to stop the soldiers from killing Alessandro, and I hadn't confessed my cowardice to the priest. I clenched my fists.

"Lucia, what's wrong?" Mamma put her arm around me.

"I forgot to confess one of my sins."

My parents looked at each other. Papa patted my shoulder. "Lucia, I'm glad you have a tender conscience. But remember, God loves you and forgives your every sin."

Mamma or Papa or both told me this every time I left the confessional, but I couldn't stop thinking of more sins that would keep me in purgatory even longer.

TWO MASTERS

Lucia
September 9, 1571

I hopped from one foot to the other. Mamma must come out of her bedchamber soon! It was the day after the Blessed Virgin Mary's birthday, and I was about to begin my schooling. Mamma had reminded me more than once that only a few lucky children enjoyed this privilege, and I could scarcely wait for her to walk me to the classroom.

Her firm voice rang out through the closed door. "Remember Giordano, I agreed to one month. If she doesn't like it, I'll take her to the convent school."

"I'm not worried. How could a girl who's been reading for years and begging for writing lessons not flourish in this class?"

Silence followed, and I thought I would burst. I rapped on the door. "Mamma, can we go now—please?"

A moment later, she closed the front door behind us, and I skipped toward Messer Datini's schoolroom. I knew better than to cross the crowded street by myself, so I marched in place until Mamma caught up. She gripped my hand. I don't know how many times I asked if we were almost there, but Mamma finally pressed her finger to her lips.

At last I opened the classroom door and poked my head inside. The empty schoolmaster's desk reminded me of a church pulpit, but cluttered with books and papers. Most of the low wooden tables still sat vacant, but Stefano, the son of Papa's friend, and seven other rowdy boys clustered around a long table. After they sharpened their quills, they poked them at each other. Mamma raised her eyebrows and kissed me goodbye.

On the other side of the room, a skinny boy sat at the back table by himself, scratching his quill across a paper. I sat on the stool next to his and noticed a cane beside him.

"What are you writing?" I strained to read the paper, but his arm blocked my view.

"A song, from the birds along my path." He kept his head down, looking at his paper. Finally, he set down the quill. "*Finito!*"

When he raised his head, I noticed how tall he was and the shadow of a moustache above his lip. He must be much older than me.

"Can I hear it?"

When he whistled, I pictured a songbird stretching its feathers in the sunshine.

"*Bravo!* I wish I could do that—I can read and write a little, and Mamma taught me to sing but not write songs. Today's my first day of school."

"I thought so." His gray eyes twinkled. "You'll learn plenty here if you work hard. Everyone says Messer Datini's the best teacher in Verona." His face turned serious and he gestured toward the other boys. "Don't let those *ragazzi* distract you."

I nodded. "My name's Lucia. What's yours? When did you join the class?"

"I'm Vincenzo, and I've been coming since Messer Datini started it six years ago."

Just then a short girl entered the classroom with two tall boys. All had dark, curly hair, and freckles, so I was sure they were siblings. She walked toward me, her brown eyes sparkling, and grinned. "I'm Elisabetta. Can I sit by you?"

I smiled back, smelling roses as she came close. If I was lucky, she'd share my interest in learning—something I hadn't seen yet from the boys across the room.

Just then, a thin man in a black robe walked to the schoolmaster's desk and opened his satchel. The room quieted. Messer Datini surveyed the classroom, introduced himself, and said a prayer. At the beginning of each subject, he told a story—some funny, some heroic, all related to the topic and with a moral we should apply to our lives. His lessons opened my eyes to new worlds—ancient Greece, the Roman Republic, the history of our own region, the Veneto, and more. By the time he dismissed us that afternoon, I couldn't wait to master Latin, Greek, history, and the Church fathers.

For the next few mornings, Vincenzo entertained me with his songs when I arrived at school, but as soon as the scent of roses announced Elisabetta's entrance, her stories and jokes made me forget about my older classmate. When the school day began, we girls whispered and sometimes even giggled.

Vincenzo always scowled at us. One day he sat at a table near the other boys, but didn't look any happier. The next day Vincenzo didn't come to class. He never returned.

I missed him and his songs. In my dreams, Vincenzo stood along a path leaning on his cane, listening to a bird's song. Then he frowned at me. I always woke up convinced he left our class because he thought we were laughing at him.

Giordano

No matter how tiring my workday, I looked forward to teaching science to my daughter in the evening. Her schoolmaster's curriculum didn't include that subject, so I happily assumed the task. After supper, Lucia joined me in my study. I pretended to be an animal or a part of the body, and challenged her to identify it.

Often, she clapped her hands and laughed, always asking me questions before she told me her guess. After I explained the answer, I praised her curiosity, reminding her that this trait had helped me become a professor. I encouraged her to keep asking me questions.

One evening, Lucia entered my study a few minutes ahead of me. I walked through the doorway and found her stretched out on the floor behind my desk, facing the corner. I stopped with one foot in mid-air. "What's wrong, Lucia?"

She didn't look up. "He was too fast for me. When I opened the door, a mouse ran across the floor. I chased him, but he got away."

I walked toward my desk.

Shaking her head, she turned toward me and faced the backside of the desk. "And Papa..."

"Sì." My shoulders stiffened, and my elbows pressed against my hips. From Lucia's vantage point, she had a clear view of the back of my desk—including the panel in front of a hidden drawer. I studied her face.

She gulped. "I forgot what I was going to say."

I pulled over a chair for her and grabbed Galen's *Anatomical Procedures* from my bookshelf.

Lucia didn't show her customary enthusiasm for my animal imitation or ask as many questions as usual. She didn't mention the hidden drawer, but if my sharp-eyed daughter had flipped up the panel, she would have seen the drawer. I had locked it, but given time, she would have found the key beneath a stack of papers on my desk. When Lucia left my study, tension drained from my shoulders.

That night, after kissing Caterina *buona notte*, I mulled Lucia's silence about the hidden drawer. Given her curiosity, she would look for the key, and if she unlocked the drawer, our family would face great danger. I rolled out of bed, lit a candle, and moved the key to a new hiding place—safe, I prayed, from Lucia's keen eyes.

Chapter 3

ANOTHER MASTER

Lucia
January 1572

Since the day I started school, I had leapt out of bed each morning as soon as daylight brightened my bedchamber, sometimes even earlier. When our class took a long Christmas holiday, I could hardly wait for the end of the twelfth night so I could return to school.

Freezing rain couldn't dampen my eagerness. By the time school ended that day, I had deciphered a long Greek passage and looked forward to sharing my triumph with Mamma and Papa at *cena*. After I said goodbye to Elisabetta at my front door, a savory aroma greeted me inside. Shedding my rain-soaked cloak and boots, I hurried to the kitchen to warm myself and beg for a sample of supper.

Mamma smiled. *"Ciao,* Lucia, I have exciting news." She set a steaming pot of stew on the table.

"Tell me, Mamma."

"Catechism class for children begins on Saturday. Papa and I have decided you're old enough to attend. You'll learn what you must believe and do as a member of the Church, and then you'll be able to take Communion, just as we do."

I straightened my spine to look more grown-up. *"Grazie,* Mamma."

For the rest of the week, I wondered what I would learn at catechism class, which of my schoolmates might attend, and who would be our teacher. Our white-haired priest, Padre Giovanni, had taken ill, and Mamma told me he probably wouldn't preach or teach again.

On that Saturday morning, I awoke before daylight and couldn't fall back to sleep. Hours later, my mother and I finally walked into the meeting room. The teacher, dressed in a hooded cloak and priest's robe, sat at a table with his back to the door. Mamma watched from the doorway while I found a seat on a bench, next to some older girls.

The teacher pulled off his cloak, rose and gazed at the adults. "Parents, come back for your children when the bells ring for *nones* (noontime)." Then he looked at us. "Ragazzi, please find a seat. My name is Padre Federico. I'm the new priest here at San Zeno Maggiore."

When I saw the two moles on his face, I couldn't breathe. This was the priest who had ordered Alessandro's burning in the piazza.

I wanted to run out the door but sat still, looking everywhere but at the priest. While the other children settled into their places, my thoughts kept returning to that summer day and Alessandro's gruesome death.

"Ciao, Lucia." I heard Elisabetta's voice before I saw her smile. My friend raced toward me, her dark curls bouncing. She hugged me, and I could only nod as she squeezed next to me on the bench. Her rose scent was my only comfort.

Padre Federico continued. "Before the Church called me here, I worked for the Holy Office of the Inquisition."

I clasped my hands and prayed God would take me up to heaven.

He continued. "Now the Church has entrusted me with another important task—teaching you proper doctrines and behavior. After you finish this class, each of you will have no doubts about right and wrong beliefs and conduct. I will begin by warning you about heresy—the wrong beliefs and practices I saw so often in my work with the Holy Office—so you can avoid these traps that might snare your soul."

That morning I heard more than I wanted to know—far more—about heresy, heretics, and punishments. Even the most unruly children sat wide-eyed. The priest closed his talk with a warning: "Ragazzi, you must avoid even the slightest suspicion of heresy. As the Holy Scripture says, flee from evil."

When he dismissed the class, I couldn't move from the bench.

Elisabetta turned to me. "You look like a ghost, Lucia."

"I feel sick." I clutched my stomach.

"You need some air." She grabbed my arm and pulled me toward the door.

That night my nightmares began again.

Chapter 4

DISCOVERY AND DILEMMA

Lucia
September 1576

A s the Blessed Virgin Mary's birthday approached, I anticipated both the end of the summer heat and the beginning of my fifth school year. But the opening day in Messer Datini's class left me restless. Now that I was nearly twelve years old and knew by heart the school routine, I could have recited the schoolmaster's annual lecture on school rules. I learned little from the hours of drill and review.

After school, I raced through my homework, reviewing Greek grammar and a few of Cicero's letters. As the afternoon light blazed through my window, I drummed my fingers on my desk and glanced at my small stack of books. I knew these volumes too well, so I wandered into my father's study to choose a new title from his collection.

Each time I entered the small room, I became a beggar in a king's treasury. This was the world of a scholar. Although my mother complained about the clutter, I relished every part of it, from the overstuffed bookshelves and stacks of paper blanketing the desk to the musty aroma of parchment.

I climbed onto Papa's chair for a better look at the volumes crammed onto his shelves. Titles in Greek, Latin, and Italian greeted me—so many choices, and now I could read them all. Each time I picked up a new book, I wondered what I would discover.

A faded volume with an illegible title on its spine stood on the top shelf. As I pulled it down, a small, shiny object tumbled onto Papa's desk. I studied the brass key and then the desk drawers. They had no keyholes, and I saw no locked boxes or chests.

Pressing my spine against the wall, I surveyed the study. On the back of the desk I glimpsed a polished wooden panel—the same one I had seen years ago. Now I flipped up the panel and uncovered a locked drawer with a keyhole. My pulse throbbed. Inserting the key, I heard a click and pulled out the deep drawer.

A single tattered book lay inside. I dug it out with my fingernails and opened to the title page: *Commentary on Saint Paul's Letter to the Galatians* by Doctor Martin Luther.

I slammed the book shut. In catechism class years before, Padre Federico had branded Luther's name into my memory. He had singled out Luther as an enemy of the faith, an arch-heretic who would burn in hell.

How had this book found its way into my father's desk drawer? Papa was a professor of medicine, not a theologian. Certainly, he couldn't be a heretic.

My throat tightened. I could almost see Padre Federico wagging his finger at me, "*Ragazza*, if you read the writings of a heretic, you contaminate your faith. You risk excommunication and the fires of perdition."

Yet I held Luther's book in my trembling hands. If I didn't report my discovery to Padre Federico, I would be guilty of a terrible sin— but handing Luther's work to the priest might endanger Papa. My feet pressed against my shoes until my toes cramped.

Maybe Papa had a good reason for keeping this book. I prayed God wouldn't send me to hell if I kept Luther's book out and asked my father why he hid this heretic's writing in his desk.

Shaking the tension from my feet, I surveyed the room. I found no clue to the mystery, but noticed the cover sheet on a stack of papers on the desk, entitled "Scientific theories: for Lucia's instruction." Papa had written this course of study just for me.

I closed my eyes and saw Papa's kind face. Then I remembered Padre Federico's words about the terrible fate of heretics. When I glanced back at Luther's book, I knew I couldn't show it to the priest. I would return the book to the drawer and try to forget about it—after I looked at it once more.

My father often had told me, "God gave you an able mind, Lucia. It's your responsibility to use it." If I could show him Luther's errors, he might at last realize how grown-up I was. How long I had dreamed of the day he would invite me to attend his lectures at the university.

The kitchen door slammed. Mamma would never do that, so I knew our kitchen maid, Anna, must have gone outside to fetch water and wood. Since Mamma didn't set foot in Papa's study unless he asked, I would have hours to myself.

Now I could learn what made Martin Luther a heretic. I stared at the title page again. This time a symbol caught my eye—a gold ring surrounding a white rose. Embedded in the rose was a red heart with a black cross in the center. How mysterious!

A creak in the floor made me flinch, and noises from the kitchen reminded me I mustn't delay. If Mamma caught me with this book, she certainly would burn it and insist I confess and do penance. How often I wished I could match her obedience and faith but not the years she had spent in a convent before she married Papa.

After reading a few pages, I knew why the Church had condemned Martin Luther as a heretic. He blamed the pope for teaching the works and traditions of men instead of the Gospel and faith in Christ. How dare Luther slander the Holy Father!

Luther insisted that not even a lifetime of good works could earn God's approval—such a different message from what our priest taught. In his weekly sermons, Padre Federico asked, "What good works have you done this week to shorten your stay in purgatory? Have you taken a vow, made a pilgrimage, or prayed to the saints? Have you bought an indulgence to speed your deceased grandfather, mother, or uncle from purgatory?"

Luther called the pope and his followers impious and filthy, full of hypocrisy and shame.

I threw the book down, locked it in the drawer and shoved the key back into its hiding place. Luther's disrespect for sacred things mustn't contaminate my faith.

I opened an illustrated volume describing herbs and their medicinal properties, but the words of Martin Luther stuck in my mind. How could he believe that God doesn't judge us by our deeds?

That night, I dreamed that Luther and Padre Federico stood at opposite sides of San Zeno's sanctuary, each bellowing condemnation at the other. I trembled as their angry voices thundered in my mind, and I awoke with a start. At least Padre Federico wasn't shouting at me in my dreams, as he did most nights.

In the morning, I tried to think of a good work that would make up for reading Luther's writings. After I returned home from school, I brought in the clean shirts, chemises, stockings, and towels that hung on a long cord next to our house. When I carried the wicker basket of folded laundry into the kitchen, Mamma and Anna smiled at me.

"Grazie, Signorina Lucia." Anna took the basket. "Now you must do your own work." She shooed me away.

Back in my bedchamber, I picked up a book, but only for a moment. My conscience still weighed on me like an ox's yoke, and I wracked my brain for a way to escape my burden of guilt.

The next afternoon, I perused Papa's library again for a new book, but my thoughts turned back to Martin Luther's strange comments. If God didn't count my good deeds, why would he let me into heaven?

I stared up at the high shelf where the key lay hidden and could almost see Padre Federico watching me, his gaze penetrating my soul. If I obeyed him, I could never finish reading Luther's argument or prove him wrong.

A moment later, I reached to the top shelf. My hands trembled as I retrieved the key and unlocked the hidden drawer. After I satisfied my curiosity, I would lock the book away forever.

I soon found the comments that outraged me the day before, but read further. One phrase caught my eye: "the afflicted and troubled conscience has no remedy against desperation and eternal death."

My breath quickened. Luther described me. Flooded by a constant stream of guilty memories—sinful thoughts, sneaking into Papa's study to read his books, curiosity I couldn't resist—my conscience never stayed clear for long. Had Luther, too, known this misery?

Then Luther offered an escape from desperation: "the promise of grace"—God's free, undeserved mercy. My heart thrashed against my ribs.

I had tried so hard to make up for my sins, and free forgiveness— without my doing a single good work—seemed too easy. I set the book down and closed my eyes. Could I dare believe Luther?

I saw only shadows when I looked around the study. After I lit a candle and picked up the book again, doubts nagged me. Padre Federico's warnings held me back. How could I trust the words of this heretic, Luther? I slowed my pace to evaluate each of his arguments.

Soon the front door creaked. I rushed to return the book and key to their hiding places. Settling back into the chair, I clutched its arms as the study door swung open.

In spite of his slender build, my father's presence filled every room he entered—especially when he wore the professorial black cap and silk cloak I saw before me. Papa's eyes missed nothing, and I worried they might glow with anger instead of affection. He had never given me permission to read in his study by myself.

When he stepped toward me, satchel in hand, I quaked inside.

Chapter 5

HEAVY BURDENS

Stefano Capriolo
September, 1576

*B*efore school began that stormy autumn morning, we boys pulled our chairs close to the fireplace to dry out after our drenching walk to class. While we warmed our hands, I told them how our goat escaped from a bear.

I hadn't finished my story when the teacher walked up behind me and tapped my shoulder with his wooden rod. "*Basta*, Stefano. Ragazzi, return your chairs to their places." He addressed the class as he walked to the front of the room. "Today we will begin with *Ars Poetica* by Horace. Take out your slates."

I groaned. Tell me about the battles and weapons of the Gallic Wars, but not poetry.

I waved my arm until the teacher nodded at me. "Messer Datini, we shouldn't study poetry. Plato and Saint Jerome said poetry's full of lust and violence. It will corrupt us."

Lucia piped up from across the classroom. "How can you say that, Stefano?" She looked at her notes. "Horace says that poetry both teaches and delights. Leonardo Bruni, the humanist, writes that anyone who lacks poetry must not be well educated. Poetry teaches love, good habits, and virtue. Petrarch, Boccaccio, and the humanists knew that poetry only corrupts people who are already evil."

Everyone laughed, and I knew the joke was on me. My brain froze. All I could do was look at the floor.

Messer Datini cleared his throat. "That will do, class. Stefano, scholars in the Dark Ages would have agreed with you, but now we are more enlightened, as Lucia has pointed out."

The other kids snickered and I shut my eyes. It was all Lucia's fault. She studied too hard and showed me up. If only our fathers weren't friends and she hadn't come to my school. My cheeks burned, and I wished I could throw her in the river.

Lucia

When I arrived home from school, the welcoming aroma of pork and onions took my mind off the school day. I set bowls and spoons on the table, then helped my mother serve *pranzo*, just as always. My hands stayed busy, but my thoughts drifted back to my sin.

Soon my father arrived and we sat down to eat. When Papa talked about his day, my mind again returned to my morning at school.

"Lucia...Lucia!" My father's voice startled me. "What did you study today?"

My parents' raised eyebrows told me I had missed something. "Sorry, Papa. I must have been daydreaming." I collected my thoughts. "The best part was a poem Horace wrote about writing poetry. Messer Datini's lessons bring poetry to life. I hope someday I can write great poems like Horace."

My parents smiled.

I shook my head. "I mean it—I want to be a poet." The meal couldn't end soon enough for me, and I cleared away my dishes as soon as my parents finished eating.

Returning to my room to finish a composition before the next morning, I could think only about what I had done to Stefano. I prayed my confession and asked for God's forgiveness. If today were Saturday or Sunday, I could go to Confession at church, but this was a Tuesday. I would have to decide on my own penance and perform it soon or I wouldn't finish my schoolwork on time. I had no coins to give the poor, no sackcloth to wear or ashes to kneel in. If I tore my clothes and confessed my sins in the piazza, all Verona would whisper about me. What could I do to free myself from guilt?

In Padre Federico's last sermon, he had told us we must model our faith after the Crusaders, who faced terrible hardships on their treks to the Holy Land. He talked about his own pilgrimage to Rome and described the marvels he had seen. His conclusion had stuck in my mind: "My heart warmed as I stood near San Pietro's tomb, in the presence of God and that great saint." He looked out over his congregation. "Alas, not everyone can undertake a long voyage, but each of you should make a pilgrimage to some holy shrine. Why, there are many shrines even in our own city."

I jumped to my feet and tiptoed through the house, peering through the doorway into the kitchen. Mamma was facing the other direction, already chopping vegetables for our evening meal. She wouldn't notice if I left, so I wouldn't have to tell her why I needed to go out. She wouldn't miss me if I came back before Papa returned for supper.

I stepped out the door and the sun's rays blazed from across the sky. Daylight would vanish in a few hours. I would have to cross the river to visit the fountain honoring the Virgin Mary. I hesitated and decided to stay on my side of the river and walk to the shrines built into the city walls.

After passing the Roman amphitheater, I followed the riverbank up to San Stefano church and turned behind it toward the hill. Padre Federico had mentioned that in the city wall above this church, two shrines contained the remains of bishops. In the distance, I saw the wall, so I quickened my pace and set off to find the shrines and complete my penance.

The hillside soon turned steep and wild, and the road became a rocky path. Dogwood bushes laden with crimson berries and wild plum bushes heavy with fruit perfumed the air. With every step, I dodged rotting fruit and berries as well as clumps of scat. I tried not to think about which large animals roamed this hill. The noises of the city faded away, and I heard only the *coo coo croo* of turtledoves and the scurrying of field mice. My feet ached.

Finally, I reached the wall and paused to catch my breath. Looking to one side and then the other, I saw no shrines. I could only guess which direction they were, and began following the wall to the right.

After a few minutes, I noticed a wide upward curve in the wall beyond me. Rushing toward the spot, I read the Latin inscription commemorating Bishop Valens. My spirits revived. I bowed low and prayed my confession aloud.

When I looked up, the sun had dropped below the horizon. I couldn't find the other shrine but heard the chirping of crickets. I turned toward home, straining to see the trail. At a fork in the path, I couldn't remember which way I had come. In the dim light, I saw no familiar sights in either direction. I imagined myself ending up as dinner for a bear or wolf. I couldn't force my feet to move, and crossed my arms for warmth.

In the distance, I saw a dark form moving toward me on the path. Too short to be human, it could be a wolf or bear running on all fours. I ran down a steep trail to escape, but slipped on loose rocks and fell. When I tried to stand, daggers of pain shot through my ankle. I screamed and fell back onto the trail.

"Hey down there! What's the matter? Where are you?" A male voice shouted from far above.

I called out in my loudest voice, "Down here on the trail. I hurt my ankle. Help me, please."

"On my way." Footsteps pounded the path. Before long, a silhouetted figure appeared in front of me. He set down the goat he held in his arms. "Lucia, is that you? What are you doing out here?"

"Sì, *eccomi*." At close range I recognized his red cowlick and green eyes—the very classmate I had embarrassed hours before. "Stefano, thank God you're here. I was afraid I'd be stranded out here all night."

Eyeing my foot, he whistled. "What a swollen ankle. You're lucky my mother sent me out to find Alba." He stroked the goat's head. "She's a crazy girl—too smart for her own good. If someone forgets to latch the gate, she pushes it open and runs up the hill looking for greener grass. One of these days I won't be able to find her, and that will be the end of our milk supply." He tied one end of a rope around the goat's neck and the other around his left wrist.

He grabbed my hands. "When I pull you up, stand on your good foot and lean on my shoulder on your other side."

He pulled me off the ground and I winced. My dangling foot throbbed. We began our descent and I tried to hop on one foot beside him.

My wobbly attempts didn't last long. "I'll fall again if I try to hop on these rocks."

He looked down the trail. "You're right. I'll carry you down the hill. But you'll need to hold the goat's leash." He untied the rope from his wrist and handed it to me. Then he reached his arms under my legs and picked me up.

The smell of goat mingled with Stefano's sweat. I would have protested his tight embrace if I hadn't feared for my life. Facing the deepening darkness with a throbbing ankle, I thanked God for Stefano's strong arms.

Finally, we reached level ground. Stefano set me down on a flat boulder and flexed his shoulders. "Don't worry, I'll carry you home. It shouldn't take too long now that we're on the road. Give me a minute to rest." He rubbed the goat's back, turned, and looked me full in the face. "By the way, you never told me what you were doing up there."

I hoped he couldn't see me blush. "You saved my life, so I owe you. But promise you won't repeat it to anyone."

He raised his brows and nodded.

I forced myself to speak. "I was looking for shrines. Padre Federico preached that everyone should make pilgrimages, and I needed to make a pilgrimage this afternoon."

His eyebrows shot up.

"Stefano, I'm sorry I embarrassed you this morning. I've felt awful ever since. I was trying to do my penance. Will you forgive me?"

He stared down at the ground.

"Please, Stefano?"

Finally, he looked up and whispered, "Sì." Without another word, he picked me up and carried me past the lamps of San Stefano church, along the riverbank, and at last back to my home.

For the next week, my greatest joy came from the scent of fresh-cut mint. The pain in my ankle kept me from walking to school or climbing up to reach Papa's key, but every morning Mamma refreshed my bedchamber with mint leaves from her herb garden.

I couldn't read Luther's book, but I had plenty of time to think about how Stefano rescued me hours after I ridiculed him. I remembered Luther's statement that God forgives us, even though we can't pay for our sins. At the time I read the passage, I couldn't believe it. As I lay in bed, I realized that if Stefano could forgive me after I sinned against him, maybe God could do the same for me, and my life could be free from constant guilt.

After my ankle healed, I slipped into my father's study again one afternoon, steeling my mind to resist heresy and deception. I took Luther's book from the drawer.

With his words, Luther painted an odd picture—Jesus Christ so full of love that he sits in heaven praying for us, not because of any works we do, but only because we believe in him. This image made no sense to me. In my nightmares, Padre Federico always accused me of pride and greed, so I certainly didn't deserve Christ's love and prayers.

A few pages later, Luther wrote that he was "covered under the shadow of Christ's wings"—like a baby chick under the hen's wing—and "living without fear under the ample heaven of the forgiveness of sins, spread over him."

I set down the book and closed my eyes. As a little girl, I had peered through gaps in our fence into our neighbors' yard, watching helpless chicks hiding under their mother's wings, just as Luther described. If I could trust his words, now I could rest secure under Christ's wings, free from fear, my sins forgiven. I wiped away tears.

Luther's ideas set my mind racing for the rest of the afternoon. As the shadows fell that evening, I could almost hear Padre Federico admonishing me: "Lucia, the doctrines of the Church have been passed down from the apostles, by the authority of the Lord himself. You must never question them!"

But the image of the chick covered under the shadow of its mother's wings pushed away the priest's warning, and my heart told me Luther's words were true.

The next afternoon, I finished my schoolwork and waited until the first shadows fell and I heard my mother preparing supper. At last I settled into Papa's desk chair to read more of Luther.

Soon a passage spoke of full and perfect joy, with peace of conscience—words that pierced my heart. I tried to imagine complete joy—no worries about sinning against God or anyone else, no need for good works to pay the penalty. Could I ever hope for such a life?

Now the debate raged not between Martin Luther and Padre Federico, but between my heart and mind. I longed to embrace the freedom Luther described, but couldn't let myself accept it until I had tested all the monk's ideas. Meanwhile, I must banish Martin Luther from my thoughts while I attended school.

After a week, I came to the final page and stood, stretching my legs. Glancing at my stack of notes, I hoped Papa would be proud of my accomplishment, not shocked by my conclusions.

I had expected to prove Luther wrong, but instead I believed him. Did I agree with Luther only because his words freed my conscience from guilt, or had his arguments persuaded me? I agonized between admitting my sympathy for Luther's ideas to my father and merely pointing out how Luther's viewpoint differed from that of the Church.

Again the front door's hinges squeaked. Now that I had finished reading Luther's commentary, I couldn't keep silent any longer, and Papa was the only person with whom I dared discuss it. So I left the forbidden book in front of me on his desk. I couldn't predict how he would react when he saw it, but this time, I didn't lock away the commentary and ignore it.

"*Buona sera*, Lucia." Papa entered the study, and the pickle scent of an anatomy professor wafted toward me. As usual, he flashed a grin and set his satchel down. "You're a busy scholar again."

"Sì, Papa, I've been reading a book I found in your desk drawer." I thrust Luther's commentary in front of him. "It fascinated me so much that I couldn't stop until I finished. Have you read it?" I whispered. "Did you know a heretic wrote it?"

Although my father wore a loose robe, I saw him stiffen. My words had upset our daily routine. He shut the study door behind him. When he turned back to me, his smile had vanished, and with it my hope of his approval.

He clutched his hands together, white-knuckled, staring at me. For the first time I could remember, my father stood speechless.

I stared back. In the silence, this image of my father—frozen, like a mouse cornered by a cat—etched itself into my memory.

Finally, he spoke. "I locked that book away before you were born, for only my eyes to see. But I should have guessed that you, my clever daughter, would someday discover my secret." His voice dropped.

"Prying into hidden things can be dangerous, Lucia, and could put our family in great peril." He stepped so close that his breath warmed my face. "Don't tell anyone what you told me."

I looked down. "I'm sorry, Papa. I'm confused. Why do you keep this book in your study? Padre Federico forbade us to read such things." I looked up at him. "The priest called Luther's works heretical."

My father gazed at me. "It's a long story, Lucia, but not a safe discussion topic."

I couldn't restrain myself. "Papa, I read this book to see where Luther went wrong, but I discovered I agree with him."

His eyes came alive again, and his arms relaxed.

"My nightmares have stopped, and at last my conscience feels clean. No more wondering if I've done enough good works for God to forgive me—what a relief, and all this because I put my faith in Jesus Christ." I looked him in the face. "Papa, my mind tells me this is too easy, but my heart tells me to believe."

His face lit up. "Sì, it's a wonderful mystery."

"Luther reminds me of you, Papa. Both of you think for yourselves and test every authority except God." I looked him in the eye. "Is Doctor Luther correct?"

He placed his hands on my shoulders and spoke in a hushed tone. "Sì, Lucia, Luther wrote the truth. If only I could tell everyone I meet, as I did when I was young."

He stepped back. "Life was so different then. Imagine, Lucia, hundreds of books flooding into Italy, new ideas spreading like the pestilence—in science and medicine, philosophy and religion."

"Oh, Papa, if only I could have lived then!"

He smiled. "When I was a student at Padova, Domenico Capriolo and I debated these ideas. I read sections of this book aloud and tried to convince him that Luther's ideas are correct." He sighed. "But he would never admit the Roman Church could be wrong. It's a wonder we're still friends."

He looked toward the door and shook his head. "Nowadays, the Church would soon put a stop to such discussions. In fact, we must talk about these things only in complete privacy—after supper, Lucia."

My father took the book from my hand, picked up the key, and locked the forbidden volume back in its hiding place.

That evening, not even the spicy aromas of basil and garlic with roast pork could interest me in supper. My mother had prepared one of my favorite meals, but I could think only of Papa's words. I picked at my food and stared at the table, waiting for my parents to stop talking long enough to finish supper.

At Mamma's nod, I excused myself, picked up my cup, spoon and bowl, and placed them in the washbasin across the room.

Papa remained seated next to Mamma. I stared at them, tapping my foot. Although Papa smiled at me, he turned back to my mother and stretched his arm around her shoulder. She beamed and her hair shone like spun gold.

At the end of every meal, Papa said the same thing: "Grazie, Caterina—another delicious meal. Your company would make the humblest meal a pleasure, so I am doubly blest." He kissed her, and she looked like the happiest woman on earth.

Pushing back his chair, he turned to me. "Lucia, shall we go to the study now?"

"Sì, Papa."

He took my arm, but looked back at Mamma. They smiled at each other and ignored me.

I pulled at his arm. "Come on, Papa." I wondered if he had forgotten his promise to discuss Luther's book with me. I forced myself to bite my tongue to keep from reminding him.

Finally, Papa shut the door of his study behind us, and we pulled chairs up to his desk.

✤

Giordano

As I followed Lucia into my study, the tight coil of her reddish-gold curls reminded me how quickly she was maturing. Her intelligence made me proud, but could she rein in her impulsiveness? I wanted to tell her the truth, but one slip of her tongue could place me or, God forbid, even Lucia herself in the clutches of the Inquisition—just as Caterina worried.

Lucia sat across the desk from me as she did each evening, but pursed lips greeted me instead of her usual bright-eyed grin. My throat tightened—I shouldn't have lingered so long in the kitchen.

"Your face tells me you're impatient to learn." With luck, her eagerness to hear what I'd taught that day at the medical school would outweigh her curiosity about Luther's book.

She rolled her eyes.

"Forgive me for keeping you waiting, Lucia."

"*Si*, Papa." She sighed. "Now can I finally ask you more about Martin Luther and his book?"

I nodded but couldn't force a smile. "What do you want to know?"

"First, how can you be sure Luther wrote this book?" She pulled out the book from under her sleeve. "Couldn't someone else have used Luther's name?"

"Good question. Luther used a special printing symbol to prove he had written books. Did you notice it?"

She nodded. "*Si*, but what does the symbol mean?" She opened to the title page.

I explained how central the heart and the cross were to Luther, how the white rose stands for spirits and angels, and the joy and peace given by faith. I concluded, "And the golden ring represents the joy of heaven that has no end."

She gazed at me. "A clever man. I'll remember his beliefs every time I see the symbol."

She cocked her head. "Where did Luther's ideas come from? He wrote about a baby chick hiding under its mother's wing, and Padre Federico told us Luther was an ignorant German peasant."

My supper churned in my gut. "Born a miner's son, but Luther was much smarter than that priest." I inhaled. "Smart enough to study the law and then the Bible as a monk and doctor of theology."

"And smart enough that you trust him more than the pope." Warmth had returned to her voice.

I couldn't help but smile. "Luther wanted to please God, but no matter how many good works he did, he felt they weren't enough."

"I felt that way, too." She fixed her gaze on me. "Papa, how did you get this book, and why do you keep it, if it's so dangerous?"

"My brother Cornelio deserves the blame or praise. At his abbot's request, he translated this book from Luther's tongue into ours."

Lucia whistled through her teeth. "My talented uncle!"

I nodded. "And brave, too. By the time Cornelio finished the translation, Luther's words had made a Lutheran of my brother and his abbot—and for that, the pope expelled them from the monastery."

Her eyes widened.

"As you said, this is a dangerous book. More than once, I've considered burning it, but it's too precious. Cornelio sent me this copy from his refuge in Venezia. I'll always treasure this book because my brother translated it but even more because it taught me we don't need to earn God's love." My fingers twitched, and I folded my hands together.

"*Capito.*" A grin lit up her face, and I knew she understood.

I exhaled. "How different my life would have been if this book hadn't inspired me to stand up against the Church."

She sat on the edge of her chair. "Tell me more."

As long as Lucia shared my belief, I could find no reason not to tell her the entire story. "Back in my university days I could speak without fear—it was glorious!" Closing my eyes, I flushed with excitement as I had back in that day. "I told all my friends about Luther's ideas, and many people accepted them."

"What happened, Papa? I've never heard anyone talk about Luther's ideas except Padre Federico."

"You're correct, these days almost no one here knows about Luther. They follow the Church's teachings like ignorant sheep, all because the pope created the Roman Inquisition to stamp out heresy. The Inquisition hounds anyone who disagrees with the Roman Church."

I stroked my beard. "Everything changed, Lucia—I lost the wonderful career I'd begun in Rome, and I had to flee to Venezia. Eventually, the only safe haven for Cornelio and me was over the mountains, outside Italy."

She stood and grabbed my hands. "You're so brave, Papa!" She shook her head. "And all because of one small book."

"Sì, one small book with ideas big enough to transform the church and stir up the pope to fight them."

When she sat down, her eyes narrowed. "Papa, you know my conscience has always troubled me. Why didn't you tell me about Luther's ideas?"

I sighed. "For years, I've longed to discuss them with you, but I had to protect you—it's a father's duty."

She shook her head. "But if Luther's ideas are true, shouldn't we tell people about them?"

Her question didn't surprise me, but I clenched my teeth and mentally debated my response. "Someday I hope we can, Lucia—but now the Inquisition would silence us, perhaps forever."

"But it's wrong to keep quiet about something so important!" She squeezed her hands into fists. "Papa, you've always taught me to tell the truth. How can I wait to speak God's truth until a safer time? Who knows if that day will ever come?"

I rolled up my sleeves and showed her my wrists. "See these scars?"

She shuddered.

"Whenever I look at them, I remember what the Inquisition did to me—it's not fit for your ears, but let this be a reminder that the Church will stop at nothing to root out heresy. I prayed for death to end my pain, but many people have paid an even greater price for holding the Bible as a higher authority than the Church. *Sola Scriptura. Solus Christus.*" Only Scripture. Only Christ.

Finally, she spoke in little more than a whisper. "So we're heretics if we believe Martin Luther?"

"*Si*, in the eyes of the Roman Church, we are heretics." I swallowed. "May God protect us."

Chapter 6

EMBOLDENED

Lucia
Late September, 1576

*E*very Sunday morning was a special occasion for me. All week long, Elisabetta and I looked forward to our pilgrimage to Mass at San Zeno Maggiore, Verona's most beautiful church. We gladly walked past closer churches so we could view the breathtaking art that Mamma had shown us years before, especially San Zeno's colorful wheel-shaped window and the golden figures etched into the bronze doors. Each week, we marveled at the doors' many panels, debating which was the most splendid scene: the ones from the Bible or those from the life of Bishop Zeno, Verona's patron saint.

Now our parents allowed us to walk to Mass without them as long as her older brothers accompanied us. Alberto counted the varieties of birds he saw each week, Massimo observed the animals along the riverbank, and Elisabetta and I enjoyed conversing without any listening ears.

When my friend knocked this morning, I threw open the front door and a gust of wind blew orange and brown leaves in my face.

"*Buon giorno.*" I smiled at my friend and her brothers.

"*Pronto, Lucia?*" Elisabetta returned my smile. Her brothers nodded and stayed back.

A glimmer of sunshine peeked through dark clouds as we strolled next to the frothing Adige River. As it roared past, I imagined the snowy alpine reaches far upstream where these waters began. I tried to picture the lands beyond the mountains—especially Saxony, Martin Luther's homeland.

My thoughts returned to my conversation with my father the previous evening. If I obeyed Papa, Elisabetta would never hear Luther's message.

I would never have a more private moment with my friend and couldn't wait another week to tell her.

"Elisabetta, have you ever felt too guilty for God to forgive you?"

She raised her brows. "I don't know. Why do you ask?"

"For years, I've dreamed that God would send me to hell. Nothing I did, no amount of confession or penance, could make him forgive me. I didn't deserve his love."

"But those were only dreams, Lucia. Why should God be angry with you after you confess and do penance?" She cocked her head.

"Try to remember the worst thing you've ever done. Do you truly believe that reciting prayers or kneeling on ashes earned God's forgiveness?"

She eyed me. "Maybe not for big sins. So you think Padre Federico is too lenient in the confessional?"

"No, but he's wrong. The Bible says Jesus died to save us from God's judgment. We only need to believe that and accept God's forgiveness."

She frowned again. "Lucia, what makes you think you're smarter than our priest? He studies the Bible all the time. How could you become an expert on the Holy Scriptures without a Bible?"

I smiled at her. "My mother grew up in a convent and learned Bible stories and verses by heart. For as long as I can remember, she's taught them to me every night."

Her blush and downcast eyes told me I had won the argument.

As we crossed Ponte Pietra, I glanced at the rushing river below and then behind us at Alberto and Massimo, who stood too far back to hear.

"And I read a book that explains Saint Paul's letter to the Galatians. The man who wrote it had a guilty conscience—like me. But when he studied the Galatian letter, he realized God gives his love as a free gift, not as a reward for our good works. That brought him joy and freedom from his guilt—and it did the same for me when I read his book."

"You read a book, and now you're ready to throw out everything Padre Federico taught us. Lucia, how can you trust that man's opinion more than the Church's teaching?" Elisabetta's voice stayed calm, but her pinched lips and somber eyes confirmed her disapproval.

I had to convince her. "He taught theology and studied the Holy Scriptures for himself. That's how he discovered the Church's errors. My mind and experience tell me he's correct."

She stiffened and lowered her voice. "Watch what you say. Padre Federico might call that heresy."

I shook my head. "How can it be heresy if it's written in the Bible?"

Elisabetta said nothing. She looked to the left at Castelvecchio, the brick fortress guarding Verona's northern entrance, while I turned my eyes toward the river and watched gulls soaring over Ponte Scaligero. We continued our walk in painful silence, finally turning away from the river and approaching Piazza San Zeno.

If my friend read the Bible, maybe she would understand the truth and freedom that God offers, just as Luther did. I didn't dare show her Luther's book, but with each step, I tried to think of another way to convince her.

The church bell signaled that Mass was about to begin. Elisabetta, Alberto, Massimo, and I hurried past the heavy outer doors. As always, the aroma of incense tickled my nose. We entered the dark sanctuary, and I glanced back at the window wheel. On that cloudy Sunday, I saw only a dim reflection of the window's glory.

Flickers of light from a side chapel caught my eye. A dozen votive candles glowed on a table in front of the altar. A wrinkled, barefoot woman grasped an unlit candle from a basket and hobbled toward the moneybox.

The ragged woman was about to deposit her coins and light the candle, but I couldn't stand by and let her waste her money. Luther had written that such offerings were useless. I rushed toward the moneybox to stop her. As the woman approached, I blocked her path.

"Signora, save your money for food. God will answer your prayers without this coin."

She frowned. "No, *signorina*, the priest told me. I must speed my husband's soul along to heaven."

I sighed. Of course this woman would trust the words of a priest more than a girl she didn't know.

Turning away, I faced a host of stares and heard her coin resound. Elisabetta's cheeks turned crimson when I walked toward her, but she stayed with me and we took our places for Mass.

The monks' choir sang *Agnus Dei*, and the soloist caught my eye. The cane at his side confirmed my suspicion.

I whispered to my friend, "Remember Vincenzo from our class? There he is!"

Glancing his direction, she nodded. "I never pictured him as a monk."

When Padre Federico began his homily, I heard yawns and saw glazed eyes. Then the priest came to his favorite topic, God's final judgment of humanity.

"Beware, all of you, every man, woman and child! Will God declare you are one of his blessed sheep and welcome you into his eternal kingdom? Or will he judge you as a goat, curse you for your evil deeds, and send you off into the eternal fire prepared for the Devil and his angels?"

I glanced around the church. All eyes—except children too young to understand—focused on Padre Federico. An old man stared, wide-eyed, at the priest. A grandmother and some young children wiped away tears.

I gazed at the wooden crucifix above the main altar. The outstretched arms of Jesus, the nails in his wrists and feet, and his slumping head reminded me of his sacrifice, the agony he suffered, and his death—out of love for sinful people like all of us. Yet Elisabetta and the old woman in the chapel couldn't accept God's free forgiveness. I wouldn't have believed it myself if I hadn't read Luther's book, but now I longed to tell everyone the truth Luther discovered in the Bible. Then I remembered my father's warning to keep silent. Which path should I choose?

When the service ended, Elisabetta started toward the back doors.

I called to her. "I need to talk to the priest. I'll join you in a moment."

She raised her eyebrows.

I turned toward the cleric. "Padre Federico, could I ask you something?"

"What is it, signorina?" He wiped his brow.

"Could you give me some Bibles in our tongue? I want to study the Holy Scriptures with my friends."

He blanched. "Have you forgotten what I told you in catechism class? Heresies and immorality flourished when people had their own Bibles. Why, it was because of such misdeeds that the pope needed to set up the Inquisition!"

His tone softened. "I can't give you Bibles. However, if you and your friends would like to meet with me, I will instruct you."

"But if I had my own Bible, I could study it every day."

"Signorina, the Church must interpret Holy Scripture. You must never forget that." His eyes flashed.

I stepped back.

"Remember the fates of those who stray from the Church's teaching. God forbid that you might become one of them." The priest spoke in a low but forceful tone.

His words numbed my tongue. Turning toward the aisle, I tripped over Vincenzo's cane. It bounced to the floor, and I gasped. *"Mi dispiace.* Are you hurt?"

Vincenzo picked up his cane and glanced at me.

"Lucia?" For an instant, the corners of his mouth rose.

I nodded.

"Don't worry about me, but take care for yourself." His voice dropped. "I heard what you asked my uncle."

"Padre Federico is your uncle?" Maybe the priest had frightened Vincenzo into becoming a monk.

"Si, that's all the more reason you should take my advice: stay out of trouble. If you want to read the Bible, join a convent."

I clenched my jaw. I shouldn't need to join a convent just to read the Bible. I opened my mouth to reply, but remembered Elisabetta. I exhaled my anger instead. *"Prego,* I need to leave. My friend is waiting outside."

I rushed out of the church. Dark clouds blanketed the deserted piazza. Far down the street, I glimpsed the silhouettes of Elisabetta and her brothers. Lifting the hem of my dress, I bolted toward them, my cloak flapping behind me in the wind.

Chapter 7

ARRESTED

Lucia
October, 1576

O ne autumn night, I lay in bed reading long after I should
have snuffed out my lamp. Suddenly I heard a commotion
at the other end of the house. Dropping my book, I pulled
myself out of bed and tiptoed into the hallway. Seconds
later, Mamma clasped my arm. We watched my father trudge by the
light of a single candle through the dark *sala* toward the front door.

"Who is it?" Papa's deep voice rang through the house.

"Open up in the name of the Holy Office of the Inquisition!" thundered a deep voice.

Mamma and I both startled.

My father froze, then glanced to his right, left, and toward the
back of the house. He sighed and opened the door. Two men in black
robes burst in and flanked him, clutching his arms.

"What is the meaning of this? How dare you disturb me at this
hour! Don't you know I am a professor of medicine at the university?"
His air of authority calmed my racing heart.

I heard a slap and saw Papa's head slump toward his left shoulder.
I couldn't breathe.

The tall man who held Papa's left arm cuffed his colleague's hand
with the blunt edge of a dagger. "Basta, Bruno! We want him to cooperate." He turned to my father. "So you are Giordano Locatelli?"

"Sì, eccomi." I could barely hear his reply.

I took a step to help Papa, but Mamma grabbed my shoulder and pointed toward my room. Wrapping her cloak around her, she strode toward the front door.

"Signori, you're making a terrible mistake! My husband fears God and attends Mass every week. He's a friend of the bishop; just ask him about Giordano's reputation." Mamma's clear voice rang through the house.

"Signora, we have our orders," declared the tall man. He turned to my father. "Come with us."

Papa's captors gave him no chance to don his cloak or boots. Mamma tossed her cloak toward his shoulders, but it slid to the floor. The soldiers marched my father out into the night.

I stared at Mamma. Then my feet flew through the house. I yanked the door open and stood on the porch. Before I could demand that the Inquisition's agents release my father, the foggy darkness had swallowed up Papa and his captors.

I clenched my fists. If only I could have stopped them.

The cool river breeze made me shiver, and I looked down at my thin gown and bare feet. A lump clogged my throat, and I slowly turned toward the door.

Back inside the house, I tried to convince myself this had been a vivid nightmare—until I saw Mamma in the sala, picking up her cloak. Extending her arms, she approached me with tears in her eyes and held me silently. I didn't want to leave her warm embrace.

She coughed and stepped back.

"Mamma, how can we help Papa?" My voice sounded puny compared to Mamma's brave words.

"Tonight, we must pray for him. In the morning, I'll ask his friends to help free him." She sighed. "But we both need our rest to give us strength for tomorrow."

While she locked the front door, I headed toward my bedchamber. The lamp still burned in Papa's study, so I tiptoed inside. When I saw my father's desk, I remembered Martin Luther's book and the fear I saw in Papa's eyes the first time I showed him the forbidden volume.

If only I had obeyed his warning instead of speaking out at church. Now they had taken Papa away. The Inquisition must have blamed my father for my rash words. Chills raced down my spine, and I snuffed out Papa's lamp.

I dove onto my bed and buried my head in the coverlet. If only I could keep my mouth shut. God help me, and God help poor Papa!

Anger burned in my throat. God shouldn't have let this happen after I tried to tell people the truth about Him. The Inquisition shouldn't have arrested Papa for what I did.

The night dragged on. I couldn't stop shivering. Every time I closed my eyes, my conscience shouted that I had betrayed Papa.

Finally, daybreak arrived, and I heard my mother stir. My feet hung heavy as anchors as I trudged into her bedchamber.

I choked out, ""Mamma, it's my fault." I tried to think of an explanation that wouldn't involve Martin Luther's book. I told her how I had asked Padre Federico for Bibles. "Mamma, his face turned white, and he told me only priests should have Bibles. Then he warned me about the terrible fate awaiting those who stray from the Church's teaching. He frightened me, so I left."

The color drained from my mother's face, and her lip quivered. "Lucia, haven't we raised you to honor your priest?"

"I'm sorry, Mamma. My questions must have made him suspicious." My throat felt thick. "If I'd known they would arrest Papa, I never would have spoken to Padre Federico. Forgive me, please."

She covered her eyes with her hand, and the seconds passed like hours. Finally, she looked up. "As God has forgiven me, I forgive you." She nestled me in her arms, and her strength revived me.

She shook her head. "I can't understand why Padre Federico would suspect your father of heresy because you asked a few innocent questions. And why would God allow this?"

I opened my mouth but didn't know what to say. I couldn't betray Papa's confidence again. He had told me not to discuss Luther's ideas, even with Mamma. If I told her everything, she would find out about my father's heresy. So I didn't mention Luther's book.

"*Allora*, there's no time to waste." She spoke with a new firmness while braiding the golden tresses I had always envied, then twisted her braid into a bun and pinned it on her head.

She glanced in my direction. "Let's pray that Professor Capriolo can secure your father's release. He has no ties to the Inquisition, but his long friendship with Giordano and connections at the medical school may help. If I leave now, perhaps I can speak with him before he goes to the university." Her voice quavered. "You'll need to walk to Elisabetta's house alone. Walk quickly and look straight ahead."

I nodded.

"You're exhausted, Lucia. Eat something; you'll need strength for the day. Come with me."

"Sì, Mamma." I followed her to the kitchen. She reached up to a hanging basket, pulled out an apple, and handed it to me.

"Grazie." Normally, I would have devoured the crisp apple, but food didn't interest me that morning.

Mamma wrapped an apple in a cloth, stuffed it into her *borsa*, and turned to me. "We can't know the future, but we can draw comfort from God's word to Joshua: *I will never leave you or forsake you.*"

She hugged me, threw back her shoulders, and strode out the door like a soldier marching into battle. Now I must show the same strength.

Giordano

The Inquisition's men dragged me through Verona's dark street, and I feared the worst. Even after fifteen years, the memory of the *strappado* made my shoulders ache. Such wrenching pain! The Venetian Inquisition's assistants had bound ropes under my armpits and around my shoulders, hoisted me up to the ceiling, and dropped me time after time until I gave the Inquisitor the answer he wanted. I wondered if I could again survive such torture.

The iron gate clanged behind us, and we entered what had probably once been a monastery. I prayed for strength. The jailer grabbed a lantern and locked me in a dark cell at the end of the hall.

After my eyes adjusted to the dimness, I saw a bucket in a corner, a straw mattress on the stone floor, a blanket wadded up on the mattress, and a tiny window near the top of the wall—just like the Venetian prison, except the smell of urine predominated here, where a salty dankness had overpowered all else in Venezia. I stretched out on the mattress, wrapped the blanket around myself, and closed my eyes. At least God had spared me that night from the torture chamber the Inquisition called an examination room.

Before long, I heard faint noises and glanced in their direction. All I could see was the glint of tiny eyes—which, from my past experience in prison, I recognized as rats. I steeled myself to strike if a rat jumped on me.

Questions about my arrest precluded sleep. Since my arrival in Verona, I couldn't have tried harder to avoid the Inquisition's attention. I had kept every Roman Church rule, even counted the bishop as a friend. What had I done wrong?

Suddenly, Lucia's words came back to me: "I want to shout Luther's good news to everyone." Panic swept over me, and I pounded my fists into the mattress.

The Inquisition might arrest her next. I had tried to convince her to stay silent about this, but I had also encouraged my impulsive daughter's independent mind.

May God grant mercy and protection!

Lucia

If my sweet Mamma could show such courage and strength, so must I. I bit into the apple—unripe, in spite of its rosy hue. As an act of obedience, I forced down the fruit and tried to focus on preparing for school.

Throughout the day, my worries about Papa constantly broke my focus on Messer Datini's lessons and even conversations with Elisabetta. After school, I hoped for good news and rest when I walked through our doorway.

"Ciao, Mamma." No response. I glanced in the kitchen. Mamma's market basket lay on the kitchen table, still filled with onions, spinach, apples, bread, and cheese. The house lay silent.

Perhaps the Inquisition took Mamma away, too. Rushing into my parents' bedchamber, I discovered my mother stretched out, face down on her bed. My throat tightened, and I ran to her.

"Mamma, what's wrong?"

She turned her face toward me, yawning. "I must have fallen asleep. I didn't sleep much last night."

My breath rushed out. "What did you find out about Papa?"

"*Niente*—nothing at all. Professor Capriolo asked the dean of the medical faculty to plead for your father's release. But no one knows what will happen."

"How long will they keep him?"

She shrugged her shoulders. "We're all at the mercy of the Inquisition, Lucia. The best thing we can do now is pray."

"Oh, Mamma, if only I could take back what I said to Padre Federico! Why didn't they take me instead of Papa?"

She put her arm around me. "The Inquisition wouldn't blame a girl your age."

But I deserved whatever punishment they might give my father. If only I could trade places with him.

A fog of worry settled over me, and I whispered many prayers for Papa's freedom. My cries to God brought me momentary comfort, and I hoped they were accomplishing more for my father.

In the intervening moments, images filled my mind with fear and worry—images of Padre Federico's stern countenance and the Inquisition's thugs who arrested Papa. My classmates' stares made me wonder if they had heard about my father and if Elisabetta might shun me.

Mamma went out every day to inquire about my father, so I often returned from school to an empty house or only the maid doing her work. Each time I walked inside, everything reminded me of Papa. I paced around the house, always lingering in my father's study. His boots, his coat, his books and papers all made me miss him more, and I felt guiltier by the day. If I told the Inquisition that Papa was innocent, perhaps they would set him free. But I didn't know who I should speak to or how to make them believe me.

Giordano

"This tribunal pronounces Giordano Locatelli guilty of spreading heresy by corrupting the faith of Verona's youth." The stout cleric directed his gaze at the Inquisitor as if I weren't even present in the examination room.

Guilty! How could they? An acid taste burned all the way up my throat. Experience had taught me that protesting the Inquisition's decisions made bad situations worse, so I clenched my teeth and kept silent.

When the jailer locked my cell door behind me, I feared I would never leave it again alive. Until this verdict, I had tolerated my always-cold extremities, the darkness and filth, consoling myself that I would soon leave. Now the possibility of a long stay underscored the severity of my situation.

With heavy steps, I paced the tiny room. What evidence could have prompted them to reach such a verdict? During my fifteen years in Verona, I had avoided anything that could be construed as heresy. In spite of my discretion, someone must have reported me to the Inquisition.

In recent years I had discussed Luther's ideas with no one but Lucia. A sudden pang halted me in mid-step. My daughter wouldn't betray me, but she must have spoken about Luther without understanding the consequences. If only she hadn't found Luther's book, hadn't asked me about it.

However intelligent, Lucia had proved too young to understand the results of her actions. God forgive me for leaving the book where she could find it. I deserved whatever price I would pay, but my family would suffer, too. Without my salary, Lucia and Caterina might starve.

Lucia

A knock sounded at the door after supper, and I almost dropped the bowl I was washing. Mamma was pouring hot water, so I shook my hands dry and raced to answer the door.

"Who's there?"

"*Eccomi*, Professor Capriolo."

I swung the door wide and sucked in my breath. Towering before me in a massive black cloak, he reminded me of the angel of death I had seen in paintings. "*Buona sera*, professor."

He doffed his cap and smoothed a mass of reddish-gray curls. Then he nodded. "*Buona sera*, Lucia. Could I speak with your mother?"

"Sì, come in and sit down. I'll tell her you're here." I ushered him into the sala, then dashed into the kitchen.

At the news of Professor Capriolo's arrival, Mamma straightened her back and walked into the sala.

Papa's friend bowed and kissed Mamma's hand. "Signora Locatelli, the dean asked me to convey the message the bishop sent him this afternoon." He shook his head. "Even though the dean wrote about Giordano's important role at the medical college, and the bishop sent a letter praising Giordano's good character, the Inquisition's secret court convicted him of inciting heresy. Recently, a priest denounced him for corrupting the faith of children with heretical teachings." He looked at the floor.

Padre Federico's stern face flashed into my mind. My stomach roiled.

"Years ago, Venezia's Inquisition court found Giordano guilty of heresy. Because of that conviction and the priest's sworn testimony, Verona's court believed his accusation."

My mother paled. "But my husband attends Mass, confesses, and takes communion every week." I heard a catch in her voice. "Aren't those signs of a faithful Church member?"

I looked at my feet.

"I would be the first to vouch for Giordano's character, but if even one person with a grudge slandered him and signed a complaint, that would raise the tribunal's suspicions. Their trials and courts are secret, and no defender can speak for the accused person. So all we can do is pray and plead for mercy." He pulled himself out of the chair and moved toward the door. "Your husband hasn't been sentenced yet, but I don't expect the Inquisition will release him anytime soon." I heard a catch in Professor Capriolo's voice.

Mamma rose from the couch and opened the door. "Grazie, Professor Capriolo." Her voice sounded husky.

He bowed. "Signora Locatelli, my wife and I will help your family in any way we can. I'll let you know as soon as I hear more." He put on his hat and walked out the door.

Mamma latched the door and walked toward me. I threw my arms around her and buried my face in her apron. She rubbed my back.

Mea culpa, mea massima culpa—this was all my fault. My conscience reminded me again and again. Because I ignored Papa's warning, the Inquisition convicted him of heresy. Professor Capriolo's words, "corrupting the faith of children," left no doubt in my mind. Padre Federico must have blamed Papa for corrupting my faith.

As I lay awake that night, I couldn't stop thinking about Papa in his prison cell. Smothering my tears, I tried not to imagine what might happen to him.

Giordano

Late the next morning, the jailer escorted me back to the examination room. I hoped and prayed the Inquisition had realized its error and would allow me to return to my family.

As soon as I entered the room, the Inquisitor held up a sheet of paper. "Giordano Locatelli, this tribunal sentences you to ten years in prison for corrupting the faith of Verona's youth with heresy. The length of this sentence will allow Verona's youth to reach mature adulthood without further infection from your heresy's poison. The Holy Office shows its mercy by sparing your life." He nodded to the jailer and turned his attention to the papers on his desk.

Ten years in prison, all because Lucia found Martin Luther's book! I squeezed my hands into fists. Back in my cell, I paced, pounding my fists into the air. With one blow, I imagined punching the Inquisitor and with the next, Luther.

As daylight ebbed away, I contemplated the implications of my sentence. My mood turned to despair. I couldn't practice medicine, conduct research, or teach my students. Even if Caterina and Lucia found a way to survive, I might rot in prison and never see them again.

I threw myself onto the mattress and called out to God for a miracle, that I might go home to my family and again practice medicine. I closed my eyes and pictured myself knocking on my front door, rushing through the doorway to embrace Caterina and Lucia. But when I looked up, my grim surroundings taunted me. My only hope lay in God's mercy.

Lucia

The next evening, just as Mamma and I finished cena, we again heard a knock at the door. When Professor Capriolo entered, his lips and gray mustache turned neither up nor down, and his olive-green eyes gave no inkling of his message.

Professor Capriolo nodded as my mother walked into the sala. "I have new information for you." After a quick glance in my direction, he turned to Mamma. "Shall we speak privately?"

"No, Lucia must hear, too." My mother linked her arm with mine. We sat on a couch across from Professor Capriolo.

"*Allora.*" He settled into a chair and clasped his hands. "I hate to bring this news, but the Inquisition's tribunal sentenced Giordano to ten years in prison." He shook his head. "I'm so sorry."

"Ten years!" I gasped. I would be a grown woman before Papa returned. How would I survive without him?

My mother's face turned pale, but she squeezed my hand and bowed her head. "May God protect and preserve Giordano, and us as well."

"Sì, may God protect your family." Professor Capriolo nodded. He gazed at us. "As Lucia's godfather, I'm responsible to care for her if her parents cannot. I haven't the means to provide for both of you, but I'll do all I can to help you get along without Giordano's salary.

Signora Locatelli, have you parents, brothers, or sisters who could help you?"

"No, I lost them all to plague or fire." She sighed. "They're waiting for me in heaven."

"Perhaps we should discuss your financial situation." His stroked his beard.

My mother nodded. "Lucia, could you clean up in the kitchen now?"

"Sì, Mamma." Walking into the kitchen, I scrubbed the bowls with a force that almost shattered them and rubbed them drier than ever with Mamma's dishtowel. All the while, Professor Capriolo's words ran through my mind, again and again. After I stacked the last cup in the cupboard, I peeked into the sala.

Mamma sat on the couch, her back straight as a board, her forehead furrowed, and her hands folded in her lap. Professor Capriolo sat in a chair across from her, nodding.

I returned to my bedchamber and picked up a book, but my mind couldn't take in the words. At last, the front door closed, and I ran to the sala. "Mamma, how will we live without Papa?"

She took my hand. "Sit down, Lucia, and I'll tell you."

I sank into the *lettuccio* next to Mamma, and she put her arm around me.

"We'll manage if we work hard and do our own washing and cooking. We'll have to let Anna go." Her confident tone returned. "I'll use the skills I learned in the convent to tutor. I can teach reading and writing, music, Latin, and devotions to the daughters of the other medical professors. Professor Capriolo will speak to the families."

She hesitated. "Lucia, there's one more thing. I'm sorry, but I can't pay for your schooling."

Her words rained down on me like blows, knocking the wind out of me for the second time that evening.

"But Papa always talks about how lucky we are to have such a school in Verona. Without Messer Datini or Papa, there's no one to teach me. Can't we find some way I can stay in school—please?"

"I can't even promise we'll have food on our table. Schooling is a luxury most people can't afford, and now we may be among them. I'm sorry." She wiped her eyes.

Although I lay in bed that night, the day's news ensured that sleep came only in short, exhausted stretches, between fits of tears and pleas to God for what I knew would be a miracle—Papa's freedom.

Chapter 8

HUMBLED

Lucia

W hen Elisabetta and I left our classroom after school the next day, my mother stood waiting outside the door. She pulled me aside.

"Lucia, I'm here to speak with Messer Datini. Please join me, and then we can walk home with Elisabetta."

"Sì, Mamma." I turned to Elisabetta. "Could you wait for me?"

She shook her head. "I'd better go with my brothers. My mother will worry if I'm delayed." She turned away.

"*A domani.*" I called after her. Until tomorrow, I hoped.

Mamma approached my teacher's desk, and I followed her.

"*Buona sera,* Messer Datini." My mother's confident voice calmed me.

My teacher bowed. "How can I help you, Signora Locatelli?"

In a clear voice, Mamma explained our situation. She concluded, "Is there anything I can do to compensate you so Lucia can continue her education?"

He creased his brow. "Lucia's presence enlivens the class, and I would hate to lose such an able student. Perhaps you could help me with cooking and cleaning."

Mamma nodded, but her eyelids drooped. "Grazie."

I knew I should offer to take Mamma's place. I took a deep breath. "Messer Datini, I'll cook and clean for you to earn my place in your class. I'll start work as soon as school ends each day. My mother has enough work of her own."

My teacher glanced from my face to my mother. "Signora, will you give Lucia your permission?"

"Sì." Mamma nodded. The corners of her lips hinted at a smile.

"Very well." He turned to me. "I'll look forward to your help on Monday, Lucia."

"Grazie, Messer Datini." My mother smiled. "Lucia and I will always appreciate your kindness."

He nodded. "*Buona sera*, signora. *Buona sera*, Lucia.

We stepped outside the classroom, and I hugged my mother. "Grazie, Mamma. I'm so glad I can stay in the class."

She smiled. "Be thankful for your teacher's generosity. I'll mention this to your father in my next letter. He'll be proud that Messer Datini thinks so highly of you that he's willing to keep you in the class." Her smile vanished, and she looked into my eyes. "Lucia, now you must guard your time and energy so you'll be able to keep up with your studies. Your new responsibilities will demand strength—and humility."

After a silent walk home, I lay on my bed, ruminating about the day's events. Suddenly the bright scent of orange mint revived me. I sat up, and Mamma handed me a cup of hot tea.

She smiled. "Fresh mint from the garden."

"Grazie, Mamma." Her years in the convent had taught her the proper herb for every need, and this special tea both refreshed and soothed me.

I sipped my tea, satisfied that my offer to work for my teacher had been the correct decision. Even so, it came at a cost, as Mamma had reminded me. I would miss walking home with Elisabetta after school and hoped my work as a servant wouldn't cost me her friendship.

⚜

The next day, Mamma prepared turnip soup, served with pears from our tree—a humble pranzo, reflecting the absence of my father and his salary. Neither of us said much. While we cleared away the bowls, I noticed she was dabbing tears with the corner of her apron.

Mamma cleared her throat. "Lucia, let's walk to Mass this afternoon. The Church's music and art will bring us God's comfort."

I flinched at the thought of seeing Padre Federico again, but remembering Mamma's sad eyes, my tongue stuck in my throat, and I couldn't say no.

A few moments later, I walked at Mamma's side toward San Zeno, wondering if the news of my father's sentence had reached the other parishioners. They might point fingers at us and whisper to each other. I recoiled. Then I thought of the price Papa was paying for my lack of discretion, and my embarrassment weighed in as only a light penalty I must endure.

"Lucia, my tutoring duties will begin on Monday. I know you'll be working for Messer Datini, but when you return home, could you bring in water and wood, so I can cook supper as soon as I arrive?"

Mamma's words released my mind from its anguish. Usually I resented her interrupting my thoughts, but not this time. "Sì, Mamma, I'll do it as soon as I get home."

"Then could you start the fire and begin to heat a pot of water?"

I grimaced at the thought of starting a fire. The smells brought back Alessandro's execution, but I couldn't refuse her. "Of course."

"One more thing, Lucia." Her face flushed. "Could you make sure the canary has water to drink?"

I shrugged my shoulders. "Sì, Mamma." I dared not suggest we dispose of Mamma's feathered singing companion, a gift from Papa.

"Grazie, Lucia." She smiled. "Your help will allow us to eat cena before bedtime."

I noticed dark circles under her eyes, and she had not yet begun her tutoring duties. I tried not to imagine life as an orphan. May God give Mamma strength!

We walked along the riverbank. At last Mamma spoke. "I want to make my confession before Mass. Will you go too?"

I ground my teeth. Padre Federico would be listening in the confessional. Mamma held my eye, awaiting my response. I had no excuse to avoid confession, and I must do nothing to cast more suspicion on my family. I nodded.

Padre Federico frightened me now. His penetrating stare made me suspect he knew all my secrets. But for the priest, Papa might be with us at this moment.

My hands turned to fists every time I thought of Padre Federico and his power over so many lives. Thanks to the priest's instruction, his congregation feared God's judgment but didn't understand God's love for them. Now his denunciation had shattered the lives of each member of my family.

All the way across the piazza, I had to force one foot in front of the other. Mamma strode toward the confessional and closed the door behind her. I waited outside, choosing my words.

When my turn came, I tiptoed inside. My fingers trembled as I shut the door. Only a dark curtain separated me from Padre Federico. I thought he would recognize my voice, so I chose my words with care. "Father, I confess the sin of sloth. I sometimes leave household chores for my mother."

"Say *Ave Maria* ten times, do another task to help your mother each day, and you will be absolved from your sin, my daughter. Go and sin no more."

I left the confessional and let out my breath. Somehow I had avoided his usual lecture about my sinful nature. Padre Federico slipped out of the back of the confessional, and I realized he must have been in a hurry to begin Mass.

The first ordeal had passed, but now I had to face the gathered parishioners. I followed my mother and attempted to blend, anonymous, into the cluster of families entering the sanctuary. I kept my eyes straight ahead, praying that she would remain in the back so no one would notice us.

But Mamma trekked down the center aisle to the front, where she could see and hear every detail of the service. With each step, my cheeks grew warmer, and I squeezed my arms tighter against my sides. I imagined every eye focused on me as if I were a condemned heretic walking toward the stake. I wondered if Mamma was punishing me for my conversation with Padre Federico.

When Mamma stopped, she nodded and smiled. The glow on her face told me our outing already had brought her joy and comfort. She must not have noticed the distress she had caused me. Didn't she feel shame that her husband was a convicted heretic, imprisoned by the very Church whose service we now attended? I stared at my shoes. Padre Federico would soon be standing at the lectern, and I could not bear his stare.

As Mass progressed, I imagined what Martin Luther might have done if he were standing in my place—perhaps he would have interrupted Padre Federico's homily and told the priest to stop frightening people into performing good works.

Luther might have done this in Saxony, but if I attempted it that afternoon in Verona, Padre Federico might personally escort me to the Inquisition's prison. So I kept my mouth shut and cracked my knuckles. When my mother frowned at me, I pursed my lips and forced out my breath.

I would go mad if I continued to listen to Padre Federico's frightening sermons, but I couldn't stop attending Mass. I needed to keep my mind on something else when I came to church, perhaps my Greek verb conjugations or the poetry I had memorized.

Padre Federico began his homily, his strident voice resounding through the church. He spoke that afternoon about Saint Peter's denial of Christ. As hard as I tried, I couldn't ignore his message.

"Not once, not twice, but three times Peter denied our Lord!"

I shut my eyes and thought at once of my silence about Martin Luther's message.

Then Padre Federico shouted out, "Hear the word of the Lord: if you deny me before men, I will deny you before the Father in heaven."

I shuddered. How could I be faithful to God but not endanger my family? For the remainder of the service, two images flashed through my mind: the small volume containing Martin Luther's ideas, and the Inquisition's henchmen dragging my father out of our house.

On Monday morning, my mother and I rose early to prepare for our new responsibilities. I opened an oak chest in the kitchen and pulled out the muslin apron a former maid had left behind. Eyeing the coarse, stained cloth, I fought back tears. This apron conferred on me the status of a servant, all because of one rash conversation with Padre Federico.

I shook my head. Shame on me! That conversation had sent Papa to prison for ten years. I deserved his fate but kept my place in Messer Datini's class. I placed the apron under my books and papers, at the bottom of my schoolbag.

Mamma and I left the house together and walked down our street. She bade me farewell and turned down a side street while I continued to Elisabetta's house. With each step, my dread increased. I still couldn't face telling her that I wouldn't be walking home with her. I put off the conversation until just before we reached the door to our schoolroom.

"Elisabetta, my mother has begun to tutor and needs my help with errands after school. I can't walk home with you any longer." My voice wavered.

"What?" She froze and shot me a frown. "I'll have to walk home with my brothers every day?"

"I'm sorry." I shrugged my shoulders and stepped inside the doorway. All through the school day, my friend's long face weighed on me.

After our lessons concluded, I packed away my schoolwork and left the classroom with Elisabetta. After a quick goodbye, I ducked around the corner, away from her curious eyes. I counted to fifty and walked back inside to begin my work.

My teacher looked up from his book and smiled. "I'm grateful for your help, Lucia. You'll know why when you see the kitchen." He stepped away from his desk, opened the kitchen door, and shrugged. "I've no time to cook or clean."

I peered into the cramped room, dark but for the light from a small oilcloth window.

"You'll find water and wood in the courtyard and food on the table. I'm not particular about how you prepare it." He walked back to his desk.

Inside the kitchen, a head of cabbage, a hambone, two bread chunks, a few carrots, and an onion fought for space on a rickety table piled high with grimy bowls, spoons, and knives. As I approached, a foul odor gagged me. I tied my kerchief around my nose, understanding at once why my teacher was so thin.

Slipping the apron over my dress, I picked up the cooking pot and threw open the door to the courtyard. While the kitchen aired out, I filled the pot from the well and gathered wood for the fire. I opened the tinderbox and tried to remember how our maid had lit a fire. After singeing my fingers, I strained to hang the heavy pot of water above the fire and then tossed in the ham bone. I tried to imitate Mamma's chopping technique with the vegetables, but bits of onion, carrot, and cabbage flew off the table.

Finally, I retrieved all the vegetables and tossed them into the pot. Every few minutes, I dipped a spoon into the broth and tested it for flavor and the vegetables for tenderness. At last I ladled my concoction into a bowl and offered it to Messer Datini.

Sipping a spoonful, he nodded. "A fine stew, Lucia, just like my grandmother's." He pointed to a bowl. "Serve yourself. I can't eat it all. And here, take the other piece of bread."

Exhaustion and hunger stilled my protest, and I savored my own cooking. Then I set to work, scrubbing the crusty dishes and throwing out forgotten remnants of past meals.

Messer Datini stepped into the doorway. "Grazie, Lucia. You've worked long and hard. Now hurry home before dark. A domani."

"Until tomorrow, Messer Datini." I took off my apron, stuffed it in my schoolbag, and put on my cloak. Flinching at every noise in the fading light, I walked home as fast as my weary legs could carry me. With all the strength I could muster, I dragged wood and water into our kitchen, took a deep breath, and started the fire. Then I collapsed on my bed.

When I arrived at Elisabetta's house the next morning, my friend shot me a frosty glance. "Lucia, I didn't know if you'd come today."

Her greeting warmed my cheeks. "It's only after school that I can't walk with you." I knew I must explain.

We set out for school—followed, as usual, by Alberto and Massimo. I searched for words that would speak truth without turning her against me further. "I'm sorry I didn't explain myself yesterday." My voice quavered. "Already I miss your company in the afternoon, but I must stay and help Messer Datini to earn my place in his class."

She raised her brows.

"Elisabetta, I made a mistake, and then something terrible happened. Now we can't pay Messer Datini." I looked her in the eye. "Do you remember when I spoke to Padre Federico after Mass a few weeks ago?"

She nodded.

"That's why the Inquisition arrested my father and sentenced him to prison. How I wish I could take back my words!"

She stopped and stared at me. "Your father's in prison?"

"Sì." I looked down, my cheeks now burning.

She reached her arm around me. "I'm so sorry, Lucia." She shook her head. "If only you'd told me—I thought you were angry with me."

All I could do was nod. If I opened my mouth, I would burst into tears.

She continued, "I can't imagine what my family would do if we lost my father. How will you and your mother get along?"

I inhaled. "Mamma's begun tutoring the medical professors' daughters. We'll get along without a maid, and I'll work for Messer Datini."

She thought for a moment. "Could I help you after school, Lucia?"

Hope surged through me for an instant. Then my better judgment took charge. "Grazie, but I must pay this penalty myself."

I never doubted Elisabetta's loyalty after that conversation, but couldn't bring myself to tell her about the stench in Messer Datini's kitchen. I also kept to myself the prickles of fear I felt during my walks home in darkness, my exhaustion after fetching water and wood, the ache in my fingers each time I had to start a cooking fire, and my revulsion at the smell of smoke and fire.

When Mamma stepped inside the house each evening, my dark mood lifted. Now she walked at a slower pace, but I still saw the joy she found in a beautiful flower or sunset and her gratitude to God as she recited a verse from the Psalms before each meal.

After supper and our cleanup, Mamma sang and brought the strings of her harp to life, just as before Papa's arrest. Since Papa began to teach me science years before, I hadn't paid attention to Mamma's music, but now her dulcet voice and the canary's accompaniment soothed me.

I watched the tension melt out of my mother's face. She taught me to read music so I could follow along and sing with her. Every day, she gave me short daily harp lessons, taking pity on my tender fingers until I developed callouses.

When the music ended, my emptiness returned. I sometimes read the poetry of others—expressions of love, bliss, grief, comfort, or heroic struggle. But more often I picked up a quill and a sheet of paper to pour out my grief in poems of my own.

A few days into this evening routine, I had just set down my quill and pushed back my chair when Mamma glanced at me.

She smiled. "Are you working on a project for school?"

I blushed. "No, I've been writing poems."

"Did Messer Datini assign this?"

"No, Mamma. But the poetry I've read in his class inspires me, and if I can't get a thought or feeling out of my mind, I try to set it into verse. By the time I figure out the poem, I'm not so angry or sad. I sleep better after I write poetry."

She nodded. "As I do after I pray." She touched my shoulder. "I would love to hear your poems."

"The one I wrote tonight tells how much I enjoy your music." I smoothed the sheet and read the poem to her.

She dabbed the corners of her eyes. "Grazie, Lucia. Such beautiful words—you're too kind. Could you read me another?"

I pulled out the poem I wrote the night before, reflecting on how much I missed Papa, wondering if he was well, and what he was doing.

Mamma's tears flowed, and she lifted her apron to wipe her face. "God gave you the gift of poetry. Give thanks to Him, and nurture His gift—use your poems to speak to God and glorify Him." She reached out her arms and embraced me.

My heart swelled. "Grazie, Mamma."

She nodded and put out the lamp. We walked in silence to our bedchambers. In this sweet moment, I forgot my sadness and mulled Mamma's words. I could imagine no calling I would enjoy more than poetry.

Then Papa's image filled my mind, and I remembered all the evenings we spent together talking about scientific theories. Guilt displaced my elation. Would Papa approve of my writing poems instead of studying science? I would give up poetry in an instant to have Papa back.

I lay in bed that night, recalling Papa's admonition that I must use my gifts, but he had also told me not to talk about Luther's beliefs. If I challenged the Church's errors, I would likely bring more calamity upon my family. Should I write poetry instead?

Muting my voice seemed a betrayal of God and my father's principles, but I knew no other way my family could survive. I looked toward the starry heavens beyond my window. "God, what should I do?"

Chapter 9

PESTILENCE STRIKES

Giordano
November 1576

*H*eavy footsteps awakened me, and the light of a torch grew brighter. Squinting, I saw two silhouetted figures approach. The lamp lingered outside my cell, a guard extended his key, and my door squealed open.

"Giordano Locatelli?" The Inquisitor's voice set my heart pounding. Even in daylight, his too enthusiastic tone grated on me. Now I locked my arms together against my chest to keep from shivering.

"Sì, eccomi." I willed my stiff limbs to obey. If I delayed, my jailer might beat me. Pushing myself up from the filthy mattress, I struggled for balance and forced my legs toward the door.

A whirlwind of questions swept through my mind in those few steps: was this midnight interruption designed to break my resistance, force me to supply a list of heretics? Would the Inquisitor's assistants subject me to the *strappado*, again wrenching my arms and shoulders out of joint? They still ached in damp cold, especially here. Or had the Inquisition's tribunal changed my sentence to death, burning at the stake like my student? May God strengthen me.

The Inquisitor stepped inside and locked his gaze with mine. "Doctor Locatelli, pestilence has struck down many in Venezia, far beyond what local physicians can treat. The medical college recommends you as an authority on pestilence, so the Holy Office wishes you to treat the afflicted. If you agree, you will depart for Venezia to-morrow—with an escort, of course. If not, you will remain here until you complete your sentence."

My breath burst from my lungs. "Of course I will serve. I cannot ignore the oath of Hippocrates." I pictured a pestilence hospital teeming with infected people. "But I must have proper supplies to protect myself from pestilence. I can't treat others if I contract the disease myself."

He frowned. "Supplies for a prisoner? Highly irregular."

I eyed him. "Without such protection, my service in Venezia would be a wasted effort, and I would have to decline." As much as I longed to leave my prison cell and practice medicine again, I couldn't take that risk. Too many physicians had died of pestilence.

At last he spoke. "What will you need?"

"At the minimum, several sacks of cedar chips, gloves, a standard bag of physician's supplies, a physician's robe, and a plague doctor's mask. The medical school's pharmacy stocks them all." I paused. "Add these things to the list: a quill, ink, and paper to inform my family before I depart for Venezia."

His gaze lingered. "I can make no promises." He turned away.

Soon both men and the lantern disappeared. I groped my way back to the mattress and huddled under my blanket. One moment I thanked God for the chance to escape my wasted existence in this rat-infested cell, treat patients again, and return to Venezia. The next moment, a mental image of the peril before me quelled my enthusiasm. I whispered a prayer for provision of my supplies and for God to sustain me in Venezia, so far from my beloved Caterina and Lucia. Even with every precaution, only God's protection could ensure I would reunite one day with my family.

Lucia

Just after Mamma and I repeated the Our Father together one evening, a knock disturbed our bedtime routine. Mamma pulled her cloak over her shoulders and strode to the door. I overheard a male voice but nothing more. A moment later, Mamma bolted the door and rushed into my bedchamber.

"Professor Capriolo brought us a letter from your father." She beamed. Breaking the seal, she unfolded a dingy paper sheet and held it close to the lamp.

I jumped out of bed. Side by side, we read:

14 November, 1576

To my dear Caterina and precious Lucia,

God be praised that you are well and have found work to keep bread on your table and Lucia in school! Through my jailer's mercy, I received your letter a few weeks ago. Now I keep it close to my heart. Since the night of my arrest, you have been in my prayers and thoughts day and night, but this is my first and last chance to write you from this prison cell.

The Inquisitor allows me to tell you that I will soon depart for Venezia. Yesterday he informed me that pestilence rages there and asked if I would offer my medical services to the many stricken citizens of that city. As a faithful successor to the great Hippocrates, I took an oath to treat all who seek my aid, so I could not refuse this request. I rejoice in my opportunity to use my knowledge and years of training after so many months of idleness.

Please pray for strength for my weak body and wisdom as I diagnose and treat these patients.

May God protect you until we meet again.

With all my love to you both,

Giordano Locatelli

PS: Don't worry about my health. I know the precautions I must take to avoid pestilence and will follow them strictly.

"What a blessing to hear from him." Mamma set the letter on my desk. Her cheerful words couldn't hide her moist eyes.

I took her hands. "His letter worries me, Mamma. He'll be far away in Venezia, around all those sick people."

She nodded. "Sì, Lucia, but at least he'll be able to use his gifts to heal people who need his help. We must pray all the more for him."

And so we did.

February 1577

Three months had passed since my father departed for Venezia, and still pestilence terrified me each time I thought about its threat to Papa. One morning my fear turned personal. As Elisabetta and I walked to school, we noticed wooden signs nailed to the doors of several houses. A huge X was painted on each sign. Underneath were printed the words: "Pestilence quarantine until," followed by a date. We hurried across the street and stared at each other. I knew from Papa's letter that pestilence had ravaged Venezia, but these signs meant the outbreak had spread to Verona.

Arriving at school, we reported what we had seen. Messer Datini told us that families with quarantine signs on their doors must stay in their homes for forty days so they would not infect others.

Concentration proved difficult that day, even on poetry. I wondered how quickly the pestilence might spread in Verona. Would we need to retreat to the countryside to avoid contagion, telling witty tales to pass the time as did the Florentine characters in Boccaccio's famous *Decameron*? By the time school ended, I could think of little else.

Rushing into Messer Datini's kitchen, I pulled on my apron. I had never cleaned or prepared his food so quickly. When he invited me to join him for the meal, I declined, eager to go home.

Even in the twilight, I noticed new quarantine signs nailed to doors as I walked home. When Mamma finally arrived at our house, I rushed out of the kitchen.

"Mamma, did you see the signs of quarantine?"

She nodded, pale-faced and without her usual smile. "Sì, Lucia. The vegetable vendor told her customers to buy extra food. Verona's health officials may close down the market and force everyone to stay in their homes to stop pestilence from spreading." She glanced down at the brimming market basket in her left hand. "So I'm carrying a heavy load and must take this to the kitchen."

As she turned away, I noticed her slumping shoulders. If only I could help her more so she wouldn't have to work so hard.

Each day brought more quarantine signs. Four days after we saw the first signs, Elisabetta and I came upon corpses in the streets as we walked to school. The bodies lay naked on pallets or boards. We averted our eyes, but not before noticing purplish-black welts around their necks, armpits and private areas. Their clothing lay in ashes next to their bodies. I covered my nose with one hand and picked up my pace.

A hay wagon rattled over the cobblestones toward us. The driver stopped his horse, and two men picked up bodies and tossed them on the wagon. I stared at a pile so high it nearly spilled out of the wagon—the bodies of old men and women, babies and young children, all now treated like refuse. I shuddered.

Wide-eyed, Elisabetta grabbed my arm. "Let's go."

I needed no further prompting. Our feet flew through the streets, and we arrived at school, panting. Three of our schoolmates didn't come to class that day. No one dared ask why or voice our suspicion that pestilence had infected them. Worry blanketed the classroom, and I thought the school day would never end.

At last, our teacher recited a closing prayer, and I hurried through my cooking and cleaning for him. I ran home as fast as I could, trying to avoid the horrifying sights I remembered from the morning. When I reached my home, I wiped beads of sweat from my face and turned the door handle.

As usual, I took my school bag into my bedchamber before gathering wood and water for our evening meal. Glancing into my parents' room, I recoiled. Mamma usually tutored girls in their homes at this hour, but she lay curled on her bed, shivering.

"Mamma! What's wrong?" I dropped my bag and rushed over to the bed.

She twisted her face toward me and whispered, "I'm freezing, then burning hot." She sank back into her coverlet.

I gasped. Mamma must never end up like the unfortunates I saw in the street. What should I do? If only Papa were here to help her, instead of treating the sick in Venezia.

"Lucia..." Mamma gasped for breath.

When I realized she wouldn't finish her sentence, I forced myself to take a deep breath and imagine what my mother would do if she found me in this condition. Closing my eyes, I pictured her at my bedside during a childhood fever. I snatched a blanket from the foot of the bed and spread it over Mamma's crumpled form. Then I ran to the kitchen for a cup of water and a damp cloth.

"Drink, Mamma!" I placed the cup at her lips. Water leaked out of her mouth into her hair, ears, and clothing. "I'm sorry, I'll get a spoon. Here's a cool cloth for your fever." I placed the damp rag on her forehead and returned to the kitchen.

When I lifted a spoonful of water to her mouth, water trickled down Mamma's chin. She turned her face away and closed her eyes. I sighed and stared at her. I could read Greek, but I couldn't put water in Mamma's mouth.

"All right, Mamma, I'll let you rest. But I'll be back soon." I trudged into my bedchamber and sat at my desk, tapping my feet. Should I stay by my mother's side or seek help from Professor Capriolo? My father's friend might know how to contact Papa. I couldn't decide which would help Mamma more.

I glanced toward my mother's bedchamber. With Mamma's life at stake, I mustn't waste time. I sprang to my feet and stepped into her room. She slept and breathed normally. Tension drained from my shoulders, and I relaxed my clenched fists. Perhaps rest would cure Mamma. I tiptoed out of the room, and images of corpses in the streets flashed into my mind.

I couldn't take a chance that Mamma would come to such an end, so I had to find Professor Capriolo. I hadn't taken off my cloak, so I hurried out the front door and ran down the dark street, around the corner, past the Roman theater and the stone bridge. I gasped for breath but forced myself to continue until I reached the Capriolos' house. I pounded on the front door and pushed my hair out of my face. The door opened just wide enough for me to see Signora Capriolo's wiry black hair and sunken eyes.

"Lucia? What a surprise." She turned away from the doorway, whispering and gesturing to someone behind her.

"*Per favore*, signora—it's important!" I called in my loudest voice.

Signora Capriolo returned to the doorway. "Forgive me for the wait, but I had to make sure Angelina and Cristina didn't run out the door." Her cheeks flushed, and she wiped her brow. "They worry me to death, and I can't keep up with them." She sighed.

"This is urgent, signora. May I come in?" I peered inside.

She opened the door and I slipped inside. "Is something wrong, Lucia?"

"It's an emergency—I must speak with Professor Capriolo. My mother is in bed, burning with fever. I don't know how to help her. We need my father's help, but I don't know how to contact him."

Susanna Capriolo shook her head in disbelief. "Not Caterina! Your saintly mother has already endured so much."

"Come with me." Linking her arm with mine, she led me past tiny shoes and stockings strewn in the sala, and through the disheveled bedchamber. She stopped outside her husband's study and rapped on the door. "Domenico, we need your help."

The door cracked open. When Professor Capriolo saw me, his brows arched. "What is it?"

"An emergency, Domenico. Lucia will explain." Susanna Capriolo pushed the door wide, prodded me through the doorway, and stepped back.

A sharp aroma struck my nostrils. Then I noticed the cup of red wine in Professor Capriolo's hand and the cluster of bottles on the floor. I felt his gaze and looked up.

Face to face with him, I searched for the right words and threw back my shoulders. "Professor Capriolo, I'm worried pestilence has struck my mother."

His eyes widened. He stood rigid, and his mouth curved down at each end. I wondered if he believed me. His stare threatened my concentration. Had he no sympathy for my family?

"My father can save her, but you must bring him back from Venezia." I looked him straight in the eye.

Professor Capriolo nodded. "No one knows more about pestilence than Giordano. He can cure your mother, if anyone can." He set down his cup, stroked his beard and looked at the floor.

Silence hung like a heavy curtain between us. I locked my jaw and shifted my weight from one foot to the other. The tension in the room seemed about to explode when my godfather threw back his auburn locks and brown beret.

He sighed and looked up. "If only I could save her myself. I owe Giordano too much to refuse this request." He glanced back at his wife. "When I look at you, Susanna, I see the beautiful woman I met only because Giordano was my friend."

Turning back to me he continued, "And you, Lucia, remind me of my debt to Giordano's family. Their warm welcome me made me feel more at home in their house than my own." He set back his shoulders. "My lectures, my writing, must wait. I will go to Venezia and bring him back." He looked at his wife, then at me, and nodded. "Sì, I must go."

I stared at my godfather, and a lump clogged my throat. I could only whisper, "*Tante* grazie, Professor Capriolo. How can I ever repay you?"

"Prego, Lucia." Domenico Capriolo's face reddened, and he turned away. "I must leave at once." He picked up his leather medical bag, threw several small cloth bags inside, and stepped past me into his bedchamber.

I turned toward the doorway and waited for Signora Capriolo to escort me out to the sala. But she stood motionless, as if she had forgotten I waited in her husband's study. She bit her lip and wiped the corners of her eyes. Without a glance at me, she closed the door to the bedchamber.

Abandoned in the study, I overheard her sniffle. "Prego, Domenico, you mustn't go to Venezia. How can you avoid the pestilence? Our family will starve if you die. Don't go, I beg you!"

"I'm sorry, but I must. I can't leave Caterina here to die while Giordano remains in Venezia. I could never forgive myself. If ever his expertise were needed, it is now." He paused. "I'll take every precaution, Susanna."

I heard nothing further except footsteps. When the bedchamber quieted, I knocked on the door. Hearing no response, I let myself out and walked toward the sala.

Professor Capriolo finished his goodbyes to his family. Then he stepped out the front door, paused, and turned toward me. "Lucia, I must confirm your mother's condition before I journey to Venezia. Walk with me to your home, and I'll talk with you about your mother's care."

"Grazie, Professor Capriolo." I could hardly believe my ears.

He glanced at me. "Lucia, you will need all your wisdom and strength to keep your mother alive until Giordano returns. I have little special knowledge of pestilence, but I can give you a few instructions about how to treat a fever. Give your mother plenty of water to drink, cool cloths to bring down the fever. If her stomach can tolerate it, give her broth to sustain her. And do you have an herb garden?"

I nodded. Thank goodness for Mamma's gardening skills.

"Then gather rosemary and juniper branches. Burn them in the fireplace to kill the sickness and keep it from spreading."

Just before we entered my house, he stopped, pulled a small cloth bag from his satchel, and handed me the strings. "You must protect yourself, Lucia. Tie these cedar chips around your neck and wear them whenever you're near your mother. Giordano told me they keep the pestilence away from those who care for the infected."

After he tied a bag of cedar chips around his own neck, I led him through the house to my mother's bedchamber. Mamma lay half-awake, trembling and moaning. Professor Capriolo pulled on gloves and rolled up one of her sleeves. He looked under her arm, sighed, and smoothed her sleeve back in place. Then he strode out of the room, stripping off his gloves.

He stopped in the sala, shaking his head at me. "The swelling under her armpit leaves no doubt. Your mother is infected with pestilence." He bowed and kissed my hand. "I must find a ship bound for Venezia. May God save us all." He raced out the door toward the Adige River.

As he headed away, my heart pounded. Now all responsibility for keeping Mamma alive fell to me until Papa returned from Venezia—and the journey would take days. I took a deep breath, recalled Professor Capriolo's instructions, and came to my senses. Straightening my shoulders, I headed for Mamma's herb garden in the courtyard.

Giordano
Venezia, Winter, 1577

From dawn to dusk, I treated men, women, and children whose family members showed signs of pestilence. After months at the *lazzaretto nuovo* on this isolated Venetian island, I no longer startled at moans, cries, or fetid odors. Instead, I fought exhaustion and the inner voice that daily ridiculed my choice to serve here. Now I trudged to the hospital kitchen before the next boatload of Venetians arrived for their quarantine.

When a nun handed me a steaming bowl of black stew, I relished my meal. I told her, "grazie," and meant it. By this time I knew the stew would silence my growling stomach and that the muddy color came from cuttlefish. Sinking into a chair, I lifted a spoon to my mouth and savored the fragrance, warmth, and rich flavor.

"Giordano, is that you?" The deep voice sounded familiar, but from the distant past.

I whirled around and saw only another physician, unrecognizable in his plague mask, gloves, and voluminous robe. "Sì, eccomi."

The man ran toward me and pulled off his mask.

"Domenico!" I could scarcely trust my eyes.

We threw our arms around each other.

"What are you doing here, my friend?"

His smile vanished. "I came on a desperate mission, Giordano." He clasped my hand. "Pestilence has struck Caterina."

I pulled away. "No—not my Caterina! Are you sure? The contagion has spread to Verona?"

He nodded. "I've seen her."

My shoulders fell. "But she's alive?"

"Sì, and your daughter cares for her day and night. I told Lucia all I know about treating pestilence and promised I'd fetch you home to treat your wife."

"But I can't leave—I'm still a prisoner."

"The Inquisitor will allow you to return to Verona to treat Caterina—if I take your place here until you come back."

My jaw dropped. "You would do that for me, Domenico?"

He nodded. "I owe you debts I can never repay. Tell me how to help these people, and pack your bag. The Inquisitor's messenger leaves for Verona in the morning—he'll escort you."

From that moment, I thought of nothing but Caterina's survival. My supper lost its appeal, and I forced down the remainder only to protect my health.

I retired early to gather strength for my journey, but Caterina's plight kept me awake long into the night. Her beauty, her goodness, her devotion to God—He couldn't let her die! He wouldn't take away the angel who loved me even more than I loved her. As the night wore on, Caterina's image blurred in my mind.

Before dawn, a red-haired youth shook me awake. "I'm Gianpietro, messenger for the Holy Office. Gather what you need for the trip and meet me at the wharf."

I left a note for Domenico, put on my cloak, and carried my physician's bag to the dinghy where Gianpietro waited. With only a small lantern to light our way, we set off across Venezia's lagoon. Gianpietro displayed the Inquisitor's safe-conduct pass at each checkpoint, but even so, health inspectors outside each town forced us to disrobe to prove we bore no signs of the contagion.

Every delay could mean the difference between life and death for Caterina. My patience neared the breaking point, and I whispered one prayer after another for Caterina's healing, for Lucia's protection from the contagion, and for strength to attend to her mother's needs.

Thanks to the Inquisitor's orders, we hired fresh horses as often as our mounts tired. As we galloped toward Verona, my quest to save Caterina overshadowed my grim memories of arrest and imprisonment there.

After we passed through the city gate, I led my escort down familiar streets to my home. He took charge of my horse and instructed me to report to the Inquisitor's office before I left Verona.

I rushed to the door and pounded it. With each moment I waited, my hands trembled more. Had my family abandoned the house or worse, perished inside? I searched my medical bag for a tool to force open the door.

Chapter 10

DIMINISHED

Lucia

In my nightmare, the Inquisition's agents pounded on the front door, about to drag my father away to prison. I dug my fingernails into the palms of my hands. Awakening, I moaned—I had just fallen asleep and now this terrible dream. Surely, I deserved some rest. When Mamma was feverish, I brought cold water and removed her coverlet. When chills seized her, I covered her. Day and night, over and over again.

As the rapping continued, I realized this was no dream. Maybe someone had come to help. I must answer the door. I rubbed my eyes and struggled to free myself from the nest of blankets on the floor beside my mother's bed. Pulling on my cloak, I staggered to the door. "Who's there?"

"Eccomi, Giordano!" His voice confirmed his identity.

I swung the door open and scarcely recognized the haggard, hollow-eyed man on the step. I stared at his bushy mustache and beard, the cheeks as pale as chalk. "Papa?"

"Sì." Flashing a wan smile, he took off his hat, clutched his medical bag, and limped toward Mamma's bedchamber. "I must help your mother."

I tried not to gawk as he passed. I saw only a trace of the commanding presence I remembered. His time in prison and medical service in Venezia had stolen his strength and vitality.

My mind snapped back to Mamma's plight. "*Si*, Mamma is burning with fever. You must save her, Papa. Thank God you're here at last!"

He reached into his bag and pulled out an odd-looking mask with a long beak. Covering his face with the mask, he pulled on his hat and strode toward the bedchamber. I followed close behind. When he reached the doorway, he paused and grabbed a large fabric square from his bag.

"Always cover your nose and mouth before you come near an infected person." He handed the kerchief to me. Then he knelt at Mamma's bedside and grasped her wrist.

I couldn't stop staring at the mask—with its long hooked beak and black circles around the eyeholes, it resembled a ghoulish pelican.

"Caterina, I'm here. I'll take care of you." Papa's voice came from inside the mask, muffled but smooth as velvet. He picked up Mamma's other wrist and held both of her hands.

My mother lay with her face away from him and didn't respond.

"Caterina!" He turned her face toward him and gasped. "No!" He placed her hands down gently and took off his mask. "Come back, my love," he whispered.

He wiped his eyes and faced me. "She's gone, Lucia." His voice was flat. "May God rest her soul." He turned his gaze back to Mamma.

"What?" I ran to Mamma's bedside. Her face was ashen, her features frozen like a statue.

"No, it can't be!" I rushed into Papa's arms. "I tried my hardest to save her, but nothing could help her." I choked back tears. "If only you'd been here, Mamma wouldn't have died!" I pulled away and glared at my father. "Why didn't you come sooner, Papa?"

"Lucia, I..." His voice broke. "I would have given anything, my very life, to save your mother. If only I could have been here when she needed me, instead of in Venezia!"

I winced. How could I have spoken such words? "Forgive me, Papa. I know the Inquisition held you prisoner, so you had no choice." I held his hands with a tight grip.

He nodded. "If Professor Capriolo hadn't come, I would still be in Venezia. He risked his life coming to that pestilence-infested city. The Holy Office allowed me to leave only when he agreed to stay and take my place attending the sick until I return."

My throat tightened. "You must go back? What will happen to me?"

He wrapped his arms around me. "I'll speak to the bishop and ask him to plead for my release. Don't worry, Lucia, I won't abandon you."

I relaxed within my father's embrace. He appeared feeble, but his strength held me up.

At last, I stood back and looked up at him. His eyes had clouded over, like a winter sky before a snowstorm. "Papa, are you all right?"

He sighed. "Every day in prison, my dream of coming home to you and Caterina helped me endure the long, empty hours. Your mother was the love of my life, and now I must wait to meet her in paradise.

"I thought the worst had passed, that I would enjoy life with my family again." He looked toward the heavens. "May God bring his vengeance down on the Inquisition for taking me away so I couldn't save Caterina!" He sighed. "We can do nothing more tonight, Lucia, but rest and gather strength for what lies ahead. The morning will bring new challenges." He picked up my blankets. "Sleep in your own bedchamber tonight, Lucia—away from this infected room. I'll sleep in the sala."

I nodded and stretched out on my bed. Huddled under my coverlet, I tried to believe I had read a story from a book instead of viewing Mamma's lifeless body and Papa's grief.

The next thing I remember, Papa stood beside me, trying to smile. "*Buon giorno*, Lucia. God be praised, I still have you, my dear daughter."

"Thank God you're here, Papa. What would I do without you?" I pulled myself into a sitting position and embraced him.

He sighed. "I must go now to arrange a Christian burial for your mother."

A faraway look came into his eyes. "Caterina always loved the rose window at San Zeno Maggiore. I'll ask the bishop if we can bury her body in the churchyard."

He placed his hands on my shoulders. "Lucia, while I'm out, please do a special favor for your mother—and for me." He looked into my eyes. "Before we bury her, put on my gloves and smooth her hair. Remember to cover your nose and mouth with the kerchief."

Now I couldn't deny Mamma's death. As my father walked out the door, I dragged myself to my feet and turned toward Mamma's bedchamber. Standing in the doorway, I tied on my kerchief and stared at her. The juices in my stomach rose toward my throat. I turned away and gasped for air—the sight of her lifeless body was more than I could bear. Then I thought about what my father had suffered because of me and the sacrifices my mother had made for me. I combed her hair and wiped her face with a cloth.

Then I returned to my room and lay down. Papa's footsteps roused me from fitful dreams. He squatted down beside me.

"Are you ill, Lucia?" I heard the worry in his voice as he examined my eyes, ears, and throat.

"No, Papa, I'm just exhausted." I yawned and pulled the bag of cedar chips from under my shift. "Professor Capriolo gave me this before he went to Venezia. I've worn it around my neck ever since."

He smiled. "Thank God. I've relied on cedar chips for years." He took my hands. "Thanks to the bishop, we can bury your mother outside San Zeno this evening. But after her burial, I must return to Venezia. The bishop begged for my release but couldn't change the Inquisitor's mind. Until the pestilence subsides I must stay in Venezia attending the sick."

"So soon, Papa?" I squeezed his hands. "Can I go with you?"

"I wish I could stay here with you." He sighed. "I'm still a prisoner and can't take care of you."

"Could I stay with Elisabetta's family?"

He shook his head. "Your godparents, the Capriolos, have offered to take you in. We couldn't impose on Elisabetta's family."

"But Papa, I know Elisabetta far better than the Capriolos." Recalling Signora Capriolo's reception when I knocked on her door, I fought back tears.

"I'm sorry, Lucia. When Professor Capriolo found me in Venezia, he reaffirmed his commitment to sheltering you at his home if Mamma and I couldn't take care of you. He's proud to be your godfather—he marveled at your courage when you asked him to fetch me from Venezia."

His gentle tone of voice offered comfort but not the response I wanted to hear. I wiped my eyes and prayed for a quick end to the pestilence in Venezia so Papa could return to me.

The next morning, cooing doves and the sunshine's warmth enhanced a dream of my happy childhood, surrounded by my books and notebooks, with my parents sleeping on the other side of my wall.

When I awakened, Papa had already left for Venezia. If he had let me go with him, I would have taken my chances with pestilence, rather than stay in Verona without him.

Without my father's comforting presence, my fresh, painful memories returned, and I cried out, "God, how could you let Mamma die?"

I strode out of my bedchamber, and my anger turned to sorrow. I wandered through the house, trying to fix the details in my memory: Papa's study full of books, the kitchen where Mamma had prepared our meals, the wall hanging she stitched with her favorite psalm. Then I noticed the empty birdcage in the corner. Mamma's canary had disappeared and with it, another happy memory. I had grown to enjoy the bird's company, had even sung with it as Mamma had.

I glanced into my parents' empty bedchamber and burst into tears. I would be glad to leave that sight behind. I ran to my room, threw myself on my bed, and wept for the things I would miss and even more for Mamma.

At last I sat up and remembered Mamma's courage and her resourcefulness after the Inquisition seized Papa. What would she do now if she were in my place?

Before I packed, I stepped into my father's study. Papa's *cassone*, a leather traveling chest, caught my eye. He wouldn't need it now, so I picked it up.

Back in my bedchamber, my eyes turned to the stack of books next to my bed. I longed to fill the chest with books and leave my clothes behind, but I could almost hear Mamma clucking her tongue, "Lucia, you must be practical." So I packed my clothing first before adding my books.

When the chest would hold nothing more, I carried it to the kitchen and set it on the table. I stuffed a burlap bag with all the remaining food: bread, cheese, apples, carrots, and cabbage.

I didn't want to be a burden to Signora Capriolo. My mother had once asked Papa why the family of a professor of medicine should be in such dire straits. Papa had shrugged, "Three *bambini* to feed."

A knock sounded at the door. "Lucia, are you there?"

I recognized Susanna Capriolo's thin voice. She couldn't wait even a moment for me to answer. I sighed. If she had so little patience for me now, what kind of life must I endure in her home?

"*Vengo*, signora," I walked toward the front door, still holding the bag of food in the crook of one arm. *Summon your courtesy, Lucia.* I could almost hear my mother's voice. I took a deep breath and swung the door open.

Struggling for breath, she clutched my arm.

"*Buon giorno*, signora; you were kind to come for me. Come in, please." I guided her to a chair. "Sit down and I'll bring you a drink of water."

Signora Capriolo nodded.

I walked to the kitchen and shook my head in amazement. Even this short walk taxed her. I wondered what had attracted my father to her so long ago.

How often Papa had boasted to us that when Professor Capriolo won away Susanna's affection and married her years before, he had done the greatest possible favor. "He left me free to find the greatest treasure among women—my Caterina, a woman without guile, whose lovely countenance is surpassed only by her inner beauty." In spite of my father's flowery language, I knew he was sincere. The memory brought tears to my eyes.

"Lucia, we need to go." When I returned with a cup of water, she explained. "Stefano is minding Cristina and Angelina. Thank God, he remains at home so he can watch them. His teacher suspended class because of pestilence." She sighed. "What troubles will my children cause without me?"

I smiled and tried to imagine Stefano taking care of his toddler sisters.

"Of course, signora. I was gathering food to bring along. I'll get my bags." Returning to my bedchamber, I put on my cloak. With my bags slung over my shoulders, I marched out to the sala.

"Pronto, signora." I consoled myself—now I wouldn't have to see where Mamma died.

Susanna Capriolo stepped outside. I followed, locking the door behind me and praying I could return soon.

As we trudged through the streets, I watched the ground, trying to avoid piles of rotting food and household goods tossed from pestilence-ridden houses. Even though my bags were heavy and their cords cut into my shoulders, I had to slow my pace for Signora Capriolo.

At last we reached the steps in front of the Capriolo home. When their mother unlocked the front door, the twins burst outside.

"Come Lucia." Angelina grabbed my arm.

"Lucia, you get to share our room!" Cristina grinned and hopped in place.

I turned to Signora Capriolo.

She nodded and gestured toward the back of the house. "Sì, put your things in their bedchamber. We'll arrange your bedding later."

I handed her my bag of food. "Here, signora—for your family."

"Grazie, Lucia." Susanna Capriolo poured out the sack's contents onto the kitchen table and smiled.

I carried my traveling chest into the cramped bedchamber. The little girls' mattresses, bedding, and clothing covered the entire floor, save one corner. With barely enough clear space to sleep, how would I find a place to read, study, or protect my precious books?

I set my cassone in the empty corner and curled up on the floor beside it, burying my face in the crook of my arm.

Stefano

Life turned awkward the day Lucia moved in with us. Every morning, she watched me head out to school but didn't say a word. I knew she had always enjoyed our class more than I did. It wasn't right that now I was the one who went while she had to stay home and help my mother. I felt bad.

The day after Lucia came, Messer Datini handed me a message for her. After cena that evening, she wrote notes to our teacher and Elisabetta. I delivered them the next morning.

When I got home from school and pulled out my homework, she asked me what I learned that day. Then she told me how her father used to teach her about medicine. She looked happy for a moment and asked if my father did the same for me. When I shook my head, she got quiet.

The next day, my father came home from Venezia. Late that evening, I was finishing an assignment in the sala. Lucia was reading across the room from me. Suddenly, we heard my parents' raised voices from their bedchamber on the other side of the wall.

"We're her godparents. It's our duty to care for her." Papa's voice boomed.

"But Domenico, how can we provide for her?"

"Stefano must be close to finishing his schooling, so we won't have to pay his teacher much longer."

"We don't know how long it will be. How can we survive until then?"

"You're a resourceful woman, Susanna. You've always found a way to feed our family."

"I let the kitchen maid go to pay for Stefano's schooling. Then I had to stop buying meat. Now what must I do, Domenico—starve my children and make them go naked?"

We heard nothing more.

My cheeks burned, and I looked at my feet. Didn't they know Lucia and I could hear them?

From the corner of my eye, I saw Lucia pick up her book and walk out of the room. She didn't say *buona notte*, didn't even look at me.

I sat there holding my book but couldn't pay attention to the words. Maybe I should quit school to help out my family, but what I really wanted was to never have to face Lucia again.

Lucia

Only my exhaustion allowed me any sleep that night. I wanted to run to Elisabetta's house or even beg for food and live by myself at home rather than stay here—but I didn't dare leave. Papa had insisted I stay with the Capriolos, and someday I would have to face him. As much as I wanted to escape, I remembered all too well what had happened the last time I disobeyed him.

The next morning, I awoke to the sound of the twins' giggling and whispering on the mattress next to me. Feigning sleep, I arose only after they ran out of the bedchamber. After washing my face and slipping on my apron, I pulled a quill and a sheet of paper out of my traveling chest, hoping to write a poem. But I had no ink and found none in the room, so I ventured out to the sala and noticed an inkwell on a desk. Since I was alone, I pulled up a chair and reached my quill into the ink.

Angelina's voice rang out. "Mamma, I'm hungry. Get me some food."

"Me too, Mamma." Cristina echoed.

The little girls tugged at Signora Capriolo's skirts as she poked her head into the sala. "*Buon giorno*, Lucia. Join us in the kitchen if you want to eat before we go to Mass."

"Grazie, signora." My concentration destroyed, I set down my quill and wondered when I would find a quiet moment to think and write.

An hour later, the twins, Stefano, their mother, and I had consumed a loaf of bread, and the family dispersed again.

Signora Capriolo brushed crumbs off the kitchen table with her hand and threw them outside for the birds. She called to her children, "Stefano, Cristina, Angelina, pronto! It's time to leave for Mass."

My stomach churned. If only I had a compelling reason to stay behind. Even though many months had passed since my father's arrest, the weekly pilgrimage to Mass still stirred up my hatred for Padre Federico and my suspicions that he had betrayed me to the Inquisition.

Now San Zeno Maggiore also brought back memories of Mamma, and with them, the pain of losing her. With Mamma's death such a fresh memory, I couldn't imagine standing all the way through Mass without bursting into tears.

Even if I explained my distress to Signora Capriolo, I couldn't count on her sympathy. At my age, I knew I shouldn't show such childish weakness. I must go with them to Mass, or they might grow suspicious of me. In spite of my father's lifelong friendship with Professor Capriolo, his family might wonder if heresy ran in the Locatelli family. I must go to Confession, attend Mass, take the Eucharist, and give them no reason to suspect that I strayed in any way from the Church's teachings.

When Stefano ambled into the kitchen, his mother disappeared into the twins' bedchamber. She returned with her daughters in tow.

"Mamma, where's Papa? Isn't he coming?" Angelina pulled on her mother's arm.

Signora Capriolo sighed. "Papa's still asleep. He must be exhausted from his trip, so we won't disturb him. He can go to Mass by himself later. *Andiamo.* Let's go." Holding a twin on each side, she turned toward the door. "Stefano?"

Stefano lurched to his feet. "Sì, Mamma." He yanked open the door. I resigned myself to following the others along the riverbank toward San Zeno Maggiore. But Signora Capriolo headed in the opposite direction.

"Where are we going, signora?" I couldn't restrain my curiosity.

"To San Stefano." She cocked her head toward me. "What did you expect?"

I shrugged my shoulders and relaxed. Now I wouldn't have to face Padre Federico and my memories of San Zeno. "My family always attended San Zeno Maggiore."

She shook her head. "Why did you walk so far? There's a church only fifty paces away. Isn't one church as good as another?"

I held my tongue. Even if I won the argument, Signora Capriolo might not care to hear about Mamma's love of the rose window and carved doors at San Zeno. Mamma's image lingered in my mind, and I blinked back tears.

When we arrived at San Stefano, I realized I had walked by the church many times without paying it any attention. As at San Zeno, San Stefano's façade featured an arch above its front entrance, but the similarity ended there. When I entered the church with the Capriolos, I saw none of the striking artwork that had drawn my family to San Zeno and little that would lift my thoughts to the Creator.

While we waited in line for the confessional, I watched parishioners queuing to enter the sanctuary. Suddenly I spotted Elisabetta with her brothers and parents. My heart hammered my ribs. I grinned and waved to catch her eye. She smiled back but stayed with her family. Then she disappeared into the dim sanctuary with them, a fleeting reminder of the life I had lost.

My hope of renewing our friendship drained out of me like water from a cracked pot. While I lived with the Capriolos, the most I could hope for was an occasional glimpse of Elisabetta.

At last we finished our confessions and entered the sanctuary. In this unfamiliar church, I could go through the motions of Mass, responding by rote with the rest of the congregation. If I focused on keeping Angelina and Cristina quiet, I might not think about my grief.

I glanced around the plain sanctuary and a crucifix caught my eye. For the first time, I saw myself in the forlorn, tortured body of Jesus. This wooden carving evoked feelings I had never dared to acknowledge, even to myself—hopelessness and a sense of God's betrayal. Jesus was perfect, yet he had suffered and died. God raised Jesus from the dead, giving him new life. Hope stirred in me that God would redeem my life as well.

A few days after Professor Capriolo's return, I realized I couldn't ask him to instruct me in science or anything else. Even Stefano rarely caught his father at home long enough to ask him questions. As far as I could tell, Domenico Capriolo came home only to eat and sleep. He was always too busy to spend time with his family—so different from my father.

As much as I envied Stefano's opportunity to attend school, I felt sorry for him. His father never seemed to notice him. The twins demanded Signora Capriolo's time and energy, so Stefano received little attention from either of his parents. Maybe he felt as lonely as I did after my father was arrested. I tried to show sympathy, but Stefano sometimes tried my patience.

Arriving home from school one afternoon, he took his schoolbooks and papers into the sala, placed them on a small table, and sat in the padded chair nearby. He insisted the twins stay out of the sala so he could study, but promptly fell asleep for the rest of the afternoon. When he woke up, the sun was setting and the room was dark.

Stefano yawned. "How long until cena, Mamma? I'm too hungry to finish my schoolwork."

"Supper's ready, Stefano, but your father's not home yet." She shrugged her shoulders and placed a loaf of bread on the table.

We waited and finally lit the lamps. The cabbage and rutabaga stew no longer steamed. Our stomachs growled, and the twins begged their mother for supper.

Glancing toward the front door, Signora Capriolo sighed. "*Mangia, mangia!* Come to the table. Your father must have a meeting at the university. We'll save him some food."

Angelina and Cristina raced to their places. Their mother and I pushed in the twins' chairs and then took our seats. Stefano sat down and stared at his father's empty chair.

Only the little girls filled their stomachs and promptly fell asleep in their chairs. Signora Capriolo, Stefano, and I startled at every noise from outside, staring toward the front door. Stefano left the table and returned to the sala.

After I carried the girls to their bed, I took my Greek book back to the sala and pulled up a chair near Stefano. I hoped he would tell me what he learned at school, but a scowl had replaced his normally jovial expression.

"Did I disturb you?"

"No, I was just hungry because supper was so late." He avoided my gaze.

"Does your father often have late meetings? I don't remember that my father did." Papa had always returned promptly, eager for supper and evenings with Mamma and me. I had always assumed every family was like mine.

"I don't know. He doesn't tell us much." He clenched his jaw and looked down at his book.

"I'm sorry, Stefano." I tried to change the subject. "What did Messer Datini teach in class today?"

At that moment, something slammed against the front door. Signora Capriolo hurried out of the kitchen and stared at her son. "Stefano, get up and see what happened! If robbers are trying to break in, you must drive them away."

He leapt from his chair and rushed to the door.

"Who goes there?" He called out in his loudest voice.

"Eccomi, your papa." Professor Capriolo slurred his words.

Stefano unlocked the door and cracked it open. When he swung the door wide, I saw his father lying across the porch step, rubbing a lump on his forehead.

"Papa, what happened?"

"I was looking for my key and tripped." He moaned. "I hit my head when I fell."

Signora Capriolo joined Stefano in the doorway. Stepping outside, each grabbed one of Professor Capriolo's arms, pulled him to his feet, and guided him inside. As they walked him through the sala toward his bedchamber, the odor of wine assaulted my nose.

I looked at my feet and wondered how Stefano and his mother must feel, and how many other evenings, how much of his family's livelihood, Professor Capriolo had wasted the same way.

A few minutes later, Stefano slunk into the sala, his eyes downcast, and sank into his chair. He picked up his book.

I glanced at him. "I'm glad your father came home."

He ground his teeth and looked at the floor. Then he blurted out, "Lucia, why do you waste your time studying Greek? What possible use can it be to a girl like you? I wouldn't study it myself if the teacher didn't insist. It takes so much effort, and what will I gain from it?"

I stared at him. "How can you mean that, Stefano? My father told me that learning Greek was like getting the key to a treasure room. Without it, you can never see the treasures, but you can enjoy each gem at your leisure once you have the key. I love to read the adventures of Homer and think about the ideas of Plato and Aristotle. Such treasures are worth a bit of effort."

"You're a strange one, Lucia. A pretty girl like you shouldn't worry about such things." He pushed back his chair and walked away.

I fixed my eyes on the book and pressed my lips together. My cheeks burned. I didn't look up until I heard the click of Stefano's door.

Had he meant his comments as a joke, a compliment, or an insult? I knew only that Stefano didn't understand me or appreciate what I valued. After what I had learned about the Capriolo family that evening, I realized I could rely only on myself. Before me loomed the life of a servant—the drudgery of cooking, cleaning, and caring for the twins. Perhaps this was further punishment for ignoring my father's warnings.

My mind went back to the evenings in Papa's study, his encouragement and challenges for my mind. Aching for his presence, I prayed for his quick return and cried myself to sleep.

Chapter 11

DEVIL'S BARGAIN

Stefano
Spring, 1577

I did it! No more listening to lectures, inking my quill, or writing about boring things.

Messer Datini told our class that three of us had completed his curriculum. On the way out the door, I turned to my friend, Giovanni.

"We're so lucky—we'll never have to come back to this classroom or answer the teacher's questions again. What will you do now? "

He grinned. "I'm going to study at Padova in the fall."

I shook my head. "You want more of this torture?"

He shrugged his shoulders. "How else can I become a lawyer? I'm lucky I'm the oldest—my younger brother will be a priest or monk, and my little sister will have to join a convent or marry whomever my father chooses. I'll get the best life, so I can't complain." He looked my direction. "What about you?"

"I don't know." The end of my school days caught me by surprise. My father had never mentioned my becoming a doctor or professor like him. I don't remember the last time he asked me about my studies.

Back at home, I blurted out my good news to my mother.

She threw her arms around me. "I'm so proud of you, son. I knew you were a bright boy." She stepped back and looked me in the eye.

"Now it's time for you to help our family. I'm counting on you, Stefano—you know we need every *soldo* you can earn."

Her words took me back to a conversation we had the morning I began my schooling, years ago. I knocked on the door of my father's study and asked him for money to pay my teacher. He sent me off to my mother, told me she managed the family's finances.

When I repeated Papa's words to Mamma, her face turned white, and I thought she might faint. She finally pulled open her bag of coins and spoke slowly. "I'll do what I must so you can attend school, Stefano. But we won't be eating meat any longer."

From that day on, our family ate Lenten meals all year long. When my mother's clothes wore out, she cut them up and sewed clothes for my sisters. The sparkle disappeared from her eyes, along with her laughter.

I had good times with friends during my school years, and Lucia livened up the dull moments. She was never afraid to ask questions. Too bad she had to stop coming. As for me, I just wasn't interested in old stories. And why did I need to learn other languages? I could read and write, and that was enough for me.

But now I had to help support my family and show Mamma she hadn't wasted her money on my schooling. If I was lucky, maybe I could make my father proud of me, too. I needed advice but didn't know whom to ask.

After Sunday morning Mass, I was about to leave the church when I saw the priest who taught my confirmation class. I told him my dilemma.

He looked at me and nodded. "My son, you have a good heart. I can see a future ahead of you, a future in the Church."

"But Padre Tommaso, I couldn't be a priest!"

He smiled and put his hand on my shoulder. "Don't worry, Stefano. Only those with a special call should become priests. But you read and write Latin, don't you?"

"Sì, Padre." I tried not to groan. Latin required so much thinking, and I wanted to forget it now that I was finished with school.

"So you can serve the Church by working for the Holy Office as a clerk. I'll speak to Father Inquisitor."

"The Holy Office—the Inquisition!" I gasped. I was no religious zealot, no spy, no torturer. "I couldn't do that work, padre."

His eyes wouldn't let me escape. "Stefano, you could help to provide for your family. What could make your parents prouder than seeing their son serving the Church?"

"But padre..." I had no passion for the Church, especially for its discipline.

He tapped my shoulder. "We'll speak again, Stefano. *Buona sera.*" With a nod, he turned and walked away.

"*Buona sera*, Padre Tommaso." I stared at the back of his brown robe until he disappeared into the confessional.

What had I done? Anyone who knew me could tell that I—fun-loving Stefano—didn't belong in the Inquisition. My gut ached. Padre Tommaso wouldn't forget our conversation. If I couldn't come up with a better idea, I would face a life sentence copying Latin for the Inquisition.

About a week later, I began my work for the Holy Office. That evening, my family's questions began as soon as I took off my boots and walked into the sala. Before I sat down to eat, my mother greeted me.

"*Buona sera*, Stefano. Tell us about your work." Mamma and my sisters gazed at me, but my father and Lucia looked down at their bowls.

I squared my shoulders. "When I arrived this morning, Father Inquisitor required me to take an oath of secrecy about all the business of the Inquisition, under penalty of death. So I can't talk about my work."

"But surely you can tell us something!" Mamma wouldn't give up.

"Well, it's not as exciting as you might suppose. I did a lot of writing, mostly copying documents." I smiled at her. "For so many years, you insisted I must practice my handwriting. Today I received my reward when Father Inquisitor told me I had a fine chancery cursive."

She reached over to squeeze my hand. "I always knew you would turn out well, Stefano."

"Grazie, Mamma." I glanced at my father. He sat stone-faced, eating his supper. Was he still disappointed I hadn't studied hard enough to attend the university, or didn't he care? I wondered how I could make him proud.

Two weeks later, I whistled on my way home from work. New coins jingled in my pocket. Father Inquisitor had complimented my work again when he paid me. Copying documents wasn't so bad after all.

I walked through the doorway, straight into the kitchen. Mamma was chopping carrots while Lucia sliced onions.

"Mamma." I reached into my pocket and pulled out the coins. "These are for you. Father Inquisitor paid me today." I thrust them into her palm. "Buy a new cloak for yourself and some meat for our family."

"O, Stefano!" She set the coins on the table and threw her arms around me. When she looked up, tears streamed down her cheeks. "I knew you'd remember me." Her eyes sparkled again.

The next morning, I was in the middle of copying a letter when a messenger burst through the doorway. He stopped to catch his breath. "A letter for the Inquisitor from the Holy Office in Venezia. The Venetian inquisitor awaits a response."

When Father Inquisitor lifted his hand in response, the messenger thrust the sealed document into his hand and stepped back. The room fell silent. Father Inquisitor broke the seal and unrolled the parchment.

"Of course, the Locatelli case..." He murmured to himself as he read. "So the pestilence has subsided in Venezia. Now what to do with him?" He turned to me. "Stefano, look up his file. How long was Doctor Locatelli's sentence?"

I dug through a stack of papers. "Father, the sentence was ten years."

"Grazie." He nodded. "And now he's served two years in Venezia, treating pestilence victims. This letter says Doctor Locatelli served with great skill and courage. Should I grant him mercy or insist on justice?"

I wondered if he meant his question only for himself. I couldn't decide if I should say anything but finally burst out, "Pardon me, Father, but his daughter is like an orphan. Pestilence killed her mother, and my family took her in. Doctor Locatelli's release would show mercy to her, as well as her father."

Both Father Inquisitor and the messenger stared at me. I couldn't miss the shock in their eyes. My gut twisted into a painful knot.

Father Inquisitor spoke in an even tone. "Grazie, Stefano. I will consider your comments."

For the rest of the workday, one moment I expected my daring comment would cost me my job, and the next, I hoped Father Inquisitor might sympathize with Lucia's plight and release her father early.

When I closed the door behind me after work, I stretched out my tight arms and legs. Father Inquisitor hadn't reprimanded me, so maybe my job was safe.

The following day, he inquired about my family and spoke with me more than usual. By the time I left at the end of the day, I began to take his good humor as a sign he might shorten Doctor Locatelli's sentence.

After cena that evening, I found Lucia sitting alone in the sala, reading as usual.

I pulled a chair next to her and whispered, "Lucia, I can't promise anything, but the Inquisitor may release your father early."

Her book slipped out of her hands and fell to the floor.

I reached down and handed her the volume.

She frowned. "Don't joke about that, Stefano. Mercy is the last thing the Inquisition would show my father."

"Don't be so sure." I shook my head. "I wish I could tell you more."

I hoped my news would make her happy, but she seemed upset—so I left the sala.

Chapter 12

NEW LIFE

Lucia

For days, I studied Stefano's facial expressions and listened to every word he spoke, hoping for clues about my father's case. Time stood still, and I prayed Stefano hadn't raised false hopes if my father would still have to spend years in prison.

One afternoon, I was washing bowls and cups when I heard a knock at the front door. Signora Capriolo lumbered to the entryway and pulled open the door.

She shrieked. "Giordano! Is it you?"

"Sì, eccomi."

At the sound of his voice, I nearly dropped the bowl I was drying. Wiping my wet hands on my apron, I rushed to the door.

"Papa!" I threw my arms around him. My body surged with energy I hadn't felt in months.

My father finally stepped back, and a grin lit up his face. "You've grown taller, Lucia. I see even more of your mother's beauty in you."

I flushed and smiled, but a sudden thought distressed me. "Are you here to stay, Papa, or must you return to Venezia again?"

"I'm free now." His face shone. "Thank God for his mercy. The Inquisitor released me early because of my work during the pestilence epidemic." He squeezed my hand. "Pack your things, Lucia. Now we can return home."

"O Papa!" I hugged him again. Then, like a slave suddenly set free, I ran to the bedchamber and tossed books, papers, and clothes into Papa's traveling chest.

My heart soared until I picked up my mother's prayer book. Papa and I would soon return home, but without Mamma, how could I dream of happiness?

Papa unlocked the front door and pushed it open. The moment I had dreamed of all these months had finally arrived, but instead of the warm, cheerful, home I remembered, I charged into a face full of cobwebs. I could only gape. Spiders had made this room their home, hanging webs from the ceiling to each chair, table, and lamp. Dust covered everything like a winter snowstorm. The stale, musty air smelled like a storage room, not the home whose fragrant aromas had greeted me.

If Mamma were here, she would have run to the courtyard and picked an arm-load of mint to freshen the house. Now her herb garden had suffered months of neglect. A pang of sadness shot through me.

"Lucia, are you all right?"

I grabbed his arm. "The house looks haunted, especially without Mamma."

He put down his bag and slipped his arm around my shoulder. "Sì, Lucia. Your mother transformed this house into a welcoming home. I'll need your help to restore it."

I nodded but choked back tears. Mamma had left a void I could never fill.

Before Papa could say more, I rushed into my bedchamber and set my bags down. I glanced into my parents' room. When I saw the empty space their bed had occupied, I clapped my hand over my eyes—too late to block the flood of memories of Mamma's illness and death. I remembered it all—from Mamma in her bed, burning with fever, to Papa heaping her clothes onto the mattress, hauling it out of the house, and burning the entire pile. He had refused my plea to save her favorite coverlet, insisting we must sacrifice it to save our lives.

When Papa appeared in my doorway, his words brought me back to the present. "Lucia, I must inform the medical college of my return. Would you buy food for us at the market? At last, we can enjoy supper together in our home."

"Of course, Papa."

He pulled a few small coins out of his pocket. "Please choose wisely. I have only the small gift my friends gave me when I left Venezia."

"O Papa, everything needs cleaning." I waved my arm at the dust blanketing my bedchamber. "Where shall I start?"

He nodded. "It's overwhelming. As soon as the medical college pays me again, we'll hire some help."

"Grazie, Papa." I counted the coins. "Papa, how long will these coins need to last us?"

He shrugged. "I'll find out this afternoon."

I thought back to the early days after my father's arrest, before Mamma began to tutor. We had eaten thin soup with only a few vegetables, and I drank extra water to keep my stomach from growling. Now I wrapped a kerchief around the coins and hid them in my pocket.

Giordano

After a few hours in Verona, I realized that a homecoming without Caterina offered only muted joy—even though I had longed to return home to Lucia since the night I last saw her before returning to Venezia.

As much as I loved Lucia, she couldn't take her mother's place, and I couldn't replace Caterina in Lucia's life either. I would do everything possible for Lucia, and I prayed that someday we could be a happy family again.

When I arrived at the medical college that afternoon, I stopped to visit my friend Domenico Capriolo at his office. He stared at me, wide-eyed. His mouth hung open, and the color drained from his face—like he had seen a ghost. When he recovered his composure, he stood and embraced me.

"Giordano, I can't believe my eyes. What are you doing here?"

"I can only thank God for his mercy. I'm as surprised as you that the Inquisition granted my freedom after pestilence subsided in Venezia. I've never heard of such an early release and must conclude that God knew my wretched state and took pity on me."

He nodded. "I'm glad for you, Giordano. So, have you come to retrieve Lucia and take her back to Venezia?"

My skin turned to gooseflesh. My friend's darting eyes and tone of voice reminded me of the Inquisitor's questioning.

"No, of course not. We've moved back into our home and will resume our life here in Verona."

He looked away.

"What's wrong, Domenico?"

He reached into the bottom drawer of his desk. In a moment, a bottle of wine and two glasses sat on his desk. He poured a glass and offered it to me, but I shook my head. He gulped it down and grasped my hand.

"Your best course would be to move to Venezia with Lucia. I hate to tell you this, but you have no future here." His voice was little more than a whisper, and I strained to hear.

"What do you mean?" I pulled back my hand and clenched it into a fist.

"Giordano, your heresy conviction ruined your reputation in Verona, and you wouldn't want to taint Lucia. You'd be better off starting fresh, especially in Venezia. You've made a name for yourself there."

"But my colleagues on the medical faculty know me. My medical reputation remains untarnished. In time, the religious issue will settle down." Why couldn't he understand?

Domenico closed his eyes. "Giordano, you must accept my deepest apologies." He sighed. "Last year, I became the new dean of the medical faculty. The governing board of the medical college insisted your departure couldn't be left vacant for ten years until your return. They ordered me to appoint someone to your chair." He shook his head. "Giordano, I had no choice—I had to replace you."

I stared at him. "Domenico, after all our years of friendship, how could you do this to me? I forgave you when you stole Susanna away and married her. I honored you as my daughter's godfather and entrusted her to your care."

He sat silent and covered his head with his hands.

I strode out of his office. Now I must tell Lucia we must leave Verona because my closest friend had betrayed me.

Lucia

After Papa and I parted, I took a deep breath. I must purchase enough food to sustain us yet make Papa's supply of coins last until he received more. I reminded myself I was nearly sixteen, with months of experience preparing meals for Messer Datini and the Capriolo family.

The vendors greeted me, and my spirits revived. The aromas of meats, cheeses, and freshly baked breads and the sight of the colorful produce—carrots, spinach, asparagus, peas, berries, cherries—all made my stomach growl. But I filled my basket only halfway, with a loaf of bread, cherries, and humble vegetables to make *minestra*.

Back in the kitchen, I devoured a few cherries before turning to the dreaded tasks—bringing in water for the cooking pot, wood for the stove, and starting the fire. I longed for the day a servant would relieve me of these chores that always left my apron soiled and wet.

At last I began to prepare our soup. As I washed spinach leaves in a bowl of water, I heard the front door open. "Papa?"

"Sì, Lucia." I strained to hear him.

He came into the kitchen and pulled up chairs for both of us. "Sit down, Lucia." He faced me, unsmiling. "We can't stay here after all. The dean of the medical college hired someone to replace me."

I gasped. "But Papa, how could that be? Professor Capriolo is the new dean—haven't you heard? He would never replace you." Papa must have misunderstood.

"I know about Professor Capriolo." He grimaced. "This afternoon, he told me the medical college had ordered him to find a replacement for me."

"Couldn't you practice medicine here, even if you're not teaching at the medical college?" I held onto a sliver of hope.

He shook his head. "All of Verona knows I was condemned as a heretic. Anyone who came to me might be suspected of heresy. Who would seek my services?"

His words struck me like a body blow. "Papa, what will we do?"

He reached across the table and squeezed my hand. His face softened, and the creases around his mouth and eyes hinted at a smile. "Don't give up hope, Lucia. We'll find a new home where we can stay together. If all else fails, we could join my brother Cornelio in Basel, away from the Inquisition's threats, but we would have to leave our homeland and speak a new tongue."

His eyes brightened. "Instead we'll settle in Venezia. My friends there encouraged me to stay and practice medicine. They assured me my medical reputation would put my services in great demand since so many physicians died during the epidemic." He paused. "It's a beautiful city, Lucia. I've grown to love it over the years, and I'm sure you will, too."

In a few short minutes, he had shattered my dream, like a precious glass splintered into a thousand pieces. "Papa, all these months that you've been away, I dreamed about returning home. Now I've been here a few hours, and we must leave."

"I'm sorry, Lucia." He squeezed my hand again. "I shared your dream and now share your sorrow. We must make the best of our circumstances and start a new life in Venezia. People bring interesting ideas and customs there from all over the world."

"No, Papa!" I ran into my bedchamber and buried my head in my coverlet. After my tears stopped, I heard noises from my father's room. Pulling myself up from the bed, I peered through the doorway. Papa had stacked his books and papers into neat piles and was loading them into traveling chests.

"You're packing already. Papa, when must we leave?"

"As soon as we can get passage on a ship, Lucia...perhaps in the morning." He shook his head. "I wish we could stay longer, but we have no income to support our life here. I'll need to borrow the fare for our passage to Venezia from a Jewish moneylender. When we sell our house, I'll pay him back."

I stared at him. My father, a professor of medicine, borrowing money—how humiliating! Even when Papa was in prison, Mamma and I hadn't asked anyone for money.

Stepping into the kitchen, I chopped onions and carrots for the soup and set out trenchers for the first and perhaps last supper I would serve in our home.

For months, I had imagined a joyful homecoming meal celebrating Papa's return. That evening, I asked him about Venezia and his time there, but every glance around the kitchen brought back memories of Mamma—the lace curtains she had sewn as a new bride, the burlap wall hanging she had embroidered with her favorite Bible verse, and the empty ceramic vase that once held flowers she grew to brighten the table—all now fresh reminders of our loss. I fought back tears.

My father must have noticed my distress. He paused from his description of Venezia's wonders. "Am I upsetting you?"

"Papa, I'm glad you're here with me." I surveyed the kitchen again. "But I miss Mamma so—everything in our house reminds me of her."

He rubbed the corner of his eye and nodded. "Sì, Lucia, this house awakens my sorrow as well as happy memories. Both of us had to leave suddenly. Now we have a brief chance to remember your mother and what she meant to us. Will you walk with me to her grave?"

After cena, Papa linked his arm with mine, and we followed the familiar route to San Zeno. Along the way, he reminisced about the first time he met Mamma. "I thought I was doing a good deed for her, rescuing her from a life of begging alms, when I took her on as my housekeeper. Instead, she rescued me from a life of loneliness. With a nun's modesty, she hid behind her habit and scarf, but her inner beauty shone through her lovely singing and lute playing, her merry heart, and her fervent spirit.

"She filled my life with so much joy that I couldn't dream of more—until God gave you to us. Even when you kept her up at night, Caterina sang her thanks to God and lullabies to you. Every time I look at you, I see the results of her loving nurture." He pulled out his kerchief and blew his nose.

I cleared my throat. "Mamma taught me to see beauty—in a flower, a bird song, or a sunset, as well as in art." I pushed away tears. "Now I realize how much she sacrificed, especially when we had to get along without you. She would return home from tutoring and spend the rest of her day teaching me how to cook and play the lute, telling me her favorite stories, songs, and prayers." I sniffled. "Why did God let her die, Papa? She of all people didn't deserve her fate."

He covered his eyes with his hand and then looked straight at me. "I agree, Lucia, of course she didn't deserve to die. I've been asking God the same question since the day we lost her. One day we'll meet Him and your mother, and He will tell us."

"Papa, forgive me for asking this..." My words spurted out. "How can you trust God after he allowed our family to suffer so much? Luther wrote that God cares for his people, like a mother bird sheltering her young under the shadow of her wing—but he didn't protect you from arrest and prison, or protect Mamma from pestilence and death."

My father spoke slowly. "Sì, God does allow trouble and pain, but He protects my heart from despair. I sense His tender presence in the midst of disappointment, affliction, and grief." He placed his hands on my shoulders. "May God bring you hope, Lucia."

He thanked me for supper and went back to his packing. After I cleared the table, I returned to my bedchamber and stared at my cassone. I hadn't found time to unpack since returning home and now had no reason to do so.

I sniffled, thinking of what that evening might have been—settling back into my life in Verona instead of anticipating a move to a distant city.

My thoughts turned to my old friend, Elisabetta. I would have no chance to see her before we departed, so I pulled out a sheet of paper and wrote a farewell letter. Sealing it with wax, I set it on the desk. Then I tried to imagine my life in Venezia. I had always dreamed of seeing that city—the queen of the sea with its canals and gondolas, ornate buildings and elegant clothing. Now I would come to know Venezia better than a visitor ever could, but all I wanted was to stay home in Verona, safe in my familiar world.

My father had always effused about Venezia—its interesting people, monuments, and its location where East meets West, where traders come from all over the world. Verona had views of the Alps, a Roman amphitheater, and many churches, but Papa called it provincial compared to Venezia. Perhaps I would enjoy the excitement and sophistication of that grand city.

Papa had warned me about Venezia's bone-chilling dampness, so I pulled open the drawers of my dresser to search for warm clothes. Next I glanced through the remaining books on my bookshelf, adding a few to my traveling chest. I remembered one more book I couldn't leave behind, so I walked into my father's study to find it.

For the first time since Papa's arrest, I reached for the hidden key and unlocked his desk drawer. Inside, I found a bulging leather bag, tied shut with a cord. I grabbed the sack and struggled to untie the cord. When it finally came loose, I drew in my breath. Coins filled the bag—a few cheap *soldi* at the top covered more gold *ducati* than I had ever seen.

I called to my father. "Look, Papa! Is this yours?"

"No, I know nothing about it." He looked inside the bag, and his eyes widened. "Where did you find this?"

"In your locked desk drawer. Who could have stashed it there, Papa?"

"Caterina must have saved her earnings while I was away. What a godsend she left us!" He threw his arms around me. "Now we can pay for our journey and our rent in Venezia."

I handed him the bag and glanced back at the drawer. In my excitement, I hadn't noticed the book underneath. Although the volume lay face down with its spine out of view, I recognized it as Martin Luther's commentary. Had Mamma noticed the book's author when she put the sack on top?

While Papa counted the coins, I slipped the commentary under my arm, walked into my bedchamber, and stared at the book's cover. I had ignored Luther's ideas and tried to forget them for many months, but now this book enticed me just as it had the first time I discovered it.

Should I take the risk and bring this dangerous book to Venezia? Recalling the suffering Martin Luther's ideas had brought my family, I found myself tempted to tear out every page of this book and throw them all into the fire. But I couldn't do it. I still believed Luther's words. His writings brought me something I found nowhere else— hope of God's love and forgiveness. I wrapped a chemise around the small volume and stuffed it beneath my clothing in a cassone.

When I arrived in Venezia, what would I do with Luther's book? I had walked away from the truth, hidden my light under a bushel. But now I could make a fresh start in a new city.

My eyelids grew heavy. The night before, I had gone to bed at the Capriolo home, weary from household chores with no inkling of what this day would bring. Tonight, back in my own home, my exhaustion came from the euphoria and disappointments of the day. I said goodnight to my father and sank onto my mattress.

Memories of happy moments in this house streamed through my mind. Finally, I imagined stepping onto a wharf in Venezia. A sudden thought jolted me wide awake. Papa's first arrest for heresy had been in that city. If I talked about Martin Luther's ideas in Venezia, the Inquisition might arrest me, too.

By the middle of the next day, the Adige River's current had whisked us downstream, far from our life in Verona. But the ship stopped when we reached the locks of the Brenta Canal as we waited for the water to rise in each lock. Without new sights to distract me, my mind returned to Verona. I wondered if I would ever return to see our home, Elisabetta, or Mamma's grave.

Finally, we reached the coast, and the salty ocean spray stung my eyes and cheeks. Rolling swells and whitecaps sent me clinging to my father with one arm, grasping the rail with the other.

Papa urged me to look at the horizon, and I watched as we headed north into calmer waters protected from wind and waves by a long, narrow strip of land to our right.

When the ship approached a wharf, my legs tingled. I could hardly wait to walk on dry land and see the sights of Venezia. But after a dozen men climbed on board, sailors untied the moorings, and the ship slipped back out into the lagoon.

I turned to my father. "Papa, shouldn't we have gotten off?"

He shook his head. "Our ship stopped in Fusina to pick up more passengers for the final leg of our journey, across the lagoon to Venezia."

I sighed.

Papa squeezed my hand. "Don't worry, it won't be long now."

As our ship approached Venezia, an old story returned to torment me. Years ago in catechism class, Padre Federico had recounted how Bianca Cappello, a teen-age Venetian girl of noble rank, had refused to marry the man her father chose for her. She eloped with a Florentine who mistreated her. Padre Federico had warned that such things could happen to us if we disobeyed our parents.

I turned to my father. "Have you heard of Bianca Cappello?"

He nodded.

"Her story scares me. I've heard she fled because her father insisted she must marry the man he chose or enter a convent." I looked him in the eye. "Papa, now that we'll live in Venezia, you wouldn't force me to marry, would you?"

"Never!" He squeezed my shoulder.

"But what if something happened to you? Would I have to enter a convent or marry against my will?"

"I can't predict the future, but every day, I ask God for his blessings for you, Lucia. I do everything in my power to protect and provide for you."

He glanced toward the horizon. "Ecco Venezia!" He pointed to silhouettes of islands.

I squinted. At last I saw fingers of land packed with buildings. Papa had warned me that pestilence had brought death and ruin on a grand scale, so I braced myself for grisly sights.

Instead the pink and white façade of Palazzo Ducale came into view, followed by the domes and spires of San Marco Cathedral. I whistled through my teeth. I had seen pictures in books, but nothing had prepared me for the massive scale of these buildings. Already, Venezia's grandeur put Verona to shame.

Our ship drifted into a mooring at Fondamenta Nuove, and sailors secured the ropes. My father guided me toward the gangplank, but my legs buckled. Papa and a nearby sailor caught me. I leaned on my father's arm and inched my way to solid ground.

"Brava, Lucia!" He smiled and steadied me. "Soon we'll see our new home."

We waited on the wharf for our luggage, and I looked out on Venezia. "Papa, tell me about where we'll be living." I could not bear to say "our house."

"Venezia's recent misfortunes have brought us the good fortune of a wonderful home. While I was treating the plague-stricken here, another physician, Filippo Soncini, worked with me. He owns a palazzo near Canal Grande and shared it with his brother's family. Sadly, that entire family perished in the epidemic.

"Doctor Soncini encouraged me to return to Venezia and move into the rooms his brother's family had occupied in the palazzo, with living quarters and an office for my medical practice. He promised to rent to me at a low price because he's eager to share his home with someone he knows and trusts. He also pledged his servants would scrub and air out our rooms to drive out all traces of contagion.

"As soon as I decided to return, I sent him a letter of acceptance." He smiled at me. "Doctor Soncini's servants will attend to us as well, so you won't need to cook or clean."

"Such luxury, Papa!" I had seen paintings of the mansions along Venezia's impressive waterway but never dreamt I would live in such a setting.

As a cloud obscured the sun, I thought of one crucial element I wouldn't find in Venezia—Mamma's presence. How could I enjoy life in a Venetian palazzo when Mamma lay in a churchyard in Verona?

At last our cassoni lay piled beside us on the pier. My father looked in vain for a porter, finally turning to one of the sailors. After Papa flashed several coins, the sailor recruited a comrade, borrowed a cart, and piled it high with our goods. Papa led the way along the pedestrian *calle*. Each time we crossed a canal, the sailors had to haul the heavy cart up and down the stairways of the bridge.

The slow pace gave me time to survey houses, churches, government buildings, and markets. I gaped at shop windows filled with lace, glassware, jewelry, cakes, or paper goods. When we approached a bookshop, I couldn't resist and ran to the window.

"We'll visit bookshops another time, Lucia." Papa's voice drew me away before I was close enough to read the titles. "Come along so you don't get lost—it's happened to me more than once. Venezia's a maze of calli and canals."

I sighed and walked toward my father. Suddenly my nostrils burned. In the canal behind Papa, I saw frothy, fetid water—so out of place near the elegant shops. Perhaps pestilence still lingered in the water. I shuddered.

As we continued our walk, new characters in distinctive costumes caught my attention. Gondoliers in black and white shirts, black hats and trousers waited along the bridges, calling out for customers. Fruit vendors and butchers with bloody aprons hawked their wares in the *piazzas*.

Shopkeepers stood in doorways with their brooms, sweeping out dust like servants in palaces. Women with painted faces and garish dresses whispered and giggled together. Sailors eyed them with interest—all such a dramatic contrast to Verona.

Mamma would have enjoyed these scenes as I would have if she had walked beside me. But as I tried to savor the sights, sounds, and scents, grief at my mother's absence constrained my delight.

Our small troop stopped at the land entrance to a palazzo, and my father knocked at the double doors. A graying, muscular man cracked them open, recognized my father, and ushered us in. After Papa introduced me, the servant doffed his cap, identified himself as Zuanne, *maestro di casa*, and welcomed us.

While Papa spoke with the house steward, I surveyed the wide central hall that extended all the way to the other end of the house. Drawings of a Venetian *portego* couldn't convey the grandeur of such a reception area. Tapestries and paintings, swords and coats of arms decorated the walls. Even in the daytime, this great room glowed with candles mounted on stands on both sides of the walls, and the aroma of beeswax permeated the hall. Couches and carved wooden chairs lined the walls, along with gilded side tables displaying lamps, vases, and candlestick holders. Above me, a fresco with a vibrant blue sky, billowy white clouds, intricate designs, and gold trim covered the high ceiling. This palazzo suited a count or king, not a girl from Verona who not long ago had worn a servant's apron.

The sailors carried our belongings into a large corner room. We followed close behind. Thanks to tall windows in the corner walls, rays of sunshine flooded the room with light. Even the windows on the interior wall added brightness. When my father told me he would see patients in this room, I envied him.

Glass windows in private homes—what luxuries these Venetians enjoyed! In Verona, oiled paper or cloth covered the window openings in every private home I had seen. Savoring the light, open atmosphere, I smiled at my father.

He winked. "These Venetians certainly know how to conserve lamp oil, don't they?"

After he paid the sailors, my father asked the maestro di casa to show me around the house while he sorted through our belongings and set up his office.

Zuanne nodded and stepped into the portego. The shiny floor—flecked with chips of colored stone—reminded me of pictures of the mosaics of San Marco cathedral. He beckoned me to follow.

I hesitated, pointing at the floor. "I don't want to damage this."

He chuckled, revealing the wrinkle lines in his face. "You'll see this flooring throughout Venezia. It's called *terrazzo*."

He led me across the portego and down a flight of stone stairs to the lower story. A fish smell made me wrinkle my nose. With few windows, the lower level reminded me of a dark netherworld, especially in contrast to the portego just up the stairs. Zuanne turned to me.

"This floor is the *andron*—the kitchen, storage rooms, and my family's rooms are all here. Come down when you need help from us or if you're hungry." He led me through a doorway where a squat woman with gray-streaked hair and a petite, wire-haired young girl leaned over a huge water-filled bowl. They scrubbed mussels and clams with brushes before tossing them into a cooking pot.

Zuanne gestured toward them. "Signorina Lucia, meet my wife, Flora, and my daughter, Valeria. Don't hesitate to ask them if you need anything."

He grinned at them. "You remember Doctor Soncini's friend, Doctor Locatelli. May I present his daughter, Signorina Lucia. Let's show her around and help her get settled."

Flora nodded. "*Piacere*, signorina." Squeezing a lemon wedge onto her palm, she rubbed her hands together, dried them on a cloth and clasped my hand. "Welcome to our home."

She turned to her daughter. "Valeria, why don't you give Lucia a tour of the palazzo? I can get along without you for a while."

Valeria's dark eyes lit up. "Sure, Mamma!" She dropped the shells and scrub-brush.

Zuanne smiled and turned to me. "I'll leave you to the care of the ladies, signorina, but call me anytime you need help."

"Grazie." As I nodded, he bowed and headed up the stairs.

Valeria dried her hands on a towel and tossed it aside. "Let's go, signorina!"

"Sì, I'm eager to see the house—but call me Lucia." The odor of fish emanated from Valeria's chapped hands. I raised my hands to my nose and savored the lemon scent from Flora's hands.

Valeria frowned and pushed her hair out of her face. "Lucia, then. I'll show you your family's rooms upstairs—they're over on the side of the portego. But if you want to see the Soncinis' rooms and meet their family, go with your father. I stay away from those boys. They tease me. You'd think they'd never seen a girl before." She clucked her tongue.

At the top of the stone stairway, we walked across the portego into a large room, empty but for a raised platform bed, several lampstands, and on one wall, a picture of the Virgin Mary holding Baby Jesus. Sunshine poured through the windows. Just outside, a narrow balcony overlooked a canal, its inky water glistening. I noticed a gold knob and realized the windowpanes, set into wooden frames, extended to the floor and formed a door.

Valeria turned to me. "I guess you'll get this room since it's smaller. I'll bring in your things."

If I opened the window door, I could stand outside on my own balcony and gaze at the canal. My eyes welled with tears.

"What's wrong? Isn't this good enough for you?" Valeria's voice rose.

I opened my mouth but couldn't tell her this elegant palazzo with a canal view was a dream I didn't deserve—because my sin sent Papa to prison, worked Mamma to her death, forced me to work as a servant for the Capriolos, and finally drove Papa and me out of our home. I cleared my throat. "It's lovely."

I glanced up at her. "Valeria, how long have you worked here?"

"I don't know when I started working, but I've always lived here since my parents work here and my grandparents did, too. Mamma tells me I used to play in the corner of the kitchen while she and Nonna prepared meals and cleaned."

"How old are you?"

Valeria shot me a puzzled look. "Fifteen or sixteen—we don't know exactly which day I was born, but it was sometime this season. Why do you care?"

I smiled. "Maybe we're the same age."

"No, the way you talk and dress, you must be much older." She stared at me.

"I'm not quite sixteen." I smiled. "Tell me about life in Venezia."

"I'm just a servant girl. What would I know about the nobles and rich people? I can tell you only the stories I've heard from my family."

"Really, it would help me understand Venezia better. And I'd like to hear what you think about what goes on—even here in this house."

She clucked her tongue again. "You want me to be your spy? You must want to denounce someone to the *bocca di leone* outside the Doge's palace. I'd betray my family and everyone who lives here if I told you what I hear."

"What is this lion's mouth? I've never heard of it. Is there a zoo in Venezia?" I must have said something wrong. "I don't want to cause trouble, only to learn more about Venezia since I'm new here."

Valeria gaped. "Surely you know about the *bocca di leone!*"

"Honestly, I don't!" Valeria's frown and downcast gaze told me I would learn no more from her. I pictured a lion's mouth stretched wide open, roaring, and then remembered the winged lion was the symbol of Venezia. I hoped Papa could explain this mystery, so I could earn Valeria's trust.

Just then my father entered from the portego, followed by Zuanne, his arms filled with Papa's belongings.

Valeria turned to me. "Show me which bags are yours, and I'll carry them to your room."

A few minutes later, she deposited my luggage in the bedchamber and started toward the door.

"Can't you stay longer, Valeria?"

"No, my mother needs me in the kitchen." She vanished before I could tell her grazie.

After Valeria closed the door behind her, a lonely silence descended like a fog. I surveyed the bedchamber—like the portego, too grand a room for me.

Opening my cassoni, I stuffed my books and papers onto my bookshelf and desk but still felt like a stranger in the bedchamber. I wandered into a short passageway and glanced into a bedchamber even grander than mine. My father, his back to me, leaned over an open cassone. Although I longed for his company, I left him to his work and returned to my room.

Placing a bottle of ink, a quill, and sheet of paper atop the desk, I wrote my impressions of the journey, our trek through Venezia, and the palazzo. Excitement, disappointment, and loneliness poured out onto the pages.

Shadows had fallen by the time Zuanne knocked to announce cena. Papa escorted me to the dining room and introduced me to Doctor Soncini and his wife, Cecelia. Such a youthful couple, neither with a strand of gray hair—unlike my father.

Doctor Soncini's dignified expression, along with the gold trim on his black velvet cloak, made me wonder if he was a nobleman. His stories of the latest goings-on in Venezia opened my eyes to the many factions in this city. Merchants, bankers, church officials, ancient families, those recently arrived, and many others competed to promote their own interests. His accounts heightened my excitement to explore the city.

When her husband paused for a sip of wine, Signora Soncini smiled at me, her hazel eyes radiating energy. "Lucia, what's your latest sewing project?"

I gulped. "I don't have one, signora. My mother used to tell me she would teach me to sew, but she died before she could do it."

She shook her head, and blond streaks glistened in her nut-brown hair. "What a shame! Do you play a musical instrument?"

"My mother taught me to play her harp, but I haven't had time to pick it up since she died. When I have a moment, I read and write poetry."

She nodded, but her raised brows spoke disapproval. For the remainder of the meal, I could only pick at the meaty, unfamiliar dishes Valeria and her mother served us. I mourned the loss of my mother and her simple yet cheerful kitchen.

After Valeria cleared the last dish, Doctor Soncini turned to us. "Shall we step out to the portego? I'll call my sons and introduce you."

We all pushed back our chairs. I linked arms with Papa, remembering Valeria's comments about the boys. If I clung to my father, perhaps they would leave me alone.

Doctor Soncini opened the door and called out, "Roberto, Carlo, Antonio, *venite!*"

A dark-haired, lanky young man emerged from the family's suite. He glanced at us but then focused his brown eyes on his father, like a soldier standing at attention. Moments later, a shorter, redheaded youth with freckles and a smaller boy with chubby cheeks and stringy brown hair joined us in the portego. The redhead held a squirming puppy, which his younger brother tried to grab.

Doctor Soncini stepped forward and turned to us. "Doctor Locatelli and Lucia, may I introduce our sons—Roberto is eighteen, Carlo is sixteen, and Antonio is eleven.

He turned toward them. "Boys, Doctor Locatelli and Lucia have moved into the other suite in our palazzo. Please show them every courtesy."

"Piacere, Doctor Locatelli, Signorina Lucia." Roberto bowed. He stared at Carlo and cleared his throat.

Carlo followed Roberto's example, but I noticed the hint of a smirk on his face when he greeted me. Then he elbowed his younger brother. Antonio elbowed him back and scowled.

"Ragazzi!" Doctor Soncini reprimanded the boys and stepped toward them. Antonio nodded and mumbled his greetings.

Doctor Soncini glanced around the room. "*Allora.* Go along now, boys."

My father spoke up. "Grazie, Filippo. Now we must return to our quarters. We've had a full day." He nodded to our hosts. "*Buona notte,* my friends."

Papa and I crossed the portego toward our rooms. Now I could understand why the younger Soncini boys didn't eat meals with their parents. But Roberto seemed more serious and responsible than his brothers.

"Lucia, why so quiet tonight?" My father interrupted my musing.

"Today has brought so many new sights and people, and I can tell our lives will be easier here in Venezia." I wanted to ask when we could read and discuss Martin Luther's writings again, but I knew I must not mention this where someone might overhear.

My father ushered me into our suite, and I looked around again. No matter how elegant, these rooms couldn't compare to the welcoming home Mamma had fashioned for us in Verona. "Papa, will we ever find happiness without Mamma?"

He shrugged his shoulders. "If God shows us mercy." Then he embraced me. "Buona notte, Lucia."

"Buona notte, Papa."

Moments later, I blew out my candle and slipped under my coverlet. I knew I should thank God for our safety and this grand palazzo, but Mamma's absence cut through my heart like a knife.

Chapter 13

LONG REACH

Lucia

O ne week later, I set a volume of Cicero's letters on my desk and stepped out to my balcony. Waves rippled across the canal, and the bright sunlight showed me that morning had turned to midday. After spending seven long days alone in my room except for meals, I doubted my father would find time to instruct me in my studies. As much as I enjoyed reading and studying by myself, I missed a teacher's encouragement and camaraderie with other students.

Opening a chest of books, I glimpsed my mother's prayer book and remembered her warm, nurturing spirit and the happy moments we had shared—but only until vivid memories of her suffering and death flooded me with fresh grief.

A knock sounded at the land door. Raised voices echoed through the portego. I cracked my door open, and a blast of cool air greeted me. Stabbing a cane across the mosaic floor, a tall man in a monk's robe followed Zuanne to my father's office.

"Giordano Locatelli?" The monk's deep voice rang out, sounding uncannily familiar.

My father opened his door just wide enough to look out. "*Si,* eccomi, but you must wait while I finish attending my patient. If you need medical assistance, I'll see you in a few minutes."

"No, you must answer my questions now." The monk threw back his shoulders and pulled a small scroll from his cloak. "I am Fra Vincenzo, from the Holy Office of the Inquisition." Unrolling the scroll, he shoved it in Papa's face.

I stared at him. Vincenzo, my former classmate who wrote down bird songs, now an agent of the Inquisition! I should have recognized him after I saw his cane and heard his voice.

Papa frowned, looked back into his study, and shut the door. "*Un momento*, signor." Then he faced Vincenzo. "Very well, young man, state your business quickly."

"Fifteen years ago, the Inquisition's tribunal here in Venezia convicted you of heresy. Why did you return to Venezia? What is your business here?" He pointed his cane at my father.

Papa didn't flinch. "I returned to Venezia to treat the sick as I did during the months of pestilence." He closed the door of his study behind him and lowered his voice. "I did everything the tribunal required of me. The Church welcomed me back, and the bishop of Verona wrote letters as proof. Shall I show them to you?"

"Sì, at once." Vincenzo stood stiff as a soldier at attention.

"Un momento." My father disappeared into his office.

Vincenzo removed his hood, wiped beads of sweat from his tonsured scalp, and covered his head again. He surveyed the portego, one painting, tapestry, and chair at a time.

With a trembling hand, I drew my door close to the frame.

"Ecco, the letters." When I heard my father's voice, I peered out. He handed the monk two vellum sheets.

Vincenzo looked through the papers. "Very well, I will report this to the Holy Office." He handed the letters back.

Papa shut his door. Before I could close mine, Vincenzo glanced in my direction. When he saw me, his mouth dropped open. "Lucia?"

I opened my door wider. "Vincenzo—what are you doing here?"

He blushed.

"Tell the Inquisition to leave my father alone!"

He squared his shoulders. "The Holy Office sent me to Venezia on an important mission. I can't let personal concerns dissuade me." He turned away. Listing to his left side, he strutted with his cane across the portego. His sharp tone and severe manner sent shivers down my spine, but his surprise and blush evoked the gentle soul who had welcomed me on my first day of school.

After Zuanne ushered him out, I shut my door and pulled the chair up to my desk. As I reached for a quill, my hand trembled. The Inquisition had noticed Papa's return already, so our move to Venezia hadn't been far enough. Vincenzo's appearance shattered my dream of a fresh start, free from threats, rumors, and sad memories.

Stefano
September 1577

Gusts of rain drenched me, and I splashed across the cobblestones on the way to my job. How could I have known I should dress for a storm this early in the fall? If only my day's work was done, and I could walk back home, dry my clothes in front of the fireplace, and savor the aroma of roasting fish. Whatever tasks Father Inquisitor might have for me, I hoped to finish them quickly.

Then I remembered—another Friday. Even before I got to work, I knew I would spend my day leafing through transcripts of the Inquisition trials held that week. By the end of the afternoon, I would hand Father Inquisitor a list with each name, hometown, date, and crime. Most of these accounts struck me as tedious, but occasionally I read stories so sad or strange I couldn't forget them.

"*Buon giorno*, Stefano." Before I hung up my hat and cloak, Father Inquisitor's greeting boomed across the room. His right hand reached up and clasped the wooden crucifix hanging from his neck, the usual sign that he was concentrating. "You're shivering, son. We need another log on the fire to take off the chill." He pushed back his chair.

I rushed toward the fireplace. "I'll take care of it, Padre—it will help warm me."

"Grazie, Stefano." His grin lit up the room. "Just what I need—more time to prepare." He settled down at his desk and turned to a *busta* filled with reports about the suspect he would question that morning.

My cheeks warmed. Unlike my own father, Father Inquisitor always complimented me on my good work. That and my salary kept me at this job.

I heaved a log on the fire, rubbed my hands together, and waited for the bough to burst into flame. At last I pulled my chair up to the desk, reached for my quill, and glanced at the transcript on top of the stack. Later, when Father Inquisitor disappeared into the examination room, I yawned and stretched my fingers.

A rap on the outside door shattered the silence, and a redheaded fellow about my age rushed in, each of his hands clutching a cassone loaded with documents.

"Gianpietro, what a day to visit!" Joking around with the Venetian Inquisition's messenger was a welcome break from my work.

"Ciao, Stefano." He panted. "Papers for Father Inquisitor. Is he here?"

"Sì, but I can't disturb him now. He's in the middle of a trial."

"Capito." Of course he understood. "It's a relief to stay inside—what a storm!" He took off his gloves and scarf, pulled a chair close to the fireplace, and propped his feet near the flames. "On the carriage ride from Padova, my fingers and toes went numb, even when I tucked them inside my cloak. I longed for the warmth of a roaring fire and a cup of hot wine. I don't even want to imagine the return trip down the river." He shuddered. "Tell me you haven't many papers, just a light load for me to carry back to Venezia."

I shook my head. "Our work never ends at the Holy Office and neither does the paperwork. You must know that."

"I can always hope." He sank deeper into the chair and closed his eyes.

I dipped my quill in the inkwell and turned back to my list.

At last Father Inquisitor stepped into the room, closing the inner door behind him. Gianpietro jumped to his feet, bowed, and picked up the cassoni.

"Padre, here are new documents from Venezia. Please sign for them, and I'll fill the cassoni with any documents you wish to send."

Father Inquisitor unloaded both chests, breaking the seal on every document and reading enough to see if it demanded an immediate response. While he answered the urgent requests, I pulled an armload of sealed documents out of a drawer and handed them to Gianpietro.

After I sealed and stamped Father Inquisitor's newly written responses, Gianpietro loaded the cassoni, bade me farewell, and rushed outside.

Father Inquisitor turned to me. "Stefano, when you finish your inventory, please file these documents from Venezia before you go home."

"Sì, Padre." I piled the load of papers on my desk and returned to the stack of trial transcripts.

By mid-afternoon, I began filing the papers from Venezia. Skimming through the documents, I filed each one into a busta. When I noticed Giordano Locatelli's name, I slowed my pace and read every word of the letter.

25 August, 1577

To the Inquisitor in Verona,

I send this report to inform you that I have begun my mission. I carefully scrutinize the activities of Giordano Locatelli, who recently took up residence in Venezia. As the Holy Office's new agent, I take personal responsibility for his case, along with those of other convicted heretics now at large in Venezia.

As you know, Doctor Locatelli attended the sick during the pestilence. After you commuted the remainder of his prison sentence, he returned to Venezia and has now set up his medical practice. I will continue to watch him and inform you of any suspicious behavior.

If you have any questions, please address them to me in care of the Holy Office in Venezia. As Padre Federico's nephew and a Verona native, I have particular ties to that city, and will do my best to make him and all Verona proud.

Your humble servant,

Vincenzo Ugoni

My spine stiffened. So the Inquisition was watching my father's best friend, even far away in Venezia. That I could barely believe. But Vincenzo—the crippled loner from Messer Datini's class—as the Inquisition's spy? Never in a thousand years would I have imagined that.

Someone screamed in the next room. I almost fell out of my chair. No matter how often I heard the noises, I couldn't get used to this part of the Inquisition's work. Give me a broom to sweep up dung from the streets, or even a shovel to dig graves, but spare me from sitting in my comfortable chair, hearing shrieks of anguish! If only my desk was in a different building, so I wouldn't have to hear the sounds from the other side of the wall.

I tried to calm myself, remembering Father Inquisitor's words on my first day at work. "My son, from time to time you may hear disturbing sounds from the examination room. Don't let that distress you—you must realize, as I have, that the Holy Office acts in love to save deluded souls from eternal peril. We seek the truth and use the gentlest procedures necessary."

He had shaken his head. "Only when a stubborn sinner refuses to cooperate does the tribunal need to use harsher measures to encourage repentance and rescue him from damnation." His brown eyes had glowed with the fervor of a man who believed in his work, and his warm manner had made me trust him.

Yet in the months that followed, every time pained cries echoed through the wall, my gut tensed, and I wondered what God must think.

I glanced once more at Vincenzo's letter and stuffed it in the front of the busta labeled with Doctor Locatelli's name. I hurried to file the other letters so I could escape from this reminder of the Holy Office's unpleasant side.

At last I donned my cloak and cap and walked out the door, relishing the fresh air, birds squawking, and shouts of boys kicking a ball in the street. But I couldn't dispel Vincenzo's image from my mind or imagine him as an agent of the Inquisition. His uncle the priest probably recommended him. I recalled his glum face, how he always sat by himself at school. Now he had made a new life for himself. I hoped Vincenzo wouldn't succeed at Doctor Locatelli's expense—for Lucia's sake as well as her father's.

Back at home in my room, I reached for a quill to write a warning to Lucia's father, but imagined the bleak future I might face if the Holy Office found out. I might lose not just my job but also my life. My family would slip back into poverty. My sisters would have no dowries and no marriage prospects. I set down the quill.

Chapter 14

GILDED CAGE

Lucia
September, 1577

*A*s much as I loved my books, when the sun's rays broke through the morning fog and brightened my bedchamber, I couldn't bear to pass another day inside. But Papa had warned me, "In Venezia, a girl who goes out alone loses her good reputation." So I opened the window-paned door and stepped out onto my balcony.

The gulls' cawing, the water lapping against the sides of the canal, and the sun's warmth on my face—all brought to mind happier days. I closed my eyes and recalled Sunday-afternoon strolls along the Adige River. Papa had carried a satchel that Mamma packed with rolls, cheese, fruit, and a bottle of wine. We always stopped to eat where we could watch the river rush by, in the shade of a tree. When a branch floated past, each of us guessed how far it had traveled—from nearby Parona, Bussolengo, or even the Alps.

Inspired by this memory, I pulled a chair out to my balcony and tucked the wooden frame of my mother's harp between my chin and waist. I hadn't played it since she died, and now I struggled to position my fingers where she taught me. Mamma's memory soothed me, and I recalled songs she used to sing and play. After a quick glance at the canal to make sure no one was passing, I slowly plucked the strings and sang one of her favorite songs, *Pater Noster*. I couldn't match Mamma's skill, but I felt her presence as I played.

A deep, resonant voice harmonized with me. Below, in the middle of the canal, Vincenzo sat in a dinghy, looking up at me. His monk's robe brought to my mind his call on my father, and my muscles tensed.

I set down my harp. Whatever his business here, how embarrassing that Vincenzo should hear my rusty attempt!

But he flashed me a grin. "What a surprise—I didn't know you played."

I shook my head. "Sorry to offend your ears. My mother was the musician. She taught me before she died, but I haven't picked up her harp since."

"Play another song—mind if I sing along?" He dipped his oars into the canal so his boat wouldn't drift away.

I flexed my cramped fingers. "I'll try, but you probably won't recognize this." Again my fingers pressed the strings, and before long, Vincenzo's voice wafted up to my balcony.

At the end of the song, Vincenzo called, "*Ancora*, another!"

"Sorry, my fingers ache. I lost my callouses years ago." The purple grooves in my fingers reminded me how much time had passed since Mamma died and how distant her memory had become. I pressed my lips together.

"Too bad." He sighed. "Keep practicing until you can play longer. Those songs bring back happy memories. My mother used to sing them while she cooked." A shadow crossed his face.

Suddenly Zuanne stepped out on the wharf and stared at Vincenzo's dinghy. "*Prego*, can I help you with something?"

Vincenzo colored. "No, *grazie*." He glanced up at me. "I'd better go."

I nodded and watched him paddle away. Our conversation and songs had dispelled my loneliness for a few minutes. How I longed for a friend in this new city, especially someone with a kind heart and a common interest.

Zuanne shot me a puzzled frown. Clearly, he didn't understand why I would talk with someone who spied on my father. But if Vincenzo and I became friends, perhaps I could persuade him to leave Papa alone. I hoped for the chance to talk with Vincenzo again.

Days later, Vincenzo hadn't returned, and Papa still hadn't taken me on his promised tour of Venezia. My room had become an elegant prison, and I dreamed of venturing out by myself. When I picked up my quill, my frustrations spilled out in the form of a poem.

Footsteps, too light for Zuanne, echoed through the portego, and I opened my door. Valeria was heading toward the land door. I sprinted across the hall to catch up with her.

"Where are you going?"

She held up a wet paper package, and its stench made me gag. "Back to the fish market. The fishmonger sold Mamma some rotten sardines early this morning. She's cooking pranzo, so I'm taking them back to demand fresh fish."

"Can I go with you? I haven't been out of the house in days, and I'm dying to see Venezia."

Valeria shrugged. "If you can stand the smells—and your clothes might get dirty."

"I'll be right back." Racing to my room, I grabbed my muslin apron from a cassone and pulled it over my head.

When Valeria saw me, she giggled.

I stopped in mid-step. "Why are you laughing?"

"Mi dispiace, Lucia, but a servant's apron looks strange on you." She looked down. "Allora, I must catch the fishmonger before he disappears." She headed toward the land door and paused only long enough to hold it open for me.

The Venetian sunshine again dazzled my eyes. I struggled to keep up with Valeria while taking in all the sights. As she had warned me, a variety of scents titillated my nose—food aromas wafting from homes, street vendors burning wood to barbecue tripe, the stench of garbage and dung in the calle. Next to the walkway, vines covered a high wall. "What's behind the wall, Valeria?"

"Palazzo Papadopoli. People say the gardens are gorgeous."

"But you've never seen them?"

She shook her head. "In Venezia, only rich people get to see much beauty, except in churches."

We kept walking, and Valeria eyed me. "Where did you get that apron? I've never seen one quite like it."

"I brought it from Verona."

"It looks like a servant used it." She furrowed her brow.

"Sì. There's a sad story behind it." I would tell her, but only if she wanted to know.

She shrugged. "That makes me even more curious."

If she knew I understood a servant's life, maybe she would trust me. But where to start? Just as I opened my mouth to tell her how my father's heresy conviction began the string of sad events, Alessandro's tormented face appeared in my mind's eye. I knew I couldn't trust Valeria with Papa's secret.

"I'm sure you remember the pestilence that killed so many people in Venezia—well, it came to Verona, too. My mother came down with it while my father was taking care of the sick in Venezia. By the time he returned to Verona to care for her..." I swallowed a lump in my throat. "She had died. Then my father had to return to Venezia, so I moved in with my godparents." I explained how I had to quit school and help Signora Capriolo with housework, cooking, and caring for her twins.

Valeria eyed me as we walked. Finally, she spoke up. "Such a fine young lady—I wouldn't have believed you had ever done a servant's work."

"I never thought I would, but look at the stains on my apron."

"You suffered so much, losing your mother and having to leave your home." She spoke with a warmth I hadn't noticed earlier. "Thank God He saved you and your father."

I choked on her words. Sì, God saved Papa and me but had allowed tragedies to rip my family apart. I wanted to argue with her but feared I would burst into tears.

Around a bend in Canal Grande, a huge wooden bridge spanned the waterway. I turned again to Valeria. "Is this the only way to cross the canal?"

"Sì, it's Rialto Bridge. Papa's grandparents told him it collapsed one day with a crowd on it, and everyone fell into the canal. They've rebuilt it several times. Now people talk about building a stone bridge to replace this one."

I shuddered at the thought of people scrambling for their lives in a canal full of bridge chunks. Then the clamor of the vegetable market greeted us. Booths lined up like soldiers in a parade, each with a colorful uniform: orange carrots, bright green spinach, purple onions, red apples, and more. Even though Venezia's islands lacked space to farm, somehow the array of fruits and vegetables rivaled what I had seen at Piazza delle Erbe in Verona. Valeria pushed through crowds of shoppers, and I struggled to keep up with her.

Strong odors announced the fish market ahead. When we arrived, I gawked at its grand scale. Blackened beams and planks hinted at long-gone structures, but the market had spread far beyond them.

To my right, a girlish voice sang, "By faith salvation freely comes. Thanks be to God. Alleluia." What a simple, beautiful expression of Martin Luther's ideas!

My spine tingled, and I glanced toward the source of the melody. Someone else in this city must have read Luther and brought their children up in the new faith.

Behind a table piled high with clams stood a matronly woman wearing a grimy apron. She cupped her hand over a little girl's mouth. The woman stared at the clams, but the girl's eyes sparkled, and I could tell a grin lurked beneath her mother's outstretched hand.

I rushed toward the table and smiled at the girl.

"What a beautiful song! Where did you learn it?"

The girl struggled to escape her mother's grasp. When at last she pulled away, she opened her mouth to answer me. Before she could speak, her mother cried, "Elena, *silenzio!*"

The woman turned away from me and turned her daughter around by the shoulders. I saw only her back.

Suddenly I remembered that Valeria had been at my side. I wheeled around. She had vanished into the maze of stalls and aisles. I couldn't retrace my steps back to the palazzo, and no one but Valeria knew where I had gone.

I took a deep breath. Surely Valeria wouldn't abandon me. I waited near the first stall we had passed, watching the vendors, counting the varieties of seafood I saw, listening in vain for another inspiring melody. I prayed Valeria would return home the same way we came.

As time passed, I wondered if she forgot about me or was avoiding me. If only I had paid closer attention to the route from the palazzo. Finally, I set out to find her.

Perched between two fishmongers' booths with her back to me, she stood conversing with someone. As I came closer, I noticed his monk's robe and cane—Vincenzo.

"Valeria!" I rushed toward her.

She turned toward me, and Vincenzo disappeared into the crowd.

"What happened to you, Lucia? One minute you walked beside me, and the next, you vanished."

I exhaled. "I stopped to look at a booth and didn't notice where you'd gone. What a relief to find you! I couldn't have found my way back to the palazzo by myself."

She took my arm. "I'll help you learn your way around Venezia. Every time we pass a landmark, I'll tell you about it so you can remember it."

"Grazie." I glanced at the spot where I saw Vincenzo, then turned back to Valeria. "I recognized the monk you were talking with—he attended my school in Verona. How do you know him?"

Her cheeks turned crimson, and she whispered. "Since you came to Venezia, I've seen him here several times. He always greets me, asks about my family, and how my work is going. Once he asked about your family and gave me a sweet."

I pressed my thumbnails into my fingers to calm myself. "What did you tell him?"

She looked at the ground. "Not much. I don't know your family well."

"Valeria, did your father tell you Vincenzo works for the Inquisition?"

She gasped, shaking her head. "I thought he was just a monk."

I shook my head. "If you say the wrong thing, they could arrest my father."

"I'm sorry, Lucia." She squeezed my hand. "I give you my word, I won't talk to him about your family."

As we headed back along Canal Grande, my worries about what Valeria told Vincenzo and what he had told the Inquisition, distracted me from learning the route. I must do something to win Valeria's loyalty.

"Valeria, I'll teach you to read and write. You'll learn so many interesting stories about the whole world."

"I'm only a servant girl. I'd have no use for such learning. Besides, when would I have time for it?"

"We could meet after pranzo in the afternoon. Don't you get a break then?"

"Only after we wash up and put away everything. By then I need to rest." Valeria looked away. "If you tried to teach me, you'd be wasting your time."

I nudged her. "I'll take that chance. Let's try it for a month. Then you can quit. Agreed?"

"I don't know." She hesitated. "I guess I could try for a month, but don't expect much."

"I'm not worried." The pleasant challenge of teaching her, as well as having a companion each afternoon, raised my spirits. I thought about the books I could use to teach her, and my excitement grew. "Let's begin tomorrow."

Valeria pointed out sights and told me stories about the families who lived in the grand mansions we passed. Free from anxiety, I relaxed and concentrated on her stories.

When we turned a corner, our palazzo came into view. I winced at the familiar sight. When I walked inside, I would have no further chance to search for inklings of Luther's faith. I wondered when I could escape again.

Valeria stepped up her pace. "Mamma must wonder where I went with the sardines."

I dragged my feet.

Valeria stopped in front of the door and looked back at me, her forehead creased. "What's wrong?"

"Nothing. I just wanted to enjoy a last look at the city." I forced my feet toward the palazzo.

Valeria pounded on the door. Zuanne raised his eyebrows when he saw me, but swung the door wide and said nothing. We walked toward the stairway, and my father emerged from his office. I gulped, hoping he wouldn't notice me.

Papa frowned. "Lucia, where have you been?"

As my father approached me, Valeria escaped down the stairs to the kitchen.

My face flushed. "I went out with Valeria. She showed me the Rialto Bridge and many grand mansions along Canal Grande. It was wonderful, Papa!" The song from the fish market flashed through my mind, but I couldn't tell him now.

"You left the palazzo without my permission?" His voice sounded sterner than I had heard it for years.

"Sì, Papa." I lowered my eyes. Trembling inside, I walked next to him in silence.

Back in our rooms, I gazed up at him. "I'm sorry, Papa. I couldn't bear to stay in this palazzo any longer. But I didn't go out by myself."

"Sì, you've been waiting weeks to see Venezia." His tone softened. "I'm sorry, I haven't forgotten my promise to show you the city, but starting my practice has eaten up my time. Where did you go?"

"To the fish market."

"Such a distinguished part of this city." He smiled. "I'll have to show you another side of Venezia."

"I can hardly wait. When can we go?"

He stroked his beard, and I saw his mind at work. "Let's plan on next Sunday. I won't be working, so we can explore Venezia together."

"Not until Sunday?" I would have to wait two more days.

He nodded.

"Grazie." I sighed. "Papa, at the fish market..."

A knock at the door stopped me.

"Prego, pranzo is ready." Valeria glanced in Papa's direction. "Doctor Locatelli, would you and Lucia like to eat now with the Soncinis, or should we save your meal for later?"

"We'll be right there." He nodded. "Grazie."

As we approached the dining room, he turned to me. "We can talk more after the meal. I have something important to ask Doctor Soncini."

Maybe my outing with Valeria had disturbed Papa more than I thought. Even the savory aroma of fish stew couldn't drive the worry from my mind.

After greeting the Soncinis, my father asked Doctor Soncini if he knew of a school I could attend.

Filippo Soncini held a chunk of bread in mid-air, glanced at me and then at my father. "When Venetian girls know enough Latin to read Psalms and devotionals, their schooling ends. If you want Lucia to continue, perhaps my sons' tutor could teach her privately."

My father nodded. "Could I speak with the tutor? Lucia is so eager to learn."

Doctor Soncini agreed to make inquiries, and I couldn't hide my smile. Instead of receiving a punishment, I might soon begin my studies again.

After we finished our meal, Papa followed me out of the dining room. I took his hands. "Grazie, Papa."

He smiled. "Prego, Lucia. I wish I could teach you myself, but you need someone who can instruct and encourage you daily. I hope you can start soon."

Again I wanted to ask Papa about the Lutheran song, but just then Zuanne announced the arrival of a patient.

I sighed. Returning to my room, I searched for a first text to instruct Valeria.

As I rifled through a stack of books, my thoughts kept returning to the song I'd heard at the fish market. If only the girl's mother had let her daughter speak while I stood before her without an escort. I might never go back by myself, and Valeria would learn the secret of my faith if I conversed with people who shared Martin Luther's faith. Valeria had warmed up to me, but I couldn't entrust that dangerous secret to her.

If I wanted to meet Lutheran sympathizers, I would have to sneak out by myself. I still didn't know my way around Venezia, where to look, whom to seek, or how to convince them to trust me. I could succeed only if God worked a miracle.

The next morning, I pondered my dilemma instead of my Greek grammar book. Even Horace's *Art of Poetry* couldn't hold my attention. Finally, a knock on my door startled me out of my brooding.

A grinning Zuanne carried a wooden cage covered with a brown cloth. "Your father asked me to bring this to you, signorina." When he pulled up the cloth, I saw a golden canary perched inside, its head tucked under its wing until daylight awakened it.

I couldn't stop looking at its vibrant feathers—so different from the drab canary my mother once owned. "It's beautiful, Zuanne!" I set down my books. "Where did you get it?"

"Your father bought it in the market from a vendor who breeds canaries for their color. He asked me to tell you she's an early birthday present. He hopes you will enjoy her." Zuanne pulled a bulging cloth bag from his pocket. "When she gets hungry, give her some of these seeds."

I clutched the bag. "Grazie, Zuanne." My birthday, the Feast Day of Santa Lucia, would arrive in a few weeks, but this seemed more than a birthday gift.

He stepped toward the door. "Signorina Lucia, if only every girl had a father like yours. He spends so many hours helping his patients, but he still remembers to care for you."

I nodded, a lump clogging my throat, and closed the door behind him. The canary made me think of Mamma—how she taught her canary to sing, and how much I missed her. Papa's gift might help relieve my loneliness, but it also reminded me of my sorrow. I vowed that whenever I looked at this canary, I would instead choose to remember my mother's joyful voice and my father's thoughtfulness to me.

Throughout the morning, I sang to the canary whenever I looked up from my reading. By the time Valeria called me for pranzo, the bird had begun to warble in response to my songs. This sunny creature lifted my spirits and brought me hope, so I named it Speranza.

⁜

"Pronto, Papa?" My knuckles rapped on his door. Weeks had passed since he first promised to show me Venezia. Now that he had agreed on this day, I couldn't wait another moment for our adventure.

"Sì, Lucia." He called through the door, then opened it and smiled. "Where shall we begin our tour?"

"I've always dreamed of visiting Piazza San Marco and Palazzo Ducale, and the view from our ship whetted my appetite. Could we go there first?"

"Of course. I'll ask Zuanne to take us." He disappeared into the portego.

By the time I slipped my cloak over my shoulders and put on my hat, my father had returned, grinning. He took my arm. "*Allora,* may I escort you, signorina? Zuanne will prepare the gondola."

Papa swept me through the portego, out the double doors and down the steps to the wharf. Zuanne stood inside the boat, grabbed my hand and helped me into my seat. My father climbed on board, Zuanne untied the gondola, and we headed down the canal.

After many days in the palazzo, the brisk salt air delighted my nose. The sun's rays and cloudless sky hinted at warmth, but I pulled my cloak snug.

Zuanne turned the gondola into Canal Grande, and ornate mansions dazzled my eyes on both sides. Gleaming white statues supported the balcony of one grand home. Marble, mosaics, and colorful frescoes adorned other *palazzi.* I grinned at my father. "What a treat for the eyes—such a different side of Venezia than I saw with Valeria! Do you know who owns these mansions?"

He shrugged his shoulders. "Only a few of them."

"I'm curious about these houses and the families who live in them." I hoped for clues about fellow believers in Martin Luther's faith.

Papa turned to Zuanne. "Can you instruct us?"

He nodded. "Sì, I'll tell you what I've heard. Take a look at this palazzo coming up on the right—Ca' Foscari. This family is so important, and their home so grand, that King Henry of France stayed here when he came to Venezia a few years ago."

When I saw its elegant *loggia*—two entire stories of open corridors supported by arches—I could imagine a king sleeping inside.

With every bend in Canal Grande and each smaller canal that joined it, my amazement grew at the vast size and beauty of this city. At the same time, I realized I could find a pearl in the murky canal as easily as Lutheran sympathizers.

At last we passed the customs warehouse on the right bank where the canal emptied into San Marco basin. Zuanne pointed far across the water. "See that building under construction over there?"

I squinted in the sunlight and saw gray sheets of scaffolding.

"Someday soon, they'll finish that grand new church, and we'll visit." His voice dropped. "Venezia's leaders were so thankful to God after the pestilence ended that they vowed to build it. They'll dedicate the church to the Redeemer. Already we honor him with the Feast of the Redeemer every summer. Boats make a bridge stretching across the water all the way from San Marco to the site of the church. The whole city celebrates."

Anger flashed through me at his mention of the pestilence and a celebration in the same breath. I turned to my father. "You told me thousands of people died of pestilence. Shouldn't Venezia grieve the loved ones it lost instead of celebrating?"

"Of course we'll never forget the dear souls God took to be with Him." He paused. "But we must show our gratitude for every mercy God gives us." He stared out at the canal.

A fresh pang of grief shot through me, and I wondered if I'd ever be able to thank God for those who survived when Mamma perished.

Moments later, Zuanne pulled the gondola up to a wharf at the Riva degli Schiavoni. I had thought nothing could surpass the sights along Canal Grande until I stepped out and surveyed the panorama before my eyes. In front of us, I recognized the Palazzo Ducale, with its façade of pink marble and white stone above two stories of open arches. To our left, the *campanile* towered over the largest piazza I had ever seen. I couldn't identify the other buildings, but stared, motionless, at the scale and beauty before me.

Behind me, my father tapped my shoulder. "*Avanti*, Lucia."

I scrambled out, my eyes still riveted to the scene before me. "Papa, I've seen drawings of this piazza, but they don't compare with this sight. What's that building across from us, to the left of the campanile?"

He nodded. "That's Biblioteca Marciana. They own a copy of every book printed in Venezia. Notice how the arches and open first floor loggia harmonize with the Palazzo Ducale? Such brilliant touches earned Jacopo Sansovino his reputation as a master architect."

The sound of chimes drew my attention to the bell tower at the far end of the piazza, but soon Papa took my arm and guided me around pigeons, beggars, vendors and their stalls, and passersby.

We stopped and Papa gestured upward, toward the grandest building of all, the cathedral of San Marco. I gaped at its façade. I had never seen a church with five sets of double doors in front. An arch embellished each door, some with mosaics in the spaces underneath. Four majestic bronze horses perched above the central doorway, each lifting a forepaw, eager to charge away.

I raised my eyes to the intricate spires atop the façade. Then I spied domes rising from the roof like giant onions, each topped by a cross. Could such a work of art also serve as a church?

Gazing at such splendor, I felt humble as an ant in its nest.

Papa squeezed my hand. "Let's go inside. We can look at the interior while we attend Mass."

I stared at him. During Papa's years in prison, I had to go to Mass and perform all the Church's rituals, but I expected we could drop this pretense now. "Do we have to stay for Mass, Papa?"

His smile vanished, and he looked past me. "Of course. It's a beautiful church. I'm sure you'll enjoy every moment inside."

I heard an edge in his voice, and I turned to see what had changed his mood. A few paces behind us, a tall monk leaned on a cane and looked at the ground. My body stiffened. Papa had recognized Vincenzo. Maybe his proximity was a coincidence, but I feared not.

Now Papa didn't have to tell me to show my loyalty to the Church. I sighed. "All right, but please give me another look at the exterior afterward."

He took my arm again, and we stepped inside the cathedral. I caught my breath. Papa's description had been too modest. Miniature golden tiles by the thousands covered the walls of the vestibule, and they were only the background. Mosaics of angels and the Virgin Mary welcomed us. My eyes lingered, and I savored each bright-colored mosaic.

The crowd pressed in, and Papa nudged me forward into the sanctuary. The walls of this vast structure dazzled my eyes. Marble lined the lower walls, topped by mosaic figures set in the golden background that continued all the way up to the ceiling and domes, soaring far above. Everywhere I turned, tiny squares of colored glass formed pictures of saints and scenes from the Bible.

I didn't want to miss anything, and I stepped on a few toes as we continued toward the middle of the church, almost directly beneath the great dome. In front of us, statues of the apostles, John the Baptist, and the Madonna perched atop a carved wooden screen. Anywhere but here in this building, this barrier separating the congregation from the altar would have been the church's prized possession.

A priest stepped up to the lectern, surveying the congregation from beneath a black skullcap. The cathedral quieted. I listened to the cleric's homily, but soon my focus turned upward, to the dome where I gazed at mosaics of Jesus ascending to heaven. I scrutinized everything else within view, trying to paint a mental picture of each mosaic. If I should be sequestered again inside our palazzo, these memories would help sustain me.

I shifted my gaze from one mosaic to the next. Then I noticed my father's eyelids drooping. I elbowed him and prayed Vincenzo hadn't noticed.

Finally, the priest gave his benediction and marched down the central aisle. I turned to my father. "What an amazing church, Papa—I can't appreciate it in one visit. Could we come back next week?"

He smiled.

While we waited for the crowd to disperse, I surveyed each arm of the cross-shaped cathedral. My gaze lingered on the splendor before me. The church's beauty surpassed anything I had seen in Verona, anything I could even imagine.

In the space of one thought, sorrow displaced my wonder. "Papa, you know how Mamma loved beauty. Did she ever see this church?"

"No, she never had a chance to visit Venezia." He sighed. "You're right. San Marco would have delighted her."

We left the church in silence. Papa led me down walkways and across bridges to show me as much of Venezia as he could before the sun sank below the horizon. I tried to concentrate on Papa's words, but an inner voice told me I should be mourning my mother's death instead of feasting my eyes on the most beautiful sights in Christendom.

Giordano

I had hoped our visit to Venezia's landmarks would dispel my daughter's melancholy, but as the afternoon progressed, Lucia's eyes dulled and her enthusiasm waned. When we stepped inside our suite, I led her into my study and placed my hand on her shoulder.

"Are you unwell, Lucia, or just fatigued?"

She creased her brow and looked at the ground. "I've been thinking of Mamma ever since we left San Marco. I still miss her. I wish she could have seen San Marco with us."

I embraced her. "I feel that way, too, but I think she would want us to enjoy Venezia even without her."

"Sì, Papa." She wiped her eyes. "But will I ever get over my sorrow?"

I cleared my throat. "I don't know, Lucia, but I hope someday the joy she brought us will outweigh our grief."

She sighed and looked into my eyes. "Papa, while we're alone, I have another question. Why did you suggest we attend Mass at San Marco? God never commanded that we attend Mass every week, but the Church did. Martin Luther wrote that God cares whether we believe in him, not if we follow rules or do good works. So why must we go to Mass?"

My throat constricted. "Good logic, but life in Venezia isn't so simple. Because this city was built on islands, people live in close quarters and watch each other. Neighbors notice visitors' comings and goings more than in Verona. The Inquisition takes advantage of this and questions people about their neighbors' activities."

Her face paled. "But you told me Venezia was such a cosmopolitan city—surely it must tolerate many types of beliefs."

"I thought so, too, when I lived here years ago. I gave Luther's books to my friends and met with them to discuss his ideas. Finally, someone warned me that the Inquisition was about to arrest me, so I fled for my life, all the way to the lands north of the Alps. I lost my medical practice and my friends."

She grimaced. Then she raised her eyes to mine. "Couldn't we practice our faith at home, just the two of us?"

"How I would enjoy that, but our neighbors would notice if we didn't attend Mass, and the servants might overhear us." I sighed. "We must never forget Doctor Soncini's kindness. He risks his family's reputation by allowing us to live in his lovely palazzo. Probably no one else in Venezia would rent to me." I shook my head. "No, we must not endanger the Soncinis."

A sudden inspiration sent me to unlock a nearby chest of books. I pulled out a thick, dog-eared volume and handed it to my daughter. "But I'll give you this to encourage you in your faith—your mother's Bible."

She gasped. "Mamma had a Bible?"

I smiled. "I gave it to her as a wedding gift. Your mother studied it and read it from cover to cover, but she hid it for everyone's protection. The sisters in the convent taught her many scripture passages, but they didn't give her a Bible she could read on her own. She would want you to have it."

She clutched it under her arm. "Grazie, Papa. I will also treasure and hide it." She looked up at me. "Papa, I've wanted to ask you this all afternoon: why do you obey all the Roman Church's teachings if you believe Luther's ideas?"

I sighed. "Do you remember the story of Nicodemus? Saint John told how Nicodemus came to see Jesus at night, so no one would see him. Sometimes we must conceal our beliefs as Nicodemus did, and surely this is one such time."

"But Papa, how long must we wait to tell people Luther's message?"

"I pray that moment will come soon, but only God knows."

Lucia frowned and held my gaze. At last she spoke, her voice little more than a whisper. "Grazie, Papa, for showing me Venezia." She turned and strode toward her bedchamber.

Our conversation planted a seed of worry in my mind. I prayed that in the years since we last discussed Luther, Lucia had gained enough maturity to keep our dangerous secret.

Chapter 15

CONNECTIONS

Lucia

J learned my stubbornness from Papa, and I would only waste my energy arguing with him. Instead I bit my lip and pulled my door shut, sinking into the mattress. Our outing hadn't led me to any other followers of Martin Luther. Even worse, Papa's cautionary words meant I couldn't converse with anyone about the topic I ached to discuss—my religious beliefs.

"Speranza, what should I do?" I opened my canary's cage door, tossed in some birdseed, and stroked her feathers. "If I talk about Luther's ideas, I'm disobeying my father, maybe endangering us both. But if I keep silent, I'll never find a community of fellow believers." After an excited chirp, she pecked at her food, and I closed the cage door.

Glancing at Mamma's harp, I remembered how she used to pick it up when she needed peace. As moonlight glimmered on the canal, I sat out on my balcony and played *Dona nobis pacem*, the song from Mass that Mamma taught me in my childhood. My frustration drained away as I plucked the strings and sang the melody.

When I heard Vincenzo's voice, I put down the harp and watched him, silhouetted in his dinghy, like a pea in its pod.

"Vincenzo, didn't I see you at San Marco this morning?"

He grinned. "Sì. Wasn't it amazing how the mosaics brought to life the saints and Bible stories, right in front of our eyes? And such heavenly music! How can people pay attention to Mass?"

I glanced at Mamma's harp. "Maybe the art and music point them to God."

He nodded.

I looked from Vincenzo down the canal toward the distant Piazza San Marco and felt a twinge inside. "What coincidences to see you only three days ago at the Fish Market, and today both at San Marco and from my balcony. What brings you here?"

He blushed. "I live nearby. I came out when I heard your harp. You don't mind, I hope."

Vincenzo's surveillance put me on edge, and my throat went dry. But I reminded myself that this friendship could help Papa. "Your voice certainly improves my music, and a familiar face makes me feel more at home in Venezia." I eyed him closely. "But Vincenzo, can you leave my father alone? He's the only family I have now. He's a good man. Don't waste your time watching him."

Vincenzo's smile faded. "Believe me, Lucia, I didn't know he was your father when I took this job. I'm not trying to take him from you, but I must protect Venezia from heresy. If he's not a heretic, the Church won't bother him."

I stared at him. Vincenzo's words proved the correctness of Papa's recent argument. I sighed and picked up my harp.

Twilight became darkness, and the breeze turned colder.

"I'm getting chilled. I'd better go in." By the time I set the harp inside and returned to shut the window-doors, Vincenzo had disappeared.

Dipping my quill in an inkwell, I sat at my desk and faced a blank page. Conversing with Vincenzo relieved my loneliness but left me with an uneasy feeling. I hoped writing verse would give me insight.

As I struggled with my poem, I groped for the candle and tinder-box on my desk. Finally, my eyes focused on the flame, and I heard a voice.

"See the light and warmth you brought to this room by lighting one candle? Now take the opportunities I place before you, Lucia—recognize each one as my gift. I have not forgotten you—I created you and know you. I hear your every cry and prayer. I see each word of poetry you write."

I caught my breath. God not only spoke to me, but His words showed He knows me better than I know myself. Joy and excitement surged through me, replacing the tension in my neck and shoulders.

Carpe diem, Horace had advised his readers—and I would seize the day, arising early the next morning to review my Greek grammar and select my favorite books—perhaps Sophocles' *The Birds*, Quintilian's *Latin Institutes of Oratory*, Cicero's Latin *Letters to Familiares*, and Augustine's *Confessions*—in hopes of meeting with a tutor. Then I would study my *Salterio*, the worn volume from which I had learned the alphabet, reading, and my prayers, to prepare for Valeria's lesson in the afternoon. Finally, I would speak with Vincenzo at every opportunity, praying for words that would change his mind.

Unwittingly, Vincenzo had confirmed Papa's admonition that Luther's writings must wait for a more opportune moment. But I still dreamed of the day when I could stand in Piazza San Marco and read Luther's book aloud.

Giordano

Lucia shut the door behind her. I wiped my brow, anticipating a solitary evening. Even before I warned her, I suspected my words would anger her, just as they would have infuriated me in my youth. After Lucia's birth, my drive to protect my family overshadowed even my loyalty to the faith of Martin Luther. I couldn't allow my daughter to risk her life, no matter how worthy the cause.

Perhaps I shouldn't have given her Caterina's Bible. Even though she was old enough now to realize the consequences of her actions, I couldn't be sure she would take my caution to heart. She needed something else to lift her spirits and occupy her thoughts. *May God bring Lucia a tutor soon.*

I sat down at my desk and glanced toward the window. In its reflection, my hardened features stared back at me. I recoiled.

Lucia possessed a zeal for her faith, something my painful experiences had drained from me. The words of our recent conversation echoed through my mind: *Papa, how can you believe Luther's ideas but still obey the Roman Church's teachings?*

How, indeed—and how long could I suppress my beliefs? A sob welled up from my chest. In my attempt to shield Lucia from danger, I had betrayed my convictions and demanded she conceal hers. What kind of father was I?

I imagined myself pounding on Lucia's door and apologizing for what I had told her. But I needed time to think of better advice, and she might not listen to me in her current state. Instead, I could write in my study, safe and comfortable, as I had planned.

An idea popped into my mind. I could go out and look for fellow believers in Martin Luther's faith—people with whom Lucia and I could discuss our beliefs and worship with clear consciences. I might attract the Inquisition's attention if I fraternized with suspicious people—I could never forget the brutality of the Holy Office—but I couldn't squander my life in fear.

Throwing on my cloak, I slipped out to the portego. Zuanne's footsteps resounded on the stone stairway, and I waited for him to reach the top.

"*Buona sera*, Zuanne."

He doffed his cap. "Doctor Locatelli, can I help you?"

My spine tingled. The portego lay deserted except for the loyal master of our house and me. I glanced around to make sure there were no other listening ears nearby. Finally, I nodded. "Sì, Zuanne.

Could you take me across the canal? I have business on the other side."

"Of course. Shall I wait and bring you home?"

"Grazie, but no—just let me out across the canal. I don't know how long I'll be. Come back and enjoy the evening with your family."

Zuanne smiled. "As you wish, Doctor Locatelli." He donned his cloak and opened the door leading out to the canal.

Moments later, I climbed out of the *gondola* and thanked Zuanne. Fighting a headwind off the canal, I set off along Riva del Carbon. When I reached the Rialto Bridge, I turned away from Canal Grande and approached the church of San Bartolomeo. Cracking the sanctuary door open, I counted only a handful of aged men and women listening to a priest's homily—a far cry from the animated congregation of German merchants I recalled from my first sojourn in Venezia. I walked back outside. Across the piazza, lanterns glowed on either side of a familiar doorway. The Black Eagle Inn had been the site of many a debate of Martin Luther's ideas. I found myself walking toward it.

Standing in the doorway, I surveyed the inn. Most of the tables sat empty that night, and I heard only quiet conversations in my native tongue. One man, a strapping light-haired merchant, obviously came from north of the mountains, but he had business on his mind. He opened a ledger and showed it to the man across from him. I overheard words like clocks, armor, and copper—not the religious discussion I had hoped to hear. Before the innkeeper spoke with me, I walked out.

In the past, my friends in the book trade had stayed at the nearby Fondaco dei Tedeschi, where they stored the books they traded. Now it was my last hope. I walked through Campo San Bartolomeo until I reached the Fondaco's shops, pausing in front of each, searching for a face I recognized. I found none.

Finally, I came upon an entrance to the building's interior. Climbing the stairway to the second-floor residences, I wandered down dark halls. Snatches of the German tongue echoed through closed doors. Overhearing the words *bücher* and *büchhandler*, I assumed book traders lodged within, so I knocked on the door.

"*Ja.*" A guttural voice responded, and the door cracked open. "*Wer bissen Ihnen?*"

I struggled to remember a few words of German. "*Ich heisse Giordano Locatelli.*"

A torrent of German followed, too fast for me to understand—but when he closed the door in my face, no doubts lingered in my mind about its meaning.

I continued my trek down the hallway but saw no one and heard no familiar voices. Finally, I gave up and descended the stairs to the first floor. I almost wondered if I had only imagined the once-vibrant congregation of Luther's followers. If such a community still existed, how could I discover it?

When I emerged from the Fondaco, a silhouetted figure caught my eye. Across the *campo*, the tall monk with a cane peered into the Black Eagle Inn. He stood with his back toward me, but his silhouette, with his left shoulder lower than the right, identified him at once as Vincenzo, the Inquisition agent who had questioned me in the palazzo. My breath quickened.

If he hadn't followed me here, I didn't want him to see me now. Instead of crossing Campo San Bartolomeo, passing in front of the church, and waiting next to the Canal Grande for a boatman to take me home, I turned at once to my right and followed a back route to the canal. Rushing past the storefronts of the Fondaco with my head down, I strode across the Rialto Bridge's damp planks and stopped beside a lamppost.

Catching my breath, I turned back toward the bridge to see if anyone had followed me. A minute or two later, I heard a rhythmic tapping against the cobblestones on the far side of the bridge. My muscles tensed. The noise grew louder.

I half-expected someone to spring toward me out of the darkness, but instead the tall man with a cane ventured onto the bridge and stopped in the middle, at its highest point. Silhouetted in the moonlight, Vincenzo looked toward the *campo* where I hid. I shrank back and prayed he wouldn't notice me in the shadows.

I heard only the pounding of my heart as Vincenzo's gaze lingered. At last I heard the tapping of his cane. Waiting until the sound grew distant, I let out my breath and began my long walk through the San Polo district.

With every shop I passed, my mind accused me: I should have realized times had changed and I might never be able to meet again with other followers of Martin Luther. Instead, I had ventured out on a futile journey, risked arrest by the Inquisition, and imperiled Lucia's future.

Lucia

After much discussion between Papa and Doctor Soncini, I took my favorite books to the portego to meet with Messer Guadagnoli, the graying former monk who tutored the Soncinis' three sons. Showing him my books, I answered his questions and told him about my studies in Verona. He declared that I had advanced beyond the level of Venezia's schools for girls and would need either a private tutor or a class with boys.

Messer Guadagnoli invited me to join his class. He cautioned that he didn't teach poetry, but he promised to look for a poetry instructor. Without a better option, I accepted his offer, only to learn that Doctor Soncini vetoed my joining the class until the tutor persuaded him that my presence would have a beneficial effect on his sons.

The next morning, I followed Messer Guadagnoli through the portego into a book-lined room, placing my books and quills across from him on the polished rectangular table. Scores of leather-bound volumes perfumed the air, reminding me of my father's study in Verona.

Loud footsteps clumped across the mosaic floor, and I looked up. With a quick nod, Roberto slipped into the chair beside me while the younger boys threw their papers on the table across from us.

The tutor opened a worn volume. "Take out the pages you copied from Augustine's *Confessions*."

I picked up my copy of the book, and the boys leafed through their papers.

Messer Guadagnoli eyed us. "Remember how the young Augustine stole pears, just for the pleasure of stealing, and threw them to the pigs?"

Roberto nodded. Carlo and Antonio snickered, and I could imagine them following Augustine's example.

The tutor continued. "In Book II, Chapter 7, Augustine discusses his sin: *What man who reflects upon his own weakness can dare to claim that his own efforts have made him chaste and free from sin, as though this entitled him to love you the less, on the ground that he had less need of the mercy by which you forgive the sins of the penitent?* Boys, can you explain the meaning of this passage?"

The selection reminded me of Martin Luther's writing, and I straightened in my chair, wondering if Messer Guadagnoli sympathized with Luther.

Carlo looked at his hands, while Antonio shrugged his shoulders.

Roberto spoke. "I suppose Augustine believed he needed God's forgiveness, even though he stole only pears."

The tutor turned to me. "Can you add anything, signorina?"

I nodded so vigorously that my head ached. "Augustine knew that good works could never earn God's forgiveness. He gives mercy as a gift to all who put their faith in him. No matter how small or large our sin, we all need God's mercy equally."

All three boys stared at me. None of them said a word.

Our teacher spoke in a hushed tone. "Grazie, Lucia."

I exhaled, wondering what he thought of my answer.

Moments later, I surpassed Roberto in a Latin drill, and my nerves calmed. Then he bested me in Greek and tried to hide a grin. In spite of my embarrassment, I appreciated the challenge from Roberto's quick mind.

In contrast, Roberto's younger brothers wasted the tutor's time with their whispers, kicks, and punches. Carlo's deep voice and beard stubble suggested maturity, but he whispered crude jokes and condescending remarks. Roberto ignored most of them, but the impulsive Antonio couldn't help but respond to Carlo's goads.

Now I understood better Valeria's comments about the Soncini boys. At the end of our lessons, the boys rushed out of the study, but I trailed behind, pondering whether I should stay in this class or study by myself.

Chapter 16

UNSPOKEN WARNING

Stefano

*J*n the months since Vincenzo's letter arrived, I had almost put Doctor Locatelli and Lucia out of my mind, trying to avoid my guilty feeling after not telling them an Inquisition agent was watching them.

I met a beautiful girl named Giulietta, and now her dainty frame, shy smile, and glowing dark eyes made me forget everything else.

But this afternoon, Gianpietro arrived from Venezia and handed me another letter from Vincenzo. I knew I couldn't ignore it, that I must pass on whatever information it contained to Father Inquisitor, so I forced myself to break the seal and read Vincenzo's message.

12 September 1577

Greetings in the name of our Lord to Father Inquisitor in Verona.

I am writing to inform you of my observations of Giordano Locatelli, lately of Venezia. Since my first letter, I have been watching the palazzo in which he lives and works, keeping a record of everyone who enters. Because some visitors are his patients, and others come to see the family with whom he shares the palazzo, I have had little success in identifying his personal friends. But his excursions hint that he may be slipping back into heresy.

Last night I pursued him to the Fondaco dei Tedeschi and Campo San Bartolomeo, where he appeared to be searching for someone. That area of Venezia swarms with foreigners from the north; some of them surely believe Luther's heresies. I will continue to follow him closely and will report often on his contacts.

I plan to watch him from a distance until he believes he can practice heresy with impunity. When he becomes careless, I will snare him, and the overwhelming evidence of his heresy will prove his guilt. This may take some time, but I will persist if the Holy Office permits me to do so.

Ever your humble servant,

Vincenzo Ugoni

I covered my eyes with my hand. Unless Father Inquisitor told him to stop, Vincenzo would keep watch on Doctor Locatelli for months or even years. If the Inquisition should imprison my father's friend again or execute him, my conscience would torment me for the rest of my life.

Frozen in my chair, I knew I should warn Doctor Locatelli—but Giulietta's face appeared before my closed eyes. If the Inquisition caught me, I would lose the woman I dreamed of marrying. The risk loomed too large. Placing the letter on Father Inquisitor's desk, I opened the next document.

Chapter 17

MODESTA

Lucia

After two weeks of waiting to hear about a poetry instructor, I had almost given up hope until Messer Guadagnoli approached me one day after class.

"My apologies, Lucia, for the delay in finding a poetry tutor I can recommend," he began. "At last I've learned of a young Venetian woman, Modesta da Pozzo, whose poetry has built her a fine reputation. She lives with her uncle, Niccolò Doglioni, and his wife at their home in San Giuliano parish. She would be happy to meet with you. I can't imagine a more appropriate tutor for you, so your father may wish to speak with her."

"Grazie, Messer Guadagnoli—she sounds perfect! I'll hope to meet her soon." Scooping up my books and papers, I hurried out of the study to talk with my father at pranzo. I would ask him to send Signorina da Pozzo a letter at once to arrange a meeting.

As I walked to the dining room, I wondered how Modesta da Pozzo had become a great poet and how she might teach me. I hoped she might sympathize with Martin Luther, but I remembered my father's warning about Venezia's system of informants. Broaching the subject of Luther without jeopardizing my safety would present a challenge.

We sat down to the mid-day meal with Doctor Soncini and his wife, and I turned to my father. "Papa, Messer Guadagnoli told me great news today!" I related the entire conversation.

He smiled at me. "*Bene*, Lucia. I'll try to set up a meeting with her."

"Grazie." I picked up my spoon and looked down at my plate.

Doctor Soncini spoke up. "My apologies for interrupting, Giordano, but your daughter's reputation may suffer if you allow such a meeting. The famous women poets in Venezia have reputations as courtesans. As far as I know, the only honorable Venetian women who write poetry are cloistered nuns."

I gasped. My teacher had just told me he couldn't imagine a more appropriate tutor. He would never recommend a woman of low morals. Doctor Soncini must be wrong. If only I had waited to tell Papa about Modesta in private.

At that moment, I didn't care what Doctor Soncini or anyone in Venezia would think of me if I visited Modesta da Pozzo. I returned to my bedchamber and pounded my fists on the mattress. My mind worked so well when I studied, but it couldn't warn me when I needed to keep my mouth closed.

The next morning I dressed quickly and opened my door slightly to hear Messer Guadagnoli's arrival. As soon as Zuanne closed the land door, I rushed out to the portego and told the tutor about Doctor Soncini's warning.

My tutor agreed to confirm the poet's good reputation, and he approached me after class three long days later. "Lucia, I'm happy to report that all of Venezia esteems the name of Signorina Modesta da Pozzo. Everyone I spoke to praised her as an upstanding woman. Her parents died when she was an infant, and the honorable Venetians of her extended family provided her nurture and a fine education. Her brilliance has impressed all who meet her." He smiled. "Signorina da Pozzo will send you a letter to set up an appointment."

"Grazie, Messer Guadagnoli." At last! I might never locate other followers of Luther, but at least I could share my passion for poetry. I wanted to hug him. Instead I grabbed my books and rushed out of the classroom to inform my father.

The next morning, Zuanne brought me a rough brown envelope addressed in a scrawl. I broke the crude seal and pulled out a letter. Beneath the coarse packaging, impeccable handwriting graced a vellum sheet.

Greetings and salutations to Doctor Locatelli and Signorina Locatelli,

It will be my pleasure to meet with you next Tuesday afternoon at the home of my uncle, Niccolò Doglioni. Please send word if this time would be inconvenient for you. Otherwise, I will look forward to seeing you then.

Best regards,

Modesta da Pozzo

My fingers trembled as I rolled the letter like a scroll and tied it with a ribbon. I pondered how to prepare for the meeting and how I would keep my mind on anything else until then.

On Tuesday afternoon, I climbed down the steps toward the gondola in such haste that I tripped on the hem of my favorite indigo gown. I screamed. If my father hadn't grabbed me, I would have fallen onto the wharf or even into the canal. Rising to my full height, I took a deep breath and stood in place until my legs stopped shaking. Now a fear of drowning added to my jitters, but I tried to push it out of my mind. Nothing must mar our visit to Modesta da Pozzo.

Zuanne shook his head. "Take care, signorina." He extended his hand to help me into the gondola and held the red-striped *palina* mooring the gondola until we had settled into our places. Then he whisked us out into the canal.

In one hand I clutched my borsa, now filled with poetry books, and with the other I held onto my seat. Even the sights along Canal Grande couldn't hold my interest that day. I tried to picture Modesta and silently rehearsed what I would say to this renowned poet, praying she would agree to tutor me.

When our gondola pulled up to the wharf in San Giuliano parish, I noticed a thin man seated in a dinghy at the next pier with his back to us. He didn't appear to be beginning or ending a journey, just sitting, which struck me as odd. When I took my father's arm and stepped out of the gondola, my excitement made me forget the man in the boat. We climbed the steps to the palazzo where Modesta lived.

My father knocked at the door. As we waited, I couldn't take my eyes off the façade's bright frescoes. A servant ushered us into an airy, sun-drenched portego. One glance at its paintings, statues, and marble fireplace confirmed my surmise about the family's wealth.

Then I noticed the corner of the portego where a young woman stretched her legs across a lettuccio upholstered of shiny gold silk. Her toes dangled beyond the cushion—an odd posture in this refined setting. Holding a quill in her right hand, she stared down at a parchment sheet balanced on the armrest.

She appeared young enough to be my older sister, so my eyes kept searching the hall. Finding no one else, I settled my gaze on the barefoot woman. She had gathered her raven hair into a tight bun, accentuating her severe features. Her dark brows knit into a frown, giving her the air of a serious scholar who would tolerate no nonsense. My jaw tightened.

A moment later, she set down her quill and smiled at us. I nodded. Slipping on her shoes, she walked toward us, offering her hand. "Piacere, Modesta da Pozzo. I've been trying to find the right word for my poem."

Papa kissed her hand. "Piacere, signorina. *Mi chiamo* Giordano Locatelli. This is my daughter, Lucia."

I smiled and shook Modesta's hand. As we pulled upholstered chairs close, she asked about my education and interest in poetry. Her eyes lit up when I told her I enjoyed writing poems. She told us about her parents' death from pestilence and her placement in a convent as a foundling.

Her story brought back the pain of my own mother's death but also gave me hope. Modesta had overcome even greater obstacles than I faced to win renown as a poet, so perhaps I could do the same.

I cleared my throat. "I hope someday for the privilege of reading your poetry."

She nodded. "I'll enjoy sharing my poetry with you, Lucia. Perhaps we could read our own poetry after we study the Latin poets each time we meet." She eyed my borsa. "May I see your books?"

I handed her my well-read volumes of Horace, Ovid, Terence, and Virgil. Glancing around the room again, I grinned. At last I could study my favorite subject—and not with a prim schoolmistress, but a young woman poet, in this elegant Venetian palazzo.

A few minutes later, she looked up at me. "Study the poems I've marked, and we'll discuss them next time we meet. I've written the name of each poem on a scrap of paper and placed it at the appropriate page."

"Grazie, signorina. I look forward to that meeting." I could scarcely believe my good fortune.

My father asked Modesta about her fee.

She shook her head. "My uncle provides everything I need, so why should I charge a fee for something I enjoy?" She smiled at me.

"Grazie." I smiled back. Tossing my cloak over my shoulders, I gathered my books and papers.

Giordano

Without warning, the double doors of the portego burst open, and a graying gentleman in a dark silk and velvet cloak strode through the grand hall. I didn't know his face, but he must have recognized me, judging from his wide-eyed glance in my direction.

"Buona sera, Zio Nicolò." Modesta nodded to her uncle.

He eyed her, pale and unsmiling. "Modesta, usher these people out at once and come to my study." Ignoring Lucia and me, Signor Doglioni proceeded deeper into the house.

I stared after him. If he didn't want us in his house, why had Modesta invited us?

Red-faced, Modesta shrugged and escorted us to the door. Outside, dark clouds shrouded the sun. As we walked down the stairway to the pier, my gaze followed Lucia's to the next wharf, where a tall man sat in a dinghy. When we boarded the gondola, he picked up his oars.

I saw a cane beside him, and my muscles tensed—Vincenzo, the Inquisition agent, again! I glanced at Lucia. She shuddered and pulled her cloak tight.

I turned to Zuanne. "Andiamo, *subito*."

He forced his wooden oar deep into the canal. The gondola sprang away from the wharf like a racehorse straining for the lead. After a few minutes, only distant silhouettes remained of the Doglioni palazzo, the dinghy, and its occupant. We rounded a curve in the canal and pulled into a side canal.

Zuanne sighed and shook his head. "I hope we've lost him. The Inquisition needs to find more work for that man. He's always bothering me, hovering around the wharf, asking me where I'm going. Of course I've never told him anything—I recognized him as the monk who disturbed Doctor Locatelli—but somehow he found out where we were going today."

Lucia turned to me, blinking back tears. "Do you think Vincenzo spread rumors about us to Signor Doglioni?" She paused. "Could that explain his rudeness?"

"That wouldn't surprise me." I sighed. "Signor Doglioni wouldn't want anything to taint his family's reputation, especially if he seeks a husband for his niece. Nothing remains hidden for long in Venezia, and he wouldn't want questions to arise about Modesta's character or friendships."

She shook her head. "I've waited so long for a poetry tutor, and Modesta was perfect." Her countenance hadn't looked so downcast since I told her we must leave Verona.

I clasped her hand. "Perhaps a solution will emerge, but Signorina da Pozzo must discover it."

Lucia stared at the ink-black water.

If only I could offer her more comfort. But now I realized my heresy conviction had cast a shadow not only on my future but on Lucia's opportunities as well. Such injustice and no clear path to right it.

Chapter 18

UNCHARTED PATH

Lucia
June, 1580

After nearly three years in Messer Guadagnoli's class, in the back of my mind, I knew that one day my education must end. At the age of eighteen I was still delighting in Greek and poetry, but most girls had married, joined a convent, or taken up domestic service. Even so, my tutor caught me by surprise when he asked to speak with me on a spring afternoon.

As soon as Roberto followed his brothers out of the library at the end of our lesson, our tutor spoke to me. "Lucia, Roberto is ready to begin his studies at the University of Padova, as you would be if you were male. You're an eager student, and I've enjoyed teaching you, but you wouldn't belong in a class with only Carlo and Antonio. I know you're ready for something new. I only wish I could recommend a specific course." He shook his head.

I nodded. Roberto and I had become amicable competitors. Without him, the class would lose its excitement and challenge.

"Whatever you decide, you must blaze your own trail. As you know, an educated young woman like yourself is rare. You're fortunate to have a mentor in Signorina da Pozzo. Perhaps she will have suggestions for you."

I nodded again, hoping my tutor's words would become a reality. Thank God that in spite of her uncle's proscription of my visits, Modesta had found a way to guide my poetry study. Shortly after Papa and I met with her, she had sent me a letter suggesting I send her my poems each week. By now, our exchange of poems and comments provided a weekly highlight.

"With your father's wise counsel, I'm confident you'll reach a good decision."

His announcement signaled the end of my life as his student and weighed on me as if he had tossed me a boulder. Now the responsibility for my life rested on my shoulders.

"Grazie. This decision will require much thought." I tried to maintain my composure. "How much longer will Roberto remain in the class?"

"Another two weeks."

I looked down at the table. In two weeks, only memories would remain of my tutor's lessons and my intellectual sparring with Roberto. I gathered my books and papers, wishing I could collect my thoughts about the future as easily. "*Arrivederci*, Messer Guadagnoli."

As I left the library, sadness overwhelmed me one moment, and fear of the future, the next. My tutor had challenged me to find my own way, but within the confines of Venetian society, that path might prove much narrower than I wished.

Pranzo seemed to last for hours. When we finally left the dining room, I asked Papa if we could talk. He nodded and we walked across the portego to our rooms. A moment later, he pulled up a chair across from mine.

"What's bothering you, Lucia? You seemed distracted during pranzo."

The concern in his eyes gave me comfort, and I told him what my tutor and I had discussed.

"Congratulations, Lucia." He smiled. "This day has come sooner than I expected. Now the world will recognize you as an adult, and you'll be free to choose your own course."

I suppressed a groan. "But what can I do? I want to use my education and continue to learn." I hoped he would offer a solution.

My father pulled a parchment sheet from his desk. "Just this morning, I received a letter from Stefano Capriolo. It reminded me how quickly the years pass. I can still picture you and Stefano as children and myself at your current age. I've been thinking about your future, too."

I turned my eyes to the letter.

To Doctor Giordano Locatelli and Signorina Lucia Locatelli

My dear friends,

I am writing to announce that Giulietta Biondi and I will exchange our wedding rings two weeks from today. Our families are neighbors. I met Giulietta outside San Stefano church one Sunday and have been courting her for the past two years. A promotion from my employer will give me the means to support her and rent a cottage near our families. I am about to begin my new position as a scribe transcribing trials before the Holy Office. I will need to review my Latin and write quickly, but Father Inquisitor assures me my skills will be adequate to keep up with the testimony.

I realize you live too far away to join us for our ring ceremony, but I wanted to let you know this joyful news since you are my family's closest friends.

Yours truly,

Stefano Capriolo

I shook my head. "I still think of Stefano as a prankster. I can't imagine him as a bridegroom--even less as a scribe for the Inquisition's trials. What an awful job!"

Papa grimaced. "Sì, his work won't be pleasant. Let's hope his marriage and family life bring him happiness." He eyed me. "Lucia, at your age many young women have already married. If I arranged a good match for you, you could count on a secure future. If you don't marry, my legacy won't support you for long after I die. You have many years ahead of you, and I fear that you, as a woman, won't be able to earn an adequate livelihood to sustain yourself."

"Papa, you know me too well to suggest such a thing!" I cocked my chin. "How could the life of a Venetian wife and mother ever compare with the world of books and ideas? I'd sooner join a convent where I could read and write than marry someone who doesn't love the scholarly life as much as I do."

He sighed. "You'll need the means and time to enjoy books and ideas. I wish I could leave an estate to support you, but the Inquisition disrupted my career too many times. I don't know how you could survive as an independent woman, let alone buy books and find time to read them. If you married a prosperous Venetian gentleman, you could devote your time to scholarship. Your servants could take care of your household and children."

I stared at him. "I'll find a way—and even if I wanted to marry, with your reputation, how could I find a husband? Besides, the dowry I'd need would reduce you to poverty."

He shook his head. "Don't worry about me. I'll get along, but after I've passed, you may not."

"Are you ordering me to marry?"

"Never, Lucia, but consider your choices with wisdom." He pushed back his chair. "We'll talk more, after you've had time to think this through. Now I must get back to my patients."

When my father walked toward the door, emptiness and desperation filled the pit of my stomach. I had hoped for advice to relieve my worries and guide my steps. Instead, Papa's words left me more anxious than before.

When I awoke the next morning, I looked forward to teaching Valeria. In spite of her initial hesitation about learning to read, her aptitude and enthusiasm for learning now inspired me.

But my stomach churned every time I thought about marrying for financial security. I recoiled at the prospect of a husband who had no interest in either my religious beliefs or the poetry and scholarship I loved. I needed a way to support myself and thought about taking on students.

At the end of our class, I drummed my toes on the floor until the Soncinis left the library. Then I asked Messer Guadagnoli if he thought I should become a teacher.

His eyes brightened. "That's a fine idea, Lucia, an excellent way to use your talents. I'll ask my colleagues if they know of nobles or citizens of Venezia who would like to educate their daughters."

My heart lightened. "Grazie, Messer Guadagnoli. You're very kind."

He shook his head. "I wish I could do more. If only Venezia offered more opportunities for a young lady of your talents."

I knew my teacher meant his words as a compliment, but they cast a pall over my mood. Not only did I face bleak prospects as a woman, but Venetians also might avoid me—just as Modesta's uncle had—if they knew my father's reputation.

I trudged back to my room and fed my canary. Even Speranza's melodic response didn't improve my mood, and I wondered who would entrust their daughters to me as a tutor.

Two weeks later, not a single letter of inquiry about tutoring had arrived. My hours in Messer Guadagnoli's class, as well as my hopes of a career, were ebbing away.

After pranzo, my father took my hand. "Lucia, you've spoken hardly a word this afternoon. What's on your mind?"

I swallowed. "I had hoped to become a teacher, but Messer Guadagnoli hasn't found any girls for me to tutor."

He cupped his chin. A moment later, he looked up at me. "I've just written the first section of my new medical treatise. Why don't you edit and copy it, get it ready for publication? I could use your bright mind and clear handwriting."

"But Papa," I sighed. "So many years have passed since you taught me about medicine. I've forgotten it all."

"You've always learned quickly, Lucia. I'm sure you'll master this project." His eyes lit up. "Let me show you my manuscript."

My father's enthusiasm and my lack of other options persuaded me. But as soon as he returned to his office, a sinking feeling came over me. Papa needed an assistant who understood his theories, not my poet's eye.

Over the next few weeks, vivid details about the prevention and cure of pestilence filled even my dreams. Finally, one evening after cena, we returned to our suite and I handed my father the precious stack of papers. "Ecco, Papa, I've finished."

He skimmed through my handwritten pages, then pulled up a chair and compared my edition of his manuscript with his original treatise.

Some time later, he turned to me, grinning. "Beautiful work, Lucia! This section is ready for publication. I'll show it to my old friend from Brescia, Francesco Ziletti, so he can publish the treatise as soon as I finish it. If he works quickly, we could save Venezia from another pestilence epidemic." He smiled again. "Why don't you come with me to Ziletti's bookshop? He runs his printing business in the back, but you could browse through hundreds of books in the front. You'd enjoy it."

I grinned. "Of course I'd like to go along, but isn't it too late?"

"Not if I know Francesco. He'll be working until his wife drags him upstairs to bed. Besides, his shop isn't far." He picked up his coat. "I'll ask Zuanne to prepare the gondola."

Outside the shop, a torch illuminated a large sign. The top of the sign featured the picture of a well, followed by the words, " *Al segno del pozzo* ." At the sign of the well. Underneath, in large letters, I read, "Ziletti Books—Publisher and Bookseller." I imagined a well gushing forth with wise sayings.

Soon my father ushered me into a bookshop unlike any I had seen before. Tall stacks of books surrounded us. Volumes of all sizes filled every nook and cranny in the shop, leaving scarcely enough room for a path from the door to the sales counter. So many choices!

No one came to wait on us. I wondered how the shop could turn a profit with such poor service. Papa rapped on a door leading to an inner room.

A red-faced man opened the door and raised his brows. "Sì?"

While Papa explained his business, I noticed the man's rolled-up sleeves and the sweat glistening on his face. As he opened an inner door, I glimpsed a large room with typesetters, printers, and bookbinders, all hard at work. Papa whispered, "Wait for me in the front," and followed his guide.

I perused one pile of books after another, searching for poetry books. At last I picked up a volume of Petrarco. I had scarcely begun to read when the door opened. A gust of wind made me shiver, but I tried to concentrate on my reading.

"So you enjoy Petrarco?"

The deep voice startled me. I summoned my courtesy, for my father's sake. "Vincenzo, what brings you here?"

The corners of his mouth turned up in a half-smile. "I, too, enjoy reading. Why did you choose Petrarco?"

"I write poetry, and what better source of inspiration than the pioneer of verse in our tongue?"

"You came here just to read Petrarco?" He cocked his head and watched me.

"I'm always eager to visit a bookshop. I never know what I'll find." I tried to project a calm that eluded me.

Vincenzo glanced toward the inner door. "But your father isn't looking for books."

My spine stiffened. "No, something nobler. He's seeking publication for his book. It will save many lives and end the scourge of pestilence."

"Really?" For an instant, his eyes lit up, but a shadow soon crossed his face. "If only he had published it earlier. My parents might still be alive."

"I'm sorry. My mother died of pestilence, too—a tragedy for her and us."

Vincenzo stepped closer. "I beg you, Lucia, warn your father to stay far from heresy." His voice turned husky. "He sounds brilliant, and I'd hate to have to arrest him. I'll have no reason to do so if he follows the Church's teachings."

My tongue froze. Finally, I nodded.

The workroom floor creaked, and Vincenzo disappeared out the front door.

A short, dark-haired man opened the workroom door, holding it for my father. "You must excuse me. I haven't a moment to spare."

Papa opened the front door, then took my arm. "Lucia, I only wish you could have heard Ziletti rave about your fine editing and clear handwriting. It made me proud."

"Grazie, Papa." My spirits brightened as we greeted Zuanne and climbed into the gondola. But in the back of my mind, I couldn't decide if I should interpret Vincenzo's words as kind advice or a threat.

Twisting a lock of hair around my little finger, I crossed the portego. At the land entrance, the door slammed shut and startled me.

"Francesco Ziletti sent this for you." Zuanne's voice rang out behind me. He strode through the hall and handed me a letter.

"Grazie, but it must be for my father." I had no business with the printer.

Zuanne smiled and pointed to my name, printed in large letters on the envelope.

Shrugging my shoulders, I thanked him. As soon as I had closed my door, I broke the seal and pulled out the folded sheet.

Signorina Locatelli,

> *Your work of editing and copying your father's treatise impressed me. Would you consider taking on similar projects for my publishing firm? Please come by my shop as soon as possible. I have a project to show you, and would like to discuss the details with you.*

> *Yours truly,*

> *Francesco Ziletti*

My spine tingled. I re-read the short note, reflecting on how this work might allow me to support myself.

After pranzo, I showed Ziletti's letter to Papa.

He looked up at me, grinning. "Ziletti's no fool. You're a talented editor, a great boon to his work."

"So I should try it?

"You won't get rich, but it's honest work you might enjoy."

"Grazie, Papa." I rushed down the stone stairway and found Zuanne in the kitchen, spooning rice and beans from his bowl. I begged him to take me to Ziletti's bookshop.

He winked at me. "So you need some new books, Lucia?"

I smiled.

Zuanne swabbed his bowl with a chunk of bread, smacking his lips after he finished. He downed his wine and handed his bowl and cup to his wife. "Grazie, Flora." Pushing back his chair, he turned to me. "Andiamo, Lucia."

When we reached Signor Ziletti's shop, I noticed Vincenzo sitting in a dinghy across the canal, so I didn't protest when Zuanne insisted on waiting for me at the wharf outside the bookshop. After a short conversation with the busy Signor Ziletti, I emerged from the shop with my first paid editing project, a manual on dance at Italian courts. The treatise even included musical notations for the harp. I thanked Mamma silently for my musical instruction.

Back home again, I climbed out of the gondola and turned to Zuanne. "Grazie, Zuanne. Now I can edit for Signor Ziletti and begin my career."

He raised his eyebrows.

"If I prepare now, I'll be able to support myself after my father can't." Thinking about that inevitable day cast a shadow over my exuberance, and my recollection of Vincenzo's presence near the bookshop made my throat tighten.

Whenever I sat down to work on my editing assignment, no matter how undecipherable the handwriting, I remembered my choices—a marriage of necessity, begging shelter in a convent, or earning my own living—and picked up my quill. When I finished the project, I pushed away my fears and asked Zuanne to send my edition back to Signor Ziletti.

The bookseller paid me what he promised for each page of my work, but, after all my hours of work, I realized editing wouldn't provide me with the means to live independently. Messer Guadagnoli hadn't found any students for me, so I sent a letter to Modesta, asking for advice.

A few weeks later, I stood before my new class of fifteen girls, silently thanking God and Modesta, who had recommended me to several families seeking a tutor for their daughters. I read Proverbs 3:7 to encourage my students: "Wisdom is supreme; therefore get wisdom. Though it cost all you have, get understanding."

The girls' varied educational backgrounds stretched my ability to challenge the advanced students and still provide basic instruction to the beginners. I needed an assistant, and soon Valeria, now fully literate, left behind her life as a servant to help me with the class.

Just weeks after my final class session with Messer Guadagnoli, my new routine—teaching, editing manuscripts, reading and writing poetry— filled my days and added coins to my borsa. In the evenings when I returned to my room after supper, I found my canary asleep with her head tucked under her wing, reminding me of Luther's image of the chick safe under its mother's wings. I read a section of Luther's book every night, longing to discuss these ideas safely with people who shared my faith. If only I could hasten that day without the Inquisition's notice.

Chapter 19

APEX

Lucia
June, 1581

*A*s much as I enjoyed my work, Modesta's letters delighted me even more in those early months after my schooling ended. Her poetic insights encouraged me, and I savored her entertaining reports on the Venetian writers' gatherings she attended. Every other week, Domenico Venier, the famous civic leader and poet, hosted a *ridotto* at his palazzo. I looked forward to reading Modesta's descriptions of each meeting—the poetry she heard, the poems of her own that she read aloud, and the witty poetic exchanges between writers. I dreamed that one day I could attend and perhaps recite my poetry.

When I opened the envelope on a sunny afternoon in June, Modesta's letter began with an announcement. In honor of her new book of chivalric poetry, her uncle would stage a *serata*, a grand evening celebration at his palazzo. He had invited authors, poets, artists, and the leading figures of Venetian society, among them painters Paolo Veronese, Palma Giovane, Jacopo Tintoretto and his daughter, Marietta; historians Paolo Paruta and Andrea Morosini; and even the doge, Nicolò da Ponte.

I turned to the next page, a personal invitation from Modesta. I thrilled at the prospect, picturing myself in the august company, until

I read her next sentence. She wrote that I must find someone other than my father to escort me. I grimaced.

Modesta followed the request with an apology, explaining that her uncle would allow me to attend only on this condition. She implored me to come, so we could meet again, and she promised to introduce me to the stellar figures about whom I had heard so much.

At once I vowed to attend this party, whatever obstacles I must overcome. Modesta had praised Domenico Venier as the most enthusiastic supporter of women authors and poets in all of Venezia, and I couldn't pass up my opportunity to meet him. Perhaps I could also meet followers of Luther.

After I read Modesta's invitation, I struggled to concentrate on the poems she included in her letter. As soon as I finished reading, my thoughts returned to the upcoming event. I wished I could set aside my teaching responsibilities to focus on my poetry, so I could recite or show my best work at the party.

First I needed to find an escort. I couldn't ask my father to arrange this without reopening the wound of Nicolò Doglioni's rude behavior. But with my limited circle of acquaintances, I could think of no appropriate young men except Roberto Soncini, who had returned home after completing his studies at Padova. Now employed in Venezia's bureaucracy, he ate meals with his parents in the dining room.

After supper that evening, I caught his eye as he stood to leave the table.

"Roberto, could I speak with you for a moment?"

His eyes widened. "Certainly, Lucia. What is it?"

I told him about Modesta's party but didn't mention the condition her uncle had placed on my attendance. I simply asked if he would consider escorting me.

"What a grand event!" A smile brightened his face. "I would be honored to accompany you, Lucia."

"Grazie, Roberto."

I waited for his response, but he just kept looking at me.

My cheeks flushed. "I must return to my studies now. Buona sera." I lifted the hem of my dress and hurried down the stairs to my room.

With my door latched behind me, I sank onto my bed. Now I could attend Modesta's party, but Roberto's long gaze embarrassed me. After his years away, he seemed like a stranger.

My mind returned to the serata. I had never attended such a festive event, and I owned no appropriate gown. My appearance normally didn't concern me, but I didn't want my clothes or hairstyle to detract from the good impression I hoped my poetry would make. I spoke to Valeria's mother, who hired a seamstress to sew me a gown and cloak for the occasion.

In the weeks leading up to the celebration, Modesta's party filled my thoughts. Imagining myself conversing with Venezia's cultural elite about their latest projects, I struggled to concentrate on reading, writing, and preparing lessons for my class.

At last, the day of the serata arrived. After Valeria's afternoon tutorial, she stayed to help me prepare for the evening, pulling my hair back into a braid, coiling it on top of my head, and weaving through a strand of tiny pearls. When she finished my coif, I donned my new dress. With its embroidered blue satin, lace-edged neckline and sleeves, this was the most elegant gown I had ever worn.

Valeria tightened the laces, stepped back, and inspected the outfit. "Lucia, if you wore a crown, the guests would mistake you for a princess tonight. The dress highlights your eyes."

"Grazie, Valeria. I couldn't have accomplished all this without your help."

She smiled. "My pleasure. Enjoy the party."

After she departed, I looked down at my dress and shoes, then into the looking glass. As a girl who always preferred treasures of the intellect to outward trappings, my reflection shocked me. I had to resist the temptation to tear off the dress and let down my hair. I didn't dare sit down for fear of wrinkling my dress, so I bent over my desk and sorted through my poems. Gathering my favorites, I rolled the sheets together, tied a ribbon around them, and slipped them into my borsa.

"Lucia." I heard my father's voice and a knock.

After I opened the door, my father raised his brows and then smiled. "Can this be the babe I cradled in my arms?" He blinked, and I saw moisture in his eyes. "Lucia, your beauty reminds me of your mother. I came to escort you to supper, but I see you have grander plans."

"Sì, Papa." My cheeks warmed. "I shouldn't risk soiling my gown with food." My appetite had vanished in the excitement. After my father left my room, I wondered how to pass the time until Roberto came for me. Finally, I inked my quill and voiced in verse my excitement, hopes, and fears about the serata.

At last, I heard another knock. This time, two faces greeted me. Roberto and my father waited in the portego while I picked up my borsa and walked out to meet them. Papa beamed, and Roberto held my gaze from the time I entered the portego.

Roberto smiled and stepped toward me, cutting a handsome profile in his fur-lined black cape, velvet tunic, and hose. "Buona sera, Lucia. You look lovely tonight."

"Grazie. I hope you'll enjoy the celebration." My nerves left me short of conversation.

My father coughed. "Shall I call Zuanne to prepare the gondola?"

We nodded. A moment later, the three of us followed him to the door. Papa kissed me on both cheeks and bade us farewell. Roberto took my arm, and we descended the steps to the gondola.

Before we left the wharf, Zuanne shook his head and smiled. "I feel like an old uncle. I remember you as a bambino, Roberto, when you used to play..." He cleared his throat. "...and your arrival in Venezia, Lucia. Now you could pass as a count and countess."

Dusk fell as he maneuvered the gondola through the canals. One by one, lamps dispelled the darkness. At last, Zuanne pulled up to a wharf. Roberto took my arm once more and escorted me to the Doglioni palazzo.

I stepped inside and caught my breath. Gilded lamps, tables laden with food and drink, musicians, and throngs of guests had transformed the portego. I scarcely recognized the hall where I had met Modesta years before.

"Welcome, Signor Soncini and Lucia." Modesta approached us, reaching out her hands. "Glad you could join us. Let me introduce you."

For the remainder of the evening, I tried my hardest to remember the name that belonged with each face. But I would never forget one wrinkle-lined visage. Modesta introduced us to a graybeard resting in a chair next to the wall, his left foot propped up on an upholstered footstool—Domenico Venier.

Roberto excused himself to speak with a friend across the room.

Signor Venier cocked his head toward me. "So how are you acquainted with Modesta, signorina?"

"We share a love of poetry. Every week, we read each other's new poems and comment on them."

His eyes lit up. "Ah, another woman poet graces our city! What kind of poetry do you write?"

"Perhaps I could show you, sir." With trembling fingers, I pulled out my sheaf of papers.

Signor Venier shook his head. "My weak eyes can't read in this light. Would you favor me by reading me your poetry, signorina?"

"Of course."

Extending his healthy foot to the leg of a nearby chair, he dragged it close and gestured for me to sit down.

I took a breath and began to read. At the end of each poem, Signor Venier's questions and enthusiastic comments spurred me on to read another. We conversed until the musicians stopped playing.

Across the portego, Roberto stood with his back to me. When he turned toward me, I saw Vincenzo next to him. My breath froze in my throat. I nodded, attempting a smile. Roberto frowned at me. My fingers pressed against my thumbs as if I were fingering my harp.

At that moment, Signor Doglioni tapped his goblet with a knife. The crowd fell silent. He introduced Modesta and her book, and applause echoed through the room. She read a few passages, and the clapping resumed.

After the room quieted, I told Signor Venier I wanted to congratulate Modesta. He nodded. I stood to bid him farewell, and he took my arm.

"Signorina Locatelli, please come with Modesta to the ridotto next week at my home. She'll tell you the details. When you arrive, I'll introduce you to our fellow writers."

My face flushed. "Grazie, Signor Venier. I'll be honored to attend." Snaking my way through the grand hall, I waited my turn to congratulate Modesta.

Roberto stood by the door. When I reached him, he followed me down the steps to our gondola, frowning and silent. Zuanne asked about the serata, so I regaled him with details all the way back to our palazzo.

Roberto nodded a terse good night, and I returned to my room. Signor Venier's affirmation still captivated my thoughts. But when I snuffed out my lamp, the image of Roberto's frown haunted me. His expression might have signaled anger at my long conversation with Domenico Venier, or perhaps Vincenzo told Roberto something disturbing about my father or me. The monk's presence also had squelched my hopes of looking for other followers of Luther. My discordant impressions of the serata battled in my mind, cursing an already short night with unsettled sleep.

For the next week, I could only nod or smile at my students' best efforts at reading and writing. The upcoming ridotto at Domenico Venier's palazzo consumed my thoughts, blotting out my worries about the final moments of Modesta's celebration.

As before the serata, I prepared by reading, writing, and revising my poetry. But I couldn't prepare poetic witticisms to recite on the spur of the moment. If my tongue stumbled, I feared Signor Venier wouldn't ask me to return—even though Modesta reassured me that only the daring engaged in poetic debates, that our host wouldn't embarrass me.

At last I rode through the canals toward Modesta's home, lacing my fingers together to quell their trembling.

Zuanne eyed me. "Are you well, Lucia?"

"Sì, I'm just excited." I didn't want to admit my fears about how Modesta's uncle might treat me. After Domenico Venier invited me to his ridotto, Signor Doglioni could scarcely refuse to let me join his family for the short journey to Ca' Venier, but he might not welcome my presence. Butterflies lingered in my stomach until I saw Modesta step out her front door.

Radiant in a green silk gown and matching cloak, Modesta hurried down to the wharf and embraced me.

"Buona sera, Lucia. I'm thrilled you can join us for the ridotto." Her broad smile calmed me.

"You can only imagine how excited I am."

We both giggled.

"Buona sera, signorina." A quick smile flitted across Signora Doglioni's face as she stepped down to the wharf.

Behind his wife, Niccolò Doglioni glanced at me, nodding. "Signorina." He turned to his wife and Modesta. "Shall we depart?"

We settled into the gondola. Gradually the knot of tension in my stomach unwound. Even so, I gave only tongue-tied responses to the Doglionis' questions.

When we arrived at Ca' Venier, Modesta and I followed her uncle and his wife out of the gondola. We linked arms and climbed the steps from the wharf to the palazzo. As we entered the grand portego, our host, Domenico Venier, strode toward us, favoring his left foot.

"Welcome, ladies and Signor Doglioni." Smile wrinkles wreathed his face. He turned to me. "Signorina Locatelli, what a pleasure to see you. I'll introduce you when everyone has arrived. Would you grace us with one of your poems this evening?"

My cheeks flushed, and I nodded. "Sì, Signor Venier." My words came out in a whisper. For all my efforts to appear sophisticated, my pounding heart surely gave me away. I fingered *Dona nobis pacem* on my thumbs.

When Signor Venier turned to greet another guest, I pulled out my sheaf of poems. Leafing through them, I placed the poem I wrote after the celebration of Modesta's book on top of the pile.

Some time later, our host called the gathering to order and introduced each person. At last I put a face to several names: among them, Maffio Venier, Domenico's fleshy, sharp-tongued nephew; Paolo Paruta, the wizened historian; his energetic young protégé, Andrea Morosini; and Andrea's brother, Nicolò Morosini.

When Signor Venier introduced a vocal trio of three monks, wedged in a corner of the room, my body stiffened. In the middle sat Vincenzo. Whether by design or coincidence, he could observe me all evening. I focused my attention on our host, to avoid Vincenzo's gaze.

Signor Venier announced my name last. He described how he met me and heard my poems at the serata for Modesta.

"Signorina da Pozzo doubtless taught Lucia much about poetry, but the young woman before you now deserves full credit for her creativity. Her poems address many topics, always with eloquence and emotion. Signorina Lucia Locatelli, please grace us with a poem."

I took a long breath. "Grazie, Signor Venier, for your gracious words." I looked around the room. "Our host took a chance—he doesn't know which poem I chose. When he spoke with me for the first time a week ago, he inspired the poem I'll read. Since then, his encouragement and knowledge of poetry have filled me with awe and gratitude. I wrote this poem about and in honor of Domenico Venier, who served Venezia with distinction, and now opens his home to enrich our literary community."

When I concluded my reading, applause filled the room. Several men rose to their feet, shouting, "Bravo!" A single voice shouted, "A toast to Domenico Venier!" Wine glasses clinked throughout the hall.

Signor Venier called out, "A toast to Signorina Locatelli!" He raised his glass, and I blushed. Surveying the room, I noticed Modesta and most others with raised glasses, smiling.

After that thrilling moment, the remainder of the evening passed quickly, a pleasant anticlimax.

Finally, the readings, toasts, discussion, and songs concluded. I stretched my legs and gazed out the windows at the lamps along the canal. Out of the corner of my eye, I saw someone walk toward me. When I turned my head, Vincenzo stood beside me.

I gestured toward the canal. "*Bella* Venezia, so lovely at night!"

He raised his brows. "But a dangerous place under the cover of darkness."

In that instant, a chill replaced the warm glow inside me. "What do you mean?"

He eyed me closely. "Evil thrives in darkness. Heresy is no exception."

I shrank away from him. "Prego?"

"What's your father doing tonight?"

I flinched. "He's probably writing in his study. That's his usual evening pastime."

His gaze lingered. "Don't you know the truth, or are you lying to protect him?"

My jaw dropped. "How can you say that?"

He lowered his voice. "Lucia, it's my job to watch him, and I've seen plenty. I'm only warning you because he's your father and a great man. If you want to save him, he must confess and repent at once."

I clenched my jaw. "Don't slander my father." I strode toward Modesta.

As we followed my friend's aunt and uncle to the door, Domenico Venier came alongside and tapped my shoulder. "Please come again, signorina. Your presence has enriched our gathering."

I tried to focus on his smiling face. "Such an honor and a pleasure for me! Grazie, Signor Venier."

I glanced around the portego and noticed several pairs of eyes watching me—the same stony faces that had stared instead of toasting me. We climbed down the steps to the wharf, and I wondered if Vincenzo had told them rumors about my father.

Waves beat the sides of the gondola, and I couldn't stop thinking this might be my only journey to a ridotto. In spite of Signor Venier's words of praise, I feared Vincenzo's whispers would exclude me from Venezia's literary community.

Like a ship rolling with the waves, my perspective on the ridotto rocked between glee and despair. Seeking another focus for my thoughts, I pulled out Luther's book after wishing my father buona notte. After reading a few pages, I turned to the Bible passage Luther had explained, from Saint Paul's letter to the Galatians: "The only thing that counts is faith expressing itself through love."

Hope rose up in my heart—even if I could never attend the ridotto again, I would still possess the most important thing, my faith. The next moment, fear and disappointment about the ridotto challenged my hope. I wrote a poem expressing my conflicting emotions. From that night, I looked forward to grappling with the truths Martin Luther discovered in the Holy Scriptures and then responding to them in poetry. As soon as the ink dried, I hid these papers beneath my chemises, next to Luther's commentary and Mamma's Bible.

I daydreamed about reading one of these new poems at the next ridotto but only until I remembered Vincenzo's remarks and the disapproving glances directed toward me at the last gathering. Any poem that raised questions about Roman Church doctrine could elicit more than hostile stares. My momentary pleasure at reading my poem aloud could lead to my arrest or my father's. The Inquisition's shadow loomed ever larger.

Signor Venier began his next ridotto with his own composition, a sonnet about a friend "stricken by the hand of invidious death." His eloquent words about life, death, and eternal life, brought my mother to mind. I blinked back tears.

When my turn came, I recited a new poem inspired by one of Luther's descriptions—how faith can allow a believer to rise up to "that heaven of grace where there is no law or sin." This phrase awed me each time I read it. I used the image of an eagle to describe this, entitling my poem, "On Wings of Eagles." Polite applause followed, but nothing like what I received at the previous gathering. Again, a few men stared at me, grim expressions on their faces.

Much later in the evening, Veronica Franco, the courtesan poet, read her own verse. After the group applauded, Domenico Venier's nephew, Maffio, shot back a vulgar poetic retort with a similar rhyme scheme. Laughter and murmuring filled the portego. Our host called the group to order and thanked us for our contributions. The guests dispersed, and I made my way across the room to Domenico Venier. The circle of men around him parted for me.

"Signor Venier, I couldn't leave without mentioning how your sonnet touched my heart. I lost my mother to pestilence, and your verse captured my feelings of loss and hope."

"Grazie, signorina." He smiled.

I stepped toward the door, and a hand clutched my arm. I whirled around. "Vincenzo, what do you want?"

"Only a moment of your time." His grip tightened.

"My escorts are waiting." I tried to pull away.

"Then I'll be brief. Your father persists in his heresy, and the Holy Office knows."

My hands gripped my elbows.

"If you give me names of his fellow heretics, the Holy Office will look kindly on you. Your reputation will grow as a loyal supporter of the Church. You'll find that advantageous here." He gestured across the room.

I lurched toward the door as fast as my feet would carry me.

Modesta stood near the door with her aunt and uncle, watching and waiting for me. Without a word, I followed them to the wharf.

Seated beside Modesta in the gondola, I heard only the rhythmic paddling of our gondolier. My friend usually bubbled with excitement after a literary evening, but that night Modesta sat in silence.

Gazing at the cloud-veiled moon, I wondered what Modesta thought of the scene she just witnessed. Anxiety about losing my friend and my reputation stole away my happy memories of the evening. Vincenzo's words ran through my mind, again and again, and I could interpret them only as a threat. I shivered and pulled my cloak tight.

Chapter 20

STIRRINGS

Lucia
January, 1582

S hortly after the new year began, Zuanne approached me in
the portego with a letter from Modesta. I tore open the envelope. Her missive began with an announcement:

Dear Lucia,

*I have wonderful news to announce. I will soon marry Filippo de
Zorzi. Each time we've met, he has asked me to read my poetry aloud.
Although he has an important position as the supervisor of Venezia's
wells and canals, he tells me that he feels honored to wed an illustrious
poet. He encourages me to continue my writing and promises to provide enough servants to manage our household so I can devote my days
to writing poetry. I couldn't wish for a more understanding husband,
and I look forward to spending my life with him.*

*My uncle and Filippo have already signed the marriage contract,
and the ring ceremony will take place on February 15. I would be honored if you could join my family and other friends for our celebration—
again, with an escort, as my uncle will be the host. I hope to hear soon
that you will be able to attend.*

I stared at her words and re-read the message. She had written in
her poems about the bondage women faced in marriage, subject to
their husbands' whims, so I doubted my friend's decision had come

without pressure from her family. If she had chosen instead to enter a convent, she could have continued her life as a scholar.

My thoughts turned to Modesta's uncle. Nicolò Doglioni had encouraged her to pursue her career as a poet. He had paid to publish her work and spent much more for the serata. Yet I would never forget how he forced Modesta to end her appointment with my father and me, forbidding any further meetings. I feared he also might have insisted that she marry.

I studied her letter again. Its jubilant tone suggested Modesta rejoiced at the prospect of her marriage. But even if she had chosen to marry, I worried that marriage would hinder her writing.

Modesta's invitation confirmed our ongoing friendship, but I wondered if she would continue to exchange poems with me after her marriage. If she had children, would their arrival signal the end of our bond of poetry and correspondence?

I penned a note of congratulations and kept my fears to myself. Before sending off my response, I would need to find an escort. Since Signor Doglioni wouldn't allow my father to attend, I would need to ask Roberto again. Although we still took meals in the dining room together with our parents, we hadn't conversed since Modesta's serata. I could only hope he had forgotten his displeasure with me.

When Roberto pushed back his chair after supper that evening, I approached him.

"Prego, Roberto. May I speak to you?"

"Of course." His polite tone gave no clue to his feelings.

"Modesta da Pozzo will marry on February 15th, and she has invited me to the ring ceremony. Would you do me the favor of escorting me?"

He studied my face.

His hesitation made my heart beat fast and loud. If he turned me down, whom else could I ask to escort me?

Finally, he nodded. "It would be my pleasure, Lucia."

"Grazie, Roberto. Buona notte." Breathing out my anxiety, I hurried across the dining room toward my father.

When we reached our suite, Papa invited me into his study.

"Lucia, I received a letter today from Stefano Capriolo. He addressed it to both of us, and I'd advise you to read it." Sober-faced, he handed me a black-trimmed envelope.

I began to read.

Dear friends,

I must announce some dreadful news. My beloved wife Giulietta died yesterday giving birth to our baby son, who also perished.

Please say prayers for the souls of my wife and son and for me. My grief overwhelms me. But for the moments when I write these letters, I am at a loss for what to do. My work gives me no respite from my sorrow. Since Giulietta and I married, I have attended and transcribed trials before the Holy Office. This work is tortuous even in happy times, as I must pay close attention to the defendants' responses. Often I must witness the methods—I cannot describe them—that the Inquisitor must use to obtain answers.

When Giulietta was alive, her sweet presence distracted my mind from these unpleasant scenes, but now I have nightmares about them and the deaths of my wife and son. I don't know how much longer I'll be able to keep up this work.

Yours truly,

Stefano Capriolo

I stared at the letter, remembering Stefano's grin and youthful pranks, then eyed my father. "How can this be? Stefano is too young to be a widower, too decent to merit such tragedy. May God rest the souls of his wife and baby and grant him peace."

He nodded. "Tragedy doesn't respect character. How well we know that. I pray Stefano will find strength and hope to survive."

I wrote a letter of condolence, to which my father added a note. After I retired that night, I lay awake thinking of Stefano's grief at his double loss. Then I thought of Modesta and caught my breath, praying that God would protect her from such a fate.

Two weeks later, Zuanne ferried Roberto and me to the Doglioni palazzo, where festoons of flowers and ribbons adorned the entryway and windows. Nicolò Doglioni had again transformed his palazzo, outdoing even the lavish decorations for the serata.

Stepping inside, I drew in my breath. Mirrors and tapestries in rich hues graced the walls. Rugs from Byzantium adorned the terrazzo floors. Spaced throughout the portego, wooden carvings and figurines of white marble underscored the host's affluence and impeccable taste. In the middle of the hall, silver cutlery gleamed on a banquet table, promising a memorable meal.

The elegant trappings made me wonder whether Signor Doglioni had spent Modesta's inheritance for her wedding celebration, and if he had broken the Venetian laws restricting luxurious furnishings, clothing, and decorations.

"Avanti, Lucia." Roberto tugged me toward the other guests. We joined perhaps thirty others seated on chairs and couches at one side of the portego. Strains of music filled the hall, and we waited for the ring ceremony to begin. On the other side of the portego, two musicians played duets on violin and viola da gamba. Their slow, grave melodies, in the very portego where I had met Modesta, added to my worries about her.

Nicolò Doglioni entered the portego, his arm linked with Modesta's, and he escorted her to the front of the gathering. Dressed in a white silk gown trimmed with lace epaulettes and collar, Modesta would have outshone a princess. Strings of pearls hung from her neck, and the jeweled comb on top of her head resembled a crown. A slender, balding gentleman clad in black velvet followed— evidently Modesta's groom, Signor de Zorzi. I eyed him for clues about his character and affection for my friend.

The music stopped. Modesta's uncle cleared his throat. "Welcome, my friends. We gather today to celebrate the wedding of my dear niece, the esteemed poet, Modesta da Pozzo, to Filippo de Zorzi, an honorable citizen and trusted official of our city. I have invited you to witness as they give their consent to the marriage and exchange rings. Signor Petrocelli, our notary, will record these events for the official records of Venezia. And now, Padre Simone."

As Signor Doglioni seated himself on a gilded couch, a heavy-set priest stood before us. The cleric spoke first to Modesta. "Signorina da Pozzo, as your family and friends witness, as well as the Church and the city of Venezia, do you freely choose to marry this man, Filippo de Zorzi, under no compulsion?"

"Sì, padre." She nodded, her face radiant, eyes glowing.

He turned to her groom. "Filippo de Zorzi, as the Church, the city of Venezia, and your family and friends witness, do you freely choose to marry this woman, Modesta da Pozzo, under no compulsion?"

Signor de Zorzi smiled and nodded. "Sì, padre."

"Very well. You may exchange rings as a token of your marriage." Padre Simone stepped aside to give us a clear view.

Soon golden bands on their fingers declared their union. Signor de Zorzi clasped Modesta's hands. They gazed into each other's eyes as if no one else were in the room.

The priest coughed, and the couple startled. "In the name of the Father, the Son, and the Holy Spirit, I pronounce you man and wife."

Modesta and her husband turned toward us, their faces wreathed with smiles. We rose and clapped our congratulations.

After the noise subsided, a younger man resembling Filippo da Zorzi, clearly his brother, carried an ornate wooden chest to the front of the room and set it on a side table next to the groom.

Filippo smiled and nodded. "Grazie, *mio fratello*." He opened the chest and drew Modesta toward it. "This chest and all its contents are for you, my bride."

Smile lines wreathed her face "My husband, you are too generous."

He placed his arm around her waist and pulled her close. Their lips joined in a lingering kiss, disturbed at last by whistling and clapping. The newlyweds grinned and walked toward us.

Signor Doglioni arose, offered them his couch, and addressed the group. "May I have your attention, my friends? My family invites you to the wedding banquet, which will commence when the other guests arrive. Please stay and join us for all the festivities."

The music resumed, this time in a spirited, joyful tone. Filippo and Modesta stepped out to dance, and others soon followed their lead.

Roberto nudged my elbow. "May I have the honor, Lucia?"

I nodded, hoping I could resurrect the dance steps my mother had tried to teach me so many years before.

Roberto took my hand and swept me out onto the dance floor. We stood across from each other, he in the men's row and me in the women's. He held my hand tight, and his strong lead saved me from embarrassment. After a few minutes, I moved with the rhythm of the music and relaxed.

When the musicians finished their piece, Roberto whispered in my ear. "Rosy cheeks become you, Lucia."

I blushed.

The music started up again. Roberto's eyes sparkled. "Shall we?"

I smiled, and he took my hand again. This time, I didn't hesitate. We danced round after round until the musicians finally stopped, and Signor Doglioni invited his guests to the table. Roberto pushed in my chair and sat beside me.

After a toast to the bride and groom, the feast began. First came fried ravioli rolled in costly powdered sugar, a delicacy new to me.

These savory, sweet morsels thrilled my taste buds. By the time I had eaten a plateful, I could have fasted for the remainder of the day.

Platters of roasted veal arrived next. Then the aroma of herbs and exotic spices announced the pièce de résistance, enormous pies. I savored the filling of meat, cheese, and eggs, and the hint of sweetness from grains of sugar. My dress began to pinch around the waist, ever tighter as the banquet progressed, but I couldn't resist sampling these choice dishes.

Finally, servants brought carafes of wine from Napoli, a sweet ending to the feast of a lifetime. I emptied my glass, pushed my plate away, and entertained myself, watching Roberto's eyes light up as servants replaced empty platters with new ones. We joked about how many days we would wait before eating again.

When the guests could eat no more, the servants returned to clear the tables. Modesta's uncle and Filippo's brother positioned themselves next to the newlyweds and pulled them out of their chairs. They escorted the couple out of the portego. The guests laughed and clapped. Soon the crowd rose to its feet, following the couple to the bridal bedchamber. Roberto took my arm, and we joined the throng. I glimpsed gilded furnishings—picture frames, leather wall hangings, a bench covered in red leather, a carved poster bed. A brief look at Modesta and Filippo seated on the brocade-covered bed sufficed for me. But the crowd and Roberto lingered. He stared at the bridal couple and then smiled at me. I looked up at him, waiting for his comment. He kept smiling.

My cheeks warmed. At last, Signor Doglioni pulled down the silk curtains surrounding the bed, shooed out the guests, and locked the door of the bedchamber. The crowd dispersed to the portego, and I relaxed. The awkward moment had ended along with the evening's public festivities.

We stepped out the doors and looked toward the canal. Zuanne hailed us from the wharf. After a quiet ride back to the palazzo, he helped me out of the gondola and stayed behind to secure it.

I noticed his drooping eyelids. "I'm sorry for the late hour, Zuanne. Your faithful service allowed me to celebrate my dear friend's marriage. Grazie."

He smiled. "Prego, Lucia—anything for you."

Roberto climbed out behind me. He took my arm and walked me through the portego to my door.

I turned to him. "*Grazie*, Roberto. I couldn't have asked for a more enjoyable evening."

He smiled. "My pleasure, Lucia—truly." He kissed my hand and held it.

Zuanne opened the canal-side door, and I started.

"Buona notte, Roberto." I pushed my door open.

"Buona notte, Lucia." Roberto stepped back slowly and turned toward the stairway.

In spite of the hour, I lay in bed reflecting on the day. The glowing faces of Modesta and her husband and their obvious affection for each other banished my fear that she married under compulsion. I wished them well.

Closing my eyes, I saw in my mind the winsome image of the man with whom I had shared this grand evening. Roberto's smiling face, vivid in my memory as when we were together, now stirred me. Perhaps the libations and merriment had cast a spell on me, but I wished for another opportunity to enjoy his company.

My better judgment called this a foolish hope. His parents would follow the Venetian custom and choose an appropriate wife for him, a woman who would add prestige and wealth to the Soncini family, would happily manage the household, and bear children to carry on his family line.

But Roberto's glances that evening hinted that he pictured me standing with him in a similar ring ceremony, enjoying a banquet, and sharing a conjugal bed. Could I have mistaken his intent?

I told myself I would be the wrong choice for Roberto. I had worked hard to carve my niche in Venezia and had little interest in domestic duties. If by some strange turn of events we married, I would live the traditional life of a Venetian wife, secure but restricted. Worse, I couldn't risk sharing my sympathies for Martin Luther with Roberto. I would have to keep my beliefs to myself for the rest of my life.

The next evening, I sat at my desk, struggling to find the right words for a poem, when my father knocked at my door.

"Lucia, may I come in?"

"Of course, Papa." How odd for him to interrupt my studies.

"We must talk—it's important." His voice sounded higher, more animated than normal.

"Sì?" Had I committed a sin or perhaps some social faux pas?

He smiled and pulled up a chair. "I see the same guilty look in your eyes that I remember from your childhood." He took my hands. "Don't worry, I didn't come to scold you."

"Tell me then, Papa."

"*Allora.*" He cleared his throat. "Lucia, Doctor Soncini just asked me for your hand in marriage to his son Roberto."

His message set off tremors of shock in my mind. "The Soncinis want Roberto to marry me?"

"It's Roberto's choice. He begged his father to ask for your hand. His parents gave their consent because Doctor Soncini and his wife have always thought highly of you. They could bestow no greater compliment." He squeezed my hand.

"But Papa, we have neither prestige nor riches. Why would the Soncinis agree to a family alliance that advances neither their status nor their wealth?"

He flashed me a grin. "Filippo told me Roberto will consider no woman but you to become his wife and the mother of his children."

I averted my eyes and tried to restrain a smile. A thrill of excitement pulsed through me as I remembered my giddiness and delight during the evening Roberto and I shared—but a small voice within me urged caution. I looked up at my father.

"What did you tell Doctor Soncini?" I couldn't breathe. My future hung in the balance.

"Since your future is at stake, of course I told him you must decide."

I exhaled. "*Grazie*, Papa. I enjoy Roberto's company and couldn't wish for a more honorable husband. The Soncinis' confidence flatters me."

He straightened in the chair. "So, is that a yes?"

I sighed. "I don't know. I need time to think and pray."

He nodded. "Somehow I knew you wouldn't make a quick decision. Of course we don't want to offend the Soncinis with a long delay, but your life is too important to make a hasty choice." He looked me in the eye. "I have confidence in your judgment. I'll stand by you in whatever decision you make." He smiled.

"*Grazie*, Papa. I wish I could tell you my answer now. Please thank the Soncinis."

"Capito." He pushed back the chair and walked toward his study.

I looked down at my half-completed poem, a lament that I must keep Luther's message a secret. I hid the paper deep in my clothing chest and reached for a blank sheet. Now, as I pondered marriage to Roberto, I needed to search my heart and soul as never before. If I wrote a poem about my dilemma, perhaps I could unravel my thoughts and feelings.

The next afternoon I set out for Modesta's new home in her husband's palazzo. Now free from her uncle's authority, she had asked me to meet her each week to discuss poetry. After Zuanne delivered me to my friend's doorstep, I waited in the empty portego, reaching into my satchel for a Latin text—my latest editorial assignment from Francesco Ziletti.

When Modesta stepped into the room grasping a ceramic bowl, I dropped my papers and rose to greet her. She cautioned me that sickness plagued her. Then she smiled at me. "Perhaps this means I'm with child, and a healthy one, if we can believe the legends."

I nodded. "May God bless you with a robust child."

We sat across from each other. I picked up my papers, looking her in the face. "I'm fortunate you've agreed to mentor me as a poet. But I also count you as my friend."

"I'm honored, Lucia." She smiled.

"Modesta, when I look at you I see a wonderful poet and a happy woman."

She blushed.

"Can I talk with you about an important decision I face?"

"Of course." She studied my face.

"You know the joy of a scholar's life, the freedom to read and write without the obligations most women endure. Yet you gave up that life to marry and bear children."

She nodded.

I summoned my courage and told her about Roberto's proposal and the choice I faced.

Modesta's eyes narrowed. "Your father left the decision to you?"

"Sì. I don't know how to answer. I have to admit the proposal thrilled me." I couldn't forget that moment. "But when I recovered my senses, I told my father I would need time to consider it."

"Did he give you advice?"

"He told me he trusts my judgment. That frustrated me so! I need wise counsel from someone who understands my situation, someone knowledgeable and discreet."

She blushed. "Your confidence flatters me."

"If I married into Roberto's family, I would never lack for anything."

"Capito."

"But I couldn't be the kind of wife Roberto wants. His proposal mentioned the joy of presiding over a house filled with our children. He doesn't understand that study and writing are the loves of my life. Life as a Venetian wife and mother would trap me. I don't want to be a bird peering out of my golden cage at a freedom I can never gain."

"So you'll turn down his proposal?" Modesta pressed me.

"My heart tells me to say yes, but I'm afraid I'll regret my decision for the rest of my life." How I wished I could explain my fear that I could never even speak the name of Martin Luther.

"Modesta, you're the only respectable woman I know who's also a successful poet. Since the day we met, I've tried to emulate you." I selected my next words with care. "I hope my questions don't offend you, but frankly, I wonder: did you choose marriage without pressure or coercion? Are you contented with your life?"

Her face froze. "If anyone else asked me those questions, I'd refuse to answer." Her expression softened. "But you have good reasons to ask."

She sighed. "You know I lost my parents before I was old enough to remember them. Even though I could have found a happy home with my grandparents, my relatives quarreled about who should raise me, so I had to spend my first eight years in a convent. All my life, I've longed for a loving family. That's why I chose to marry and why I'll center my life around my children."

Her eyes shone. "Even though I love to write, I'd give it up in a moment for my family. When I married, I hoped to have children and expected I'd have less time to write." She smiled. "Filippo is the perfect husband for me. Before we married, he told me my lively mind and skill in expressing myself drew me to him. The extra servants he hired give me the time I need for writing." She folded her hands in front of her belly. "I'm sure I could write more if I hadn't married, but I would never sacrifice the joy of my own growing family."

I mulled her words. "Such a clear choice." I sighed. "In my lonely moments, I wish for a husband, a man who understands and loves me for who I am, who encourages me to pursue my aspirations—someone like my father. But security and status mean little to me. Am I the only woman in Venezia who feels this way?" I brushed away tears.

Modesta offered me her kerchief. "Venetian girls assume their fathers will decide their fates—a convent or a husband chosen by their family. However difficult our choices, you and I can be grateful."

I recognized the truth of her words, but when I pictured the reactions of Papa, Roberto, and his father, fear and dread blanketed me.

I cleared my throat. "I must refuse Roberto's proposal." I searched her face for a reaction.

Modesta's expression remained solemn. "Sì, if you believe this marriage would be wrong."

"Grazie, my friend." I exhaled. "Could you read your poetry now?"

On the ride back to the palazzo, mental images of Roberto and his family, all enraged by my decision, banished all thoughts of poetry from my mind. I prayed my choice wouldn't cost us the home I had come to love or someday leave me a beggar.

Chapter 21

CLOSED DOORS

Giordano Locatelli

J had just pulled my chair up to my desk that morning when Lucia rapped on my door. As she entered my study, her haggard visage told me she hadn't slept.

"Papa, I must talk with you." Her flat voice heightened my concern.

"Of course." I latched the door and pulled a chair close to mine. "What's on your mind?"

"I can't accept Roberto's proposal." She choked back a sob. "My heart tells me to marry him, reminds me how he enjoys a scholarly discussion, how he captivates me. And if I married him, I would never have to worry about starving." She wiped her eyes. "But the one topic I can't discuss with him is the most important to me." Her voice rose. "Papa, if I married Roberto, I could never read or talk about Martin Luther's ideas again. I must follow my conscience."

I clasped her hand. "So Luther's book has complicated your life once more. Sometimes I wish you had never seen it." I shook my head. "Roberto is a good man from a fine family. You could enjoy a pleasant life if you kept your faith to yourself."

"For the rest of my life?" She looked me in the face.

"How will you support yourself after I die? Your inheritance won't last long."

"God provided for Mamma and me when you couldn't. He'll take care of my needs again."

I scrutinized her face for any sign of second thoughts. "Are you certain of your decision?"

She nodded, teary-eyed. "Sì, Papa."

I sighed. "*Allora*, I'll tell Doctor Soncini."

"Grazie, Papa. How I wish I could explain my decision to Roberto, so he won't misunderstand my reasons."

Not to mention what Roberto's father would think. I pressed my lips together to keep this thought to myself.

"Papa, tell Doctor Soncini whatever you must. Tell him I've decided not to marry." Lucia addressed me with her customary strong voice. "Probably it's the truth. You don't need to warn me that I won't receive another proposal in this city. Please tell Doctor Soncini I'm grateful for his family's kindness, that I don't mean to insult them. Above all, tell him I'm thankful for Roberto's kindness. I will always hold him in the highest esteem." She burst into tears and rushed out.

I stared at the door Lucia had just shut. My daughter had showed her courage, and now I must demonstrate mine. But my shoulders and wrists ached, and I longed to pull my cloak over my head and sleep, like a bear in hibernation. Instead, I pushed back my chair and walked out to the portego to look for my friend and benefactor.

Filippo Soncini welcomed me into his study. Already dressed for the workday in boots and a black cloak, he motioned me toward a chair and took his place on the carved bench behind his reading desk. Surrounded by gilded woodwork, jeweled vases, and bronze figurines, he had the air of a king seated on his throne. He swung away the brass lamp-arm and flashed me a broad smile. "Buon giorno, Giordano. I can guess why you've come."

"Sì, Filippo." I nodded. "About your proposal." I breathed deeply. "My daughter asked me to convey her gratitude for considering her as Roberto's bride. She has great respect and affection for him." I paused. "If she were to marry, she would choose Roberto, without a doubt."

His arms stiffened, and his smile vanished. He stared at me, finally clearing his throat. "*If* she were to marry—what do you mean? Will you send her to a convent?"

"No." I sighed. "Lucia has a mind of her own, an independent streak. She wishes to continue her teaching and poetry writing and realizes she won't be able to do those things if she marries."

"So she refuses our proposal?" His face reddened.

My throat constricted. "With great reluctance and the highest regard for your family—sì."

"Giordano, you insult me!" His voice rose. "I could have made this proposal to a far better family than yours, but I bowed to Roberto's pleas." He exhaled, his tone calmer. "Our household will never be at peace unless you persuade Lucia to change her mind. How else can our families share this palazzo?"

I shook my head, wishing I could accommodate this friend who had risked his reputation for me. "Filippo, I can never repay your kindness to me and Lucia. But I raised my daughter to make her own decisions. I won't overrule her now in the most important choice of her life." I thought for a moment. "Perhaps Lucia and I could take our meals in our rooms until you deem it appropriate for us to rejoin your family in the dining room."

Filippo nodded, still frowning. "A small concession." He rose and showed me to the door. "If rumors of your refusal escape this palazzo, my family will be the laughingstock of Venezia."

"My friend, after all you've done for me, I would never tarnish your reputation. I give you my word that neither Lucia nor I will speak of this to anyone." Mourning the loss of Filippo's goodwill, I trudged back to my study and wondered how much longer we could call this palazzo our home.

⚜

Lucia
February 17, 1582

On an overcast Saturday morning, I peered out my window and hoped the fog over the canal and the haze in my heart would soon clear. A knock at my door ended my musing, and Zuanne handed me a letter from Modesta. I expected a warm greeting, followed by her poems and comments on mine. Nothing prepared me for the message I read.

My dear Lucia,

I must force myself to write these dreadful words: Domenico Venier died yesterday. My uncle told me the news, and I knew I must inform you.

May God rest his soul and grant us comfort in our loss.

Modesta

I gasped and threw down the parchment. Then I read the letter again. I still couldn't believe Signor Venier had died, and just the day after Modesta's ring ceremony. In spite of his age and infirmity, he had exuded life and vitality. If only God had granted me more time to attend his ridotti and absorb his wisdom.

This news pushed everything else from my mind, including the class I was to teach that morning. Valeria finally knocked on my door.

"Lucia, are you ready to leave?"

"Sì, just a moment." I tossed a cloak over my shoulders, grabbed my bag of books and papers, and followed her out to the gondola.

I taught the lesson by rote, adding none of my usual anecdotes or comments. Valeria answered the students' questions. I watched, but my thoughts drifted far from the scene before me.

As the students filed out, Valeria stopped me just inside the doorway.

"You're so quiet today. What's wrong?"

I steadied my voice. "A great man, a gifted poet, died—Domenico Venier. He encouraged me and the entire community of writers in Venezia. I learned the news earlier this morning."

She linked her arm with mine. "I'm sorry for your loss, Lucia."

I nodded. "Such a kind man. He praised my poetry and included me in his gatherings of writers. Those meetings were my high points this past year. Signor Venier's death brings grief not only to me but to Venezia as well."

"I'll say a prayer for his soul and for you, too."

We walked in silence to the waiting gondola.

When we arrived at our palazzo, I had no appetite and couldn't bring myself to join Papa and the Soncinis for pranzo. In the privacy of my bedchamber, my pent-up grief erupted into tears.

I heard rapping on my door.

"Lucia, are you ill?"

At the sound of my father's voice, I reached for my kerchief and wiped my eyes.

"No, Papa." I opened the door.

"I missed you at pranzo." He studied my face. "What's troubling you?"

I sighed and told him the news.

He shook his head. "The patron of Venetian poets—now I understand your grief." He stretched his arm around my shoulders.

"My sadness is doubled. I've lost both the kind soul who encouraged my poetry and his ridotti at Ca' Venier."

He pulled a chair next to mine. "But you've begun to meet with Signorina da Pozzo."

"Sì, I enjoy studying and sharing poetry with Modesta, but it can't replace the ridotti. Signor Venier gathered the entire literary community and encouraged each person to read their poems and learn from others. Papa, I've lost the audience for my verse and the chance to listen to brilliant poets." I grimaced. "I can't bear the thought of returning to the life I knew before I met Signor Venier."

"Are there similar groups you might join?" He held my gaze.

"Not for respectable women. Neither Modesta nor I would venture into the home of a courtesan, however great a poet. The Morosini brothers host a group at their palazzo, but they haven't invited women."

"I'm sorry, Lucia." He rubbed my shoulder. "I'll keep my ears open." He pushed back his chair and walked toward his office.

Domenico Venier's death had snuffed out my opportunity to become a famous poet, just as Papa's arrest years before had squelched my passion to spread Martin Luther's ideas. I could think of no way to revive my poetry career, and my sense of purpose ebbed away.

I glanced across my room at my canary. Already, she had tucked her head under her wing. Again the sight reminded me of Martin Luther's image of shelter under God's wings.

If only I could find a community as passionate about the faith of Luther as Domenico Venier's group had been about poetry. I longed to discuss Luther's ideas openly instead of hiding my beliefs in poetry. But my youthful attempts had gone so wrong and still haunted my nightmares. Now, the possibility of capture or death for my father or me loomed even larger. I couldn't risk Papa's life again.

September, 1586

Nearly a decade had passed since we settled in Venezia, and at last my father had finished his treatise on the prevention and cure of the pestilence—years later than either of us expected, due to the demands of his ever-growing medical practice.

"Bravo, Papa!" I gave him a quick hug, then stepped back and smiled. Although his beard and hair had turned nearly white during our years in Venezia, my father's eyes emanated vitality and contentment.

We stepped outside to celebrate the momentous occasion with an evening stroll on the calle. A breeze sent waves lapping the canal's banks, and aromas of fried fish greeted us at nearly every house we passed. Papa told me he would show the treatise to Francesco Ziletti as soon as I edited the final chapter. When we returned to the palazzo, my father handed me his fresh pages.

I dipped my quill in ink and began my editing. Papa's urgency to publish his treatise impelled me to set aside all my projects. After my teaching duties each day, I began working on the remaining pages as soon as I finished pranzo. A few days later, I handed my edition to my father.

I expected Papa's completed project would bring him joy, but during supper the next evening, a fire burned in his eyes and his feet tapped under the table. Normally a witty conversationalist, my father spat out his responses when anyone spoke to him, and left most of his stew in the bowl.

After cena, instead of linking his arm with mine for our usual stroll back to our rooms, he ignored me and rushed down the stairs.

Just before he reached our suite, I called out, "What's wrong, Papa?" I ran to catch up with him.

Slamming our suite's door behind us, he scowled. "Friendship counts for nothing these days." He snorted. "Francesco Ziletti wouldn't stop talking about his production delays and contracts with other authors—said he couldn't print my book for two years!"

My mouth dropped open. "Didn't you tell him how many lives it could save?"

"Of course, but he just suggested I try one of the larger publishers, Giolito, Giunti, or Manuzio." He threw up his hands.

"Certainly one of them will print your book."

He sighed. "I hope you're right. I wish I could print it myself. Then every physician and medical professor could read it today. Imagine if pestilence no longer threatened the world. Cities wouldn't be decimated; families wouldn't suffer loss."

He shook his head. "But I'm skeptical. I've approached these Venetian publishers before, with no success. If they turn me down again, I must look elsewhere. That will require more time and risk."

I knew he didn't mean financial risk. The new doge, Pasquale Cicogna, had allowed the Inquisition free rein in our city since he took office the previous year. People spoke of his fast friendship with Sixtus V, formerly Venezia's Inquisitor before his recent election as pope. Every time I spoke with Francesco Ziletti, the printer frightened me with stories about the Inquisition's tightening grip on Venezia.

The threat of losing my father left me without a response.

Giordano

An entire afternoon away from my practice—such a waste of time and effort! I slammed my office door, my temples pounding. No one understood my urgency. If pestilence struck before my book's publication, again thousands would die, needlessly. I wiped my brow. Someday Venezia's publishers would regret their cowardice but not soon enough to save those lives. I must find a way to get my book into the hands of physicians.

Pacing my office, I considered my choices. Again and again I passed the darkened window, the door, and the rejected manuscript on my desk. I longed to circulate my book in Venezia but had neither the time nor the neat handwriting to copy my treatise by hand for each physician. In any case, a handwritten manuscript wouldn't garner the respect of a published book. If I found a publisher outside Venezia, my book would take months or even years to reach the eyes of physicians. Each choice contained a flaw.

I sank into my chair and remembered Martin Luther's frustration at the Church's resistance to the Bible's teachings. In response, he composed a list of ninety-five theses to identify the Church's errors and set forth truth. I would follow his example. Grabbing my quill and a sheet of paper, I wrote my grievances. Then I stretched out my cramped legs and closed my eyes.

Lucia

Valeria told me my father had requested supper in his office, so I ate with her family in the kitchen and returned to our empty suite.

The evening passed, and he still hadn't returned. I couldn't concentrate on my reading, let alone think about sleep. Finally, I crossed the portego and knocked on his office door. He peered out at me, wide-eyed. His hair stuck out as if he had just awakened.

"May I come in?"

The door opened, and I saw a tray of food, untouched, on his desk.

"Papa, what's the matter?" I had never seen him in such a mood.

He sighed. "I wasted my day visiting my old publishers and every printer that Francesco Ziletti recommended—all for naught. In every case, they sounded interested but told me they couldn't publish it soon because of backlogs and contracts."

"Oh, Papa. I'm sorry." I touched his shoulder.

He made fists. "I wonder if Vincenzo told them about my heresy conviction in Venezia years ago. They would never admit it, but they must fear that if they publish my book, the Inquisition will shut down their presses and arrest them."

I spoke softly. "Surely a reasonable publisher who knows your medical reputation will seize the chance to print your book."

He grimaced. "Reasonable publishers have turned into cowards."

"Surely someone can help you, Papa."

He grabbed a sheet of paper from the corner of his desk and thrust it in front of me. "Read this; I've followed Martin Luther's example and written theses. If I post them, maybe printers and Church officials in Venezia will come to their senses."

I studied his document.

Out of concern for the public welfare, Giordano Locatelli, physician and lately professor of medicine at the University of Verona, proposes a discussion of the following theses in Venezia. He requests that those who cannot be present to debate orally will do so by letter.

In the summer season, pestilence struck and killed thousands of innocent people in our patria, leaving families and cities devastated.

Scientists and physicians strive to find out the cause of this plague and ways to prevent and cure it.

Yet the pope, church doctors, and Roman Inquisition restrict this research, thereby prolonging this dangerous situation.

Publishers and printers also contribute to this needless danger by refusing to publish information about new discoveries that could prevent and cure pestilence.

New laws must require publishers to disseminate this information, under penalty of banishment from Venezia.

For the good of humanity, the Church must rescind its decrees against scientific experimentation and dissection.

I tried to calm my voice. "Papa, your message couldn't be clearer. But I beg you, take the advice you've given me: be cautious. If you post this, the Inquisition will arrest you. Who will defend you then?"

He stamped his foot. "What else can I do? My book is like a baby desperate to be born, but we have no midwife, not even Francesco Ziletti. It will perish unless we can find a way to bring it out."

"Papa, what about the publishers you've worked with outside Venezia?"

"I must publish it here, before the pestilence strikes again." His eyes flashed. "Thousands of lives are at stake."

"Per favore, get some sleep before you decide." I opened the door and glanced back at him. "Buona notte, Papa."

He stared at me, and I walked to my room.

✧

Giordano

Lucia's words left a bitter taste in my mouth. Try as I might, I couldn't stop them from echoing in my mind: beyond Venezia and its dangers, someone who knows me would publish my book. Logic told me she spoke the truth.

I had no reasonable choice but to seek a distant publisher. Pestilence struck in the summertime, so physicians must learn about my discovery as soon as possible, before the summer heat ushered in the contagion. Once I had been acquainted with many leading figures in the publishing world. I had worked with several printers who might wish to publish another of my books.

Pestilence had killed my printer in Verona, and the Inquisition's threats would likely intimidate other Italians as they had the Venetians—but not publishers across the Alps. I thought at once of my co-religionist and fellow Italian, Pietro Perna. Our shared convictions had made us fast friends and gave me confidence that he would again shepherd a book of mine through his publishing firm in Basel. Publication would take longer than in Italy, so I mustn't waste a moment.

Moments later, I set down my quill and reread my letter. The next thing I remembered was a knock on my office door.

"Eccomi, Lucia. May I come in, Papa?"

"Un momento, Lucia." I opened the door. As usual, my daughter's grin made me smile. I beckoned her inside.

"You look exhausted, Papa. Did you sleep last night?"

My face flushed. "Sì, but only after I realized I should follow your advice." I looked her in the face. "Lucia, forgive me for my rudeness. You came to help me, but I took out my anger and frustration on you. I'm sorry."

"Of course, Papa." She hugged me.

I linked her arm in mine and led her to my desk. "I just finished writing a publisher in Basel." I showed her the letter.

When she saw its intended recipient, her face turned pale. "You're asking Pietro Perna to publish your book?"

"Sì. He's an old friend. I'm sure he'll do it."

"But all of Venezia knows he's a heretic—including the Inquisition. If you correspond with him, the Holy Office will suspect you again." She shook her head. "Papa, they're looking for any excuse to arrest you. Why else would Vincenzo keep spying on us?"

"My book must find a publisher. Pietro knows me, and I must take advantage of this. I have no choice, Lucia."

She held my gaze. "Please take every precaution, Papa."

I nodded, walked her to the door, and embraced her before she left. Not an easy conversation, but now Lucia knew why I would endanger myself and jeopardize her future. Grazie a Dio, she still loved me.

Chapter 22

HOPE

Giordano

Weeks passed before Zuanne handed me a letter from Basel. I broke open the seal, expecting a personal note as well as a publication offer from Pietro Perna. Instead, a stranger's handwriting told me my old friend had died, and his heirs couldn't publish my book.

I threw the letter down and pounded my fists on my desk, mourning both Pietro's death and the loss of a publisher. I struggled to concentrate on my patients' complaints that afternoon.

When we entered our rooms after supper, Lucia took my hand. "Papa, you've been so quiet. Have I offended you?"

I dropped her hand. "Of course not." Before I could say more, she broke in.

"Are you working on a new book?"

"I'm still looking for a way to publish my manuscript." I shook my head. "Pietro Perna's family sent me a letter. He's dead, so that door has slammed shut."

"I'm sorry, Papa." She squeezed my hand.

"Lucia, the world needs to hear about my discovery soon. I've tried all the easy avenues for publication, and now I must do something drastic."

My daughter's brows shot up, but she said nothing. After a quick embrace, she returned to her studies.

I dared not tell her about my latest idea for finding a publisher. I knew she would try to dissuade me, but I saw no alternative to pursuing my old connections in the book-smuggling network. I had hesitated because such a choice might endanger me and jeopardize Lucia's wellbeing.

The debate in my mind kept me awake for hours. Should I risk my life and Lucia's in order to save many more lives? Tossing in my bed, I prayed for God's wisdom.

Lucia

"Pestilence soon... summer heat... Perna dead... Ziletti and the Venetians... many deaths on their consciences."

My father's cries carried through the wall between our bedchambers, awakening me before daybreak. Throwing off my coverlet, I pulled on my cloak and knocked on his door. "Papa, what's wrong?"

He greeted me with a wild-eyed stare. "Pestilence could break out again before physicians can read my book and learn how to treat that dread disease." The dark lines under his eyes and his rumpled clothes told me he hadn't slept.

I reached my arms around him. "You've had a nightmare, Papa. May God grant you peace and sleep."

"Grazie, Lucia. Buona notte." He sighed and turned toward his bed.

"Buona notte, Papa." I closed the door and shuffled back to my room. I had never seen my father in such a condition. As I slipped under my coverlet, I prayed God would send angels to protect him.

Giordano

The next morning, I awakened with tense muscles, my mind as anxious as the night before. I pulled my Bible from underneath the mattress, and the pages fell open to Saint John's gospel. Jesus' words jumped out at me from the page: "Unless a kernel of wheat falls to the ground and dies, it remains only a single seed. But if it dies, it produces many seeds." This verse offered a challenge instead of comfort. I wrestled with my decision throughout the morning.

When I walked from my office to pranzo, a vivid image of a sheaf of wheat filled my mind. I stopped and closed my eyes. I was the grain of wheat and must prepare to die, but I would bear fruit, perhaps saving thousands from falling victim to pestilence.

After supper that evening, I set out for the Merceria's bookshops. Years before, this area near Piazza San Marco served as a meeting place for those who defied the Inquisition. I waited at a corner, hoping to see a familiar face, wishing I had stayed home with Lucia. Passersby stared, so I stepped into a bookshop.

"Prego, signor?" A bespectacled young man approached me.

"Sì, could you help me?" I scrambled to think of a request, a reason for my presence in the bookshop—something that sounded innocent, yet would signal my intention to anyone who distributed books that the Church had listed on its Index of Prohibited Books. At last, I thought of an author—controversial, but the Church hadn't banned all of his books. "Do you have any books by Erasmus?"

His eyebrows shot up. "Are you looking for a particular title?"

"No, show me whatever you have."

"Un momento." He frowned and disappeared into the back of the shop.

Moments later, a gray-haired version of the young man walked toward me, then exhaled and turned back toward the doorway.

"He's no agent of the Inquisition, Cristoforo. It's not a trap." He turned again and approached me.

"Do my eyes deceive me, or are you the illustrious Doctor Locatelli who lived in Venezia some time ago?"

"Sì, eccomi—grazie." I extended my hand. "I'm sorry, but I don't remember you."

"Giacomo—it's an honor to make your acquaintance. We've never met, but years ago, other booksellers pointed you out and told me about you." He lowered his voice. "We worried so much after the Inquisition arrested you and some of our fellow booksellers. The Holy Office confiscated our merchandise and threatened to put us out of business. We banded together to protect each other. Even now, we still worry." He shot me a quizzical look. "Why are you looking for the works of Erasmus?"

"Actually, I'm looking for a source for the works of Erasmus and other writers from lands to the north, a means of contact with publishers beyond the reach of the Inquisition. I have a book ready for publication. I've discovered a way to avoid the ravages of pestilence. It has nothing to do with religion, but I can't find a printer here in Venezia who will risk publishing my writings."

He eyed me closely. "And you think I can help you?"

"I hope so." Our gazes met. We sized each other up, each wondering if we would suffer because of our conversation.

He broke the silence. "Come back tomorrow at this time, and I may have an answer for you—but enter through the back door."

"Grazie. A domani!" We clasped hands again.

"Buona notte." He turned toward the back room.

Energized by our conversation, I let myself out the front door. Then I noticed two men outside a nearby shop. They stared at me, whispering. My neck hair bristled. The Inquisition might arrest me before my book could reach the hands of a publisher. I quickened my steps.

Lucia

After supper, my father claimed he needed to stretch his legs. He left the palazzo and didn't return in time for our customary evening conversation about the day's events. His long outings became a habit, so I filled my evenings preparing lessons and editing, pouring my loneliness into poetry.

I hoped Papa was spending the evenings looking for a publisher or perhaps meeting with other physicians to discuss medicine, but I worried he might be involved again with followers of Luther. I yearned to ask him what he was doing during his absences, but fear held me back until one morning when he emerged from his bedchamber grinning, with a spring in his walk.

I could think of only one reason for his exuberance. "Papa, have you found a publisher?"

"An acquaintance may be able to connect me with a publisher outside Venezia." His eyes sparkled.

The Inquisition could be plotting to snare my father. "Be careful, Papa. No matter how great your scientific discovery, your life is worth more. I don't want to lose you again." I quaked inside.

He nodded, and we parted ways.

I sympathized with him, but a cold unease blanketed me, thick and penetrating as Venetian fog.

Giordano

I ate a quick supper and set out for the bookshop again. This time I hid my manuscript in a leather satchel under my cloak. I knocked on Giacomo's back door.

"Who goes there?" The door didn't budge.

"Eccomi, Giordano Locatelli."

Giacomo opened the door. I hurried inside, and he bolted the door behind me. He shook his head. "These days, I can't be too careful." He ushered me to a chair. "Now about your book. My associates assure me that its subject and your reputation will create a fine market in the northern lands. If I had your manuscript in hand, I could send it off with a colporter after his next delivery."

I couldn't hold back a smile. "I hoped for just such an answer. Ecco!" I drew my cloth bag out of my cloak and showed him Lucia's edition.

"Excellent." Giacomo nodded, thumbing through the pages. "If you leave it with me, I'll take every precaution to ensure it reaches a publisher in the north. I'll send word to you as soon as I hear back."

I nodded and rose from the chair.

"Before you go, Doctor Locatelli..." Giacomo held my gaze. "I have friends who have asked whether you still have an interest in religious matters. If you do, they would like to renew your acquaintance."

I snapped to attention. At last, a chance to gather again with believers in the faith of Martin Luther, after my fears and failed attempts. But I remembered the men who watched me the previous night. "How can I know the Inquisition won't trap me?"

Giacomo's voice dropped. "If the Holy Office arrests you, they'll catch me, too—I belong to the group. If you come to my shop Sunday afternoon, I'll escort you to our meeting. We know they suspect us because we're booksellers, so we take pains with secrecy."

I reached forward and clasped his hand. "Grazie, Giacomo. You have no idea how long I've waited to gather with men who share my faith."

He nodded. "Until Sunday, then."

Lighthearted, I stepped out the door. Those few short minutes with Giacomo had replenished my store of hope—for a community of fellow believers, as well as for my book's publication.

Chapter 23

MERCY

Giordano

J had walked only a few paces when a man clutching a large traveling chest dashed past me and pounded on the door I had just closed. Before Giacomo could let him inside, a tall man in a black cloak lunged for the cassone. A cane clattered onto the cobblestones so I recognized Vincenzo even before I saw his face. The first man twisted his body to protect the chest from Vincenzo's grasp but found no place to escape. A canal lay in front of him. The two men struggled for the cassone, and it hurtled through the air. The chest hit the water and came unlatched. In an instant, water filled the cassone, and it vanished into the canal's dark water.

A thud and a scream drew my attention to Vincenzo. He lay on the cobblestones, rubbing his ankle. The other man stared at him, then back at the canal. Neither man said a word, but each shook his head. Vincenzo now had no evidence against the man he chased, and the colporter had lost his entire cargo of books on the verge of delivering it.

I turned away, but another scream riveted my attention back. Vincenzo grasped his cane and struggled to stand, but his ankle gave out, he crumpled on the ground, and his cane bounced beyond his reach. By this time, the colporter had raced away. Vincenzo lay alone, moaning.

A lust for revenge rose up in me. My hands tightened into fists. At last I could requite the torture and injustices the Inquisition had inflicted on me. I surveyed the calle—deserted, save the monk and me. If I kicked Vincenzo, battered his body with blows, or just shoved him into the canal, his threats to my freedom would vanish with his body. No witnesses could accuse me. I shut my eyes.

Bless those who persecute you... Repay no man evil for evil...Blessed are the merciful, for they will be shown mercy. These verses from Holy Scripture came to mind, and I couldn't ignore them. A man writhed in pain nearby, and I knew what I must do. Drawing in my breath, I picked up Vincenzo's cane and walked toward him.

His wide eyes watched my every step. As I approached, he shielded his face with his hand. "Don't kill me, I beg you. Have mercy on a wounded man."

My hands still shook as I reached down and eased Vincenzo's shoe from his swollen right foot. With my hands under his arms, I hoisted him to his feet. "Put your hand around my shoulders."

He leaned on me to support his right side and placed his cane to his left.

"I'll help you to the nearest church. You can rest there until you're strong enough to walk home."

We trudged down the cobblestones, Vincenzo wincing with each step. When we reached San Giovanni Novo church, the sacristan led us to a small room in the rectory. Vincenzo stretched out on a mattress, and I propped his swollen foot on a folded blanket.

Reaching beneath my cloak, I pulled my cloth bag from my shoulder and took out a small sack of chamomile leaves. Placing a handful in a basin, I poured in enough water to form a paste, and rubbed it onto Vincenzo's ankle. "This should take away some of the swelling and tenderness." He moaned, and I saw lines of pain on his face.

I reached back into my bag and placed a pinch of seeds in a cup of water, forming a poppy seed elixir, the costliest sedative and pain medication I possessed. I stirred the mixture and pressed it to Vincenzo's lips.

He swallowed the liquid, licked the inside of the cup, and looked up at me. "Grazie."

"Prego." I forced myself to grant him the same courtesy I gave all my patients. "I can do nothing more to help you now. I'll leave some poppy seeds here for you. Have someone mix them with water when you can't endure the pain. Keep your foot up, and don't walk on it until the swelling goes down and the pain goes away."

I walked out of the rectory as the sun sank below the horizon. Hurrying down a dark calle, I reflected on what had transpired that evening. My book had reached Giacomo's hands, but now I wondered if and when publishers in the north would see it. Without a doubt, the Inquisition knew about Giacomo's role in smuggling prohibited books. He offered my only link to Luther's sympathizers but further contact with the bookseller might cost me my life. I mopped my brow.

Chapter 24

Desperate measures

Lucia
October, 1586

As was his custom on Saturday afternoons, my father left the *palazzo* on that cloudy day to call on his patients, so Valeria and I walked with her parents to Confession. Without the sun's rays, the sea breeze made me shiver. Valeria's parents stopped outside to greet neighbors, but she and I entered the church and waited in line for the confessional.

While my friend took her turn, I stood at the front of the line and reflected on what I should tell the priest.

"Signorina Locatelli." A low-pitched voice whispered into my right ear.

I whirled my head toward the sound.

Vincenzo stood just to my right, his cane in his left hand and a sheaf of music in his right hand.

"Don't hide your secrets. God already sees them. Better now to clear your conscience." Now his eyes and voice revealed a hint of warmth. "The Holy Office looks kindly on those who confess their sins freely."

I locked my arms together.

Valeria opened the confessional door and walked toward me. Vincenzo stepped away, but I couldn't escape his searching eyes. I walked into the confessional with leaden feet, wondering if somehow he had discovered Martin Luther's book or my poems about it. The priest in the confessional might bring in the Inquisition, and soon they might drag me off to prison.

Inside the booth, sweat moistened my palms, but the priest asked no unusual questions. When I came out, Vincenzo had disappeared. His outburst seemed nothing more than a bad dream, but I couldn't put it out of my mind. Neither Valeria nor I spoke as we waited for her parents.

Our walk back to the palazzo took an agonizingly long time, perhaps because my friend and I spoke only in response to her parents. As soon as they headed down the stone stairs to their quarters, a grim-faced Valeria whispered, "We must talk, Lucia."

I led her into my bedchamber and closed the door.

She pursed her lips. "While you were in the confessional, the monk with a cane asked me if your father had done anything odd or suspicious."

My throat tightened.

"When I told him no, he grabbed my arm and told me I must denounce your father to the Holy Office of the Inquisition if I noticed him doing anything peculiar, or the Church would excommunicate me."

Trembling, I said nothing.

Her eyes bored into mine. "I wish I could forget the rumors about your father, Lucia, but I can't. I'm afraid the Church will banish me."

"My father has a good reputation with the Church now. Otherwise he couldn't take communion. So the Church won't condemn you because you know him." I knew she believed what the Roman church taught. She didn't just perform the rituals as I did.

"Are you sure?" She frowned.

"Sì, Valeria." I took her hand and squeezed it. "Don't worry."

Her weak attempt at a smile showed I hadn't put to rest her fears—hardly likely, since my own heart quaked.

Valeria walked out of my room, and I whispered a prayer for my father's safety.

Chapter 25

LAGOON DRAMA

Giordano
February, 1587

Winter had descended on Venezia in full force. A gust of wind churned the water, sending ice-cold spray into our dinghy. Shivering, I gripped both sides to steady myself.

Marsilio closed his Bible. "May God grant us peace and protection until we meet again." Giacomo and I nodded to him and our other three friends in the boat alongside ours. Giacomo untied the rope holding the two boats close, and we parted for the homeward journey. I flexed my fingers and toes to keep them from freezing on this coldest day of winter, longing for a time when we could worship indoors again without jeopardizing our lives.

Every Sunday afternoon, we rowed in small boats to the end of Canal Grande, crossing San Marco basin to the far side of San Giorgio Island. Sometimes we even journeyed out to the Lido to escape prying eyes and encourage each other in the faith of Martin Luther.

Once we would have thought these precautions extreme, but two years before, the Inquisition arrested several members of our group after our meeting in a Venetian home. Because they carried Bibles and Luther's writings, the Inquisition dealt harshly with our friends. Now the few of us who still met together took pains to prevent such a thing from happening again.

That afternoon, Giacomo's boat led the way through Canale della Grázia. Fog hid the swath of water stretching before us, but wind chops slapped the sides of our dinghy and signaled we had entered San Marco basin.

Suddenly a shout broke the silence. "Giordano Locatelli?"

The hair on my neck stood up. I turned around. Behind us, a gondola had pulled in front of the other dinghy. Inside the gondola sat a tall man thrusting a cane into the dinghy. Vincenzo again. My pulse raced.

At the bow, a burly man stretched a rope from the gondola to the small boat, lashing the vessels together. As he climbed into the dinghy, a silver cross swung from a chain around his neck. He, too, must be an agent of the Inquisition.

Giacomo picked up the pace, propelling our boat forward with the strength of a man half his age. The sounds of oars ploughing through the water, and waves splashing the sides of the dinghy drowned out any conversations in the boats behind us.

I glanced at my friend. "Turn back, Giacomo, we must help them escape!" My stomach turned at the thought of losing Alberto, Lorenzo, Ferdinando, and especially Marsilio, our leader. All had become my close friends over the years we gathered together.

Giacomo shook his head. "Don't you understand? Giordano, you're the one the Inquisition wants. We can only pray those thugs don't search our friends thoroughly or torture them to gather more evidence against you."

Bile surged into my throat. I would never be able to face my friends after abandoning them to the Inquisition, but I knew Giacomo was right.

Our boat flew through the open water and up Rio Canonico Palazzo, stopping only when we reached the wharf behind Giacomo's bookshop. We rushed out of the dinghy. Without a word, my friend disappeared into his bookshop and bolted the door.

I hurried down the calle toward home, the afternoon's events churning in my mind. Vincenzo's pursuit shattered my hope that he might reciprocate my act of mercy. I doubted my freedom would last much longer, and I shivered all the way home.

Chapter 26

STEADFAST

Stefano
March, 1587

J stood on the ship's wave-splashed deck watching gulls soar. Honestly, I couldn't tell if fear or the chill breeze made me tremble. At the very least, Padre Carlo would have dismissed me from my position if he knew why I journeyed to Venezia. More likely, the new Inquisitor would have sent me to the executioner.

One week earlier, Padre Carlo asked me to compile a list of persons convicted of heresy in the recent past but now freed. Of course, I couldn't omit the name of my father's friend, Giordano Locatelli. His case had been the talk of the town: the famous professor at the medical college, sentenced to rot in prison, then to tend the sick in Venezia during the pestilence.

When the Inquisitor asked me to check on the whereabouts and recent activities of each person on the list, my worries grew. There could only be one reason: Padre Carlo wanted to snare as many of them as possible. This would be an easy way for him to build up his reputation, since these people were obvious targets—already convicted and identified as heretics or enemies of the faith.

Vincenzo had been sending us reports about Doctor Locatelli for years, but the previous Inquisitor never took them seriously. He thought Vincenzo made up stories to keep his job with the Holy Office. Because of our family's long friendship with the Locatellis, I didn't show these reports to the new Inquisitor. As far as I knew, all of Venezia held Doctor Locatelli in high esteem for his medical skills. If he had stayed clear of heresy during his ten years in Venezia, he should face no censure from the Holy Office.

To protect myself, I would need to pass on Doctor Locatelli's name to the Holy Office in Venezia, but first I would tell my father's friend about this new investigation. I could never face Lucia if the Inquisition arrested her father again before I warned him.

So I dug out my stash of coins and boarded a ship bound for Venezia—an adventure for me, since I had never explored further than the outskirts of Verona. The grand city intrigued me but not as much as the prospect of seeing Lucia again.

Lucia—her name had haunted my dreams after she moved to Venezia with her father. Like a fool, I didn't appreciate her when she lived with my family, but when she left I couldn't forget her wavy reddish-gold hair, deep blue eyes, and quick mind. After my wife died in childbirth, I began to wonder what had become of Lucia. I hoped our paths would cross again.

When I stepped off the ship in Venezia, a gondolier promised to deliver me to the address I read him. He soon moored the gondola in front of a grand palazzo. I sucked in my breath.

"You're sure this is the place?"

"Sì, signor." He nodded.

"Grazie." I handed him a coin and stepped onto the wharf. Climbing the wide steps, I stood before carved double doors. The brass knocker clanged, and my heart pounded. Doctor Locatelli might revile me for my work with the Inquisition. How I hoped he would hear me out and heed my warning.

An elderly servant answered my knock, ushered me inside, and promised to announce my arrival. I looked around the hall while I waited, whistling through my teeth. Paintings, statues, tapestries, furniture, a mosaic floor—Doctor Locatelli must enjoy success in his medical career.

I recalled my mother's struggles to feed and clothe our family. Looking down at my mud-stained boots and worn cloak, I wondered if Doctor Locatelli and Lucia would scorn me as a rustic.

Just then, the servant returned. "Signor Capriolo, Doctor Locatelli must attend patients all afternoon. He sends his apologies and asks if you could speak instead with his daughter, Signorina Lucia, so as not to keep you waiting."

"Of course." My heart skipped, but I wondered how Lucia would respond to my warning.

"*Allora*, please be seated. I will announce your arrival to Signorina Locatelli." Left to my thoughts once again, I pulled a sheaf of papers from my valise, but I couldn't focus on the words.

Finally, after all these years of waiting, I saw Lucia. Instead of the cherub I remembered, she glided into the portego like a queen arriving at court, with a crown of reddish-golden braids gathered on top of her head. Her skirt trailed behind her. What fools these Venetians, that no gentleman had claimed her as his bride!

"Signorina Lucia." I scrambled to my feet and bowed so low that I lost my balance.

Lucia smiled, and her eyes twinkled. When she reached out her hand, I smelled violets. "Signor Capriolo, welcome to our home. What brings you to Venezia?"

"Call me Stefano, please. I hope I'm still a family friend." I looked around the room. "Could we speak in a more private place?"

She led me into the library and closed the door. Her eyes burned into mine. "What's on your mind, Stefano?"

I sucked in my breath. "I hate to tell you, but I must. Lucia, if your father isn't already in danger, he will be soon. Even though I'm only a clerk for the Holy Office in Verona, I know an agent has been watching your father for years here in Venezia. Now the new Inquisitor is paying close attention to these reports, insisting that agents investigate every person convicted of heresy in his territory—especially your father."

Her face turned white.

"If your father has a spotless reputation in Venezia, he'll have no problem with the Holy Office." I wanted to stop and reassure her further. But my memory of the letters, and the worried look in her eyes told me I must continue.

"I'm not here to ask you anything, Lucia. But any questionable acquaintances, anything he's done that even looks suspicious could cost him his life."

She looked at the floor and then up at me. "Exactly my worry." I strained to hear her. "Stefano, I don't know everything my father has done. I can't say how the Holy Office would judge him. But if he's in danger, what should we do? Doesn't the Inquisition have agents everywhere?"

I inhaled. "The Inquisition's agents work in every city and town that speaks our tongue. But not in the lands to the north, beyond the mountains. Heresy thrives there. If he were my father..." My cheeks warmed. "I mean, if you have any worries about your father, I would encourage him to gather his gold ducats and head north before agents of the Holy Office knock at your door again."

She nodded, her lips downturned. "Grazie, Stefano. I won't forget your kindness, traveling all this way to warn us. How can we repay you?"

My heart battered my chest, but I knew better than to voice my feelings. I stared at my boots and cleared my throat. "It's my pleasure to assist your family. As a great favor to my family, please pray for my father's health. We're all worried."

"I'm so sorry; of course we'll pray for him." She paused. "Could you join us this evening for cena? I know my father would be glad to see you after he finishes attending his patients."

"Grazie, Lucia." I couldn't hold back a smile. "How I wish I could accept your invitation. But my ship departs later this afternoon. I mustn't linger. Please give my regards to your father. May God protect you both."

"Godspeed to you, Stefano. Tante grazie." She clasped my hand.

I nodded, gazed at Lucia one last time, and turned toward the door. The scent of violets stayed with me as I walked down to the wharf.

Giordano

After a long afternoon, my last patient left my office. My stomach growled, and I wasted no time in following him toward the door. Passing the window, I saw only dim silhouettes outside. I hurried across the portego, looking forward to a hearty meal and lively conversation.

"Lucia, eccomi, your papa. Will you join me for cena?" I knocked on her door.

The moment she opened the door, her tight lips and wide eyes told me my hope for a pleasant evening would go unfulfilled.

"Come in, Papa." She pulled the door shut. "You must flee Venezia! Stefano came all the way from Verona just to warn us of the peril you face."

I grabbed a chair to steady myself.

"A new Inquisitor is investigating everyone convicted of heresy in his territory. Any evidence of new heretical activity means they'll arrest you again." She sighed. "Vincenzo frightens me now. He wouldn't keep watching you if he hadn't found—or made up—something incriminating to tell the Holy Office." She eyed me closely. "Imagine how the Inquisitor's reputation will grow if he arrests you, Papa."

My gut roiled. Drawing in my breath, I looked up at her. "I'll consider this matter now, Lucia. Go ahead to supper without me."

She took my arm. "No, Papa, you need to keep up your strength. Come with me now. You can make up your mind after cena."

Forcing one foot in front of another, I walked with her to the dining room. But my mind traveled back to my past encounters with the Inquisition—relentless questions, excruciating pain from the *strappado*, cold, lonely prison cells. At my age, I might not survive such ill treatment.

Perhaps I should follow Stefano's advice and escape while I could. But that would mean leaving behind my patients and my fellow believers in Martin Luther's faith, abandoning my quest to loosen the Roman Church's grip on Venezia.

We reached the dining room. I tried to concentrate on the food and conversation but couldn't banish anxiety from my mind. After supper, I sat at my desk considering Stefano's warning. After bidding Lucia good night, I mulled pros and cons of leaving Venezia in the wee hours of the night. My thoughts wavered between safety and conviction.

Finally, I pushed back my chair and stood in front of the window. Hints of brightness glimmered through a wall of clouds. Dropping to my knees, I prayed that as the moon penetrated darkness, God would break through my confusion and light my path. Moments later, my chin sank to my chest, and I stumbled into bed.

Lucia's door swung open just as I emerged from my bedchamber in the morning. She cornered me before I could walk out of our suite. "So Papa, will you leave?" Her cheeks flushed, and her gaze locked with mine.

I nodded. "I'm going to my office to meet my patients."

"You know what I meant." She frowned. "Will you take Stefano's advice?"

"It's a difficult decision, Lucia." I lowered my voice. "I haven't made up my mind yet."

"Papa, there's no time to lose. You must leave at once." Her eyes flashed.

My spine stiffened. "This decision is too important. I can't rush into it."

She pursed her lips. "You mustn't delay. Your life depends on it, Papa—and you're the only family I have left." She dabbed a corner of her eye with her kerchief.

"I'll do my best, Lucia." I stretched out my arms to embrace her, but she shrank back.

"No, Papa. Only your decision to leave can comfort me now." She ran to her bedchamber.

Lucia's rebuff stung every time I thought about it. By evening, I realized I must make amends and reach a decision. I vowed to make up my mind somehow that night, but first I must visit Giacomo, the bookseller. I had promised to come by his shop that evening to look at his new merchandise. After supper, I set out on foot as foggy darkness set in.

Arriving in back, I knocked ten times. The ageing bookseller cracked the door, then shooed me inside. He locked the door.

"Buona sera, my friend." He pointed to a stack of books on a table. "These just arrived from Basel. Take a look."

"Grazie, Giacomo." I never tired of reading forbidden books by religious reformers and scientists, all smuggled into Venezia under the eyes of the Inquisition. Glancing inside every volume, I took care to look beyond each title page. My years of involvement with book smugglers had taught me how often printers inserted false title pages to fool customs inspectors.

I sorted the books into three piles. I would keep a few for my own medical research or spiritual encouragement, some I would pass on to my medical friends and those in my religious circle, and the remainder I would leave with Giacomo. That evening I also found a volume of poetry written by an Italian woman—a surprise that I knew would please Lucia. Giacomo tallied up my bill. As usual, only a few coins remained in my pocket when I left the shop.

I strolled beside canals and crossed bridges. Before long my bag's leather strap dug into my shoulder, but my joy at acquiring these titles overshadowed the discomfort. I faced my favorite dilemma—deciding which books to give to which friends.

Out of the corner of my eye, I glimpsed a man watching me from a doorway. In the fog, I couldn't see his face, but his stooped posture and cane gave away his identity. Ducking around a corner, I altered my course and remembered Lucia's warning. My heavy heart outweighed the load on my shoulder, and I prayed again for God to show me if I should flee.

My circuitous route took me past Palazzo Morosini. Andrea Morosini, a fine young scion of this family, had visited my office for medical care. He had expressed interest in religious reform, so I delivered a copy of Luther's *Treatise on Christian Liberty* into his hands. Although surprised at my appearance, he thanked me for the book and pledged to discuss it with me the next time we met.

As I walked out the door, I heard a low, yet clear voice. "Well done, good and faithful servant." Whirling around, I saw no one. I stood frozen, finally concluding that God had spoken, providing the answer I needed. My heart pounded its approval. As much as Lucia would protest, I knew without a doubt that I couldn't flee Venezia and leave my fellow believers with no source of printed materials to bolster their faith.

If the Inquisition should catch me, so be it. My ancient body wouldn't survive long under torture. I would soon fly to paradise and reunite at last with my beloved Caterina. Sì, I would stay in Venezia and remain faithful. I must tell Lucia my decision as soon as I reached our suite.

Moments later, I squared my shoulders and knocked on my daughter's door. "May I come in?"

"Sì, Papa." She spoke softly, her brow creased.

"After much consideration, I've reached a decision." I took her hands in mine. "Lucia, I must stay here in Venezia. I can't abandon the people in my care."

She squeezed my fingers. "You're too loyal for your own good. Please reconsider!" Tears welled up in her eyes. "I fear for you, Papa."

Her plea tested my sense of God's direction. I looked into her eyes. "My life remains in God's hands. He'll watch over the future as he has the past. I must obey him, Lucia."

She opened her mouth but said nothing. Turning away, she covered her face with her hands.

I reached my arm around her shoulder, but she shook her head and waved me away. I walked toward the doorway. "I'm sorry to cause you pain, Lucia. May God grant you peace. Buona notte." I slipped out of her room and closed the door.

Lucia

The next evening, Papa and I walked down the stairs after cena, pausing in front of arched windows to watch the fiery sky turn crimson and fade to black. I savored this moment in a bittersweet way, mindful that we might not share many more sunsets. My distress at his decision had turned to a dull but always present anxiety.

We returned to our suite, and I headed toward my bedchamber.

"Wait a minute, Lucia." Papa tugged at my elbow. "There's news you must hear. Filippo Soncini signed a marriage contract, so Roberto will wed in a few months. Filippo offered our suite to the couple, so if they choose to move in, we'll need to find new lodgings."

I gaped at my father. My grief at giving up Roberto cut through me like a knife, compounded by the threat of losing our home. More pressing concerns had swept this possibility from my mind.

He rubbed my shoulder. "Mi dispiace. I didn't want to upset you, but you must be prepared."

His comfort revived me. "*Si*, Papa. I expected Roberto would marry one day, but I'm startled anyway."

He squeezed my shoulder. "Come with me. I have something for you." He ushered me into his study, offering me a chair. Unlocking his desk drawer, he pulled out a book. His face lit up and he handed it to me.

I read the title: *Orations, Dialogues, Letters, and Poems of Olimpia Morata*. I smiled at him. "Grazie, Papa. Another woman poet from our patria. I'll enjoy reading this."

But the imprint—Basel, 1558—revealed this book was published in a land where heresy flourished. An uneasy feeling lodged in the pit of my stomach. This book might be on the Index of Prohibited Books, proof that Papa again had involved himself with heretics. I looked him in the eye. "Where did you find this book?"

He smiled. "A friend passed it on to me. I hope you like it." He pressed his lips together.

His words heightened my misgivings. I wanted to examine the book in the privacy of my bedchamber.

"Any gift you choose is sure to please me." I bussed his cheeks and he bussed mine. "Buona notte, Papa. I'm sure this book will provide me with an interesting evening."

"Buona notte, Lucia."

I shut the door of my bedchamber and set Papa's gift on my desk, recalling my other book from over the mountains, written by Martin Luther. Excitement and the thrill of danger coursed through me. My curiosity again prevailed over caution, and I turned the pages.

In a customary dedication, the editor praised Olimpia Morata's pious and immortal soul, but lamented the loss of much of her writing in a fire after the siege of Schweinfurt, her home in Franconia.

Perhaps Olimpia had left Italy for the same reason my uncle Cornelio departed years before. Her story piqued my curiosity.

I read her first poem and smiled. Like me, Olimpia preferred poetry to traditional feminine pursuits. Thanks to her poem, I pictured her as a spirited young woman with a quill in her hand, even though she and my mother would have been the same age. Her other poetry stirred both my admiration and surprise. I couldn't wait to show these poems to Modesta.

Olimpia's story emerged as I perused her letters, and I discovered parallels to my own life. Not only a scholar, Olimpia believed in Martin Luther's ideas and encouraged her friends to do the same. Her family, like mine, suffered persecution by the Church because of its sympathy for Luther. My heart beat faster.

Olimpia's passion to tell others about Luther came into full view in her letters, and the exhortations she wrote to her friends showed her courage. As I read through them, guilt settled over me because I fell far short of her bold example.

Zuanne's voice resounded from the portego. I stuffed the book under my coverlet. If the Inquisition discovered this work in my room, I knew they would arrest me. Even after I realized Zuanne was singing to himself, I couldn't relax.

Had Papa intended this book as an antidote for his bad news, an example for me to follow, or was Olimpia's reputation as a poet the only reason for his gift? I worried that someone might overhear our conversation if I asked him now, in the nighttime quiet. I could endanger both of us.

Prudence told me to ask my father to lock this volume away with his gold coins or even toss it into the canal. But the kinship I felt with Olimpia Morata wouldn't allow me to part with her writings.

I had no doubt that Modesta, too, would delight in reading Olimpia's poems, so I would choose a few of my favorites to show her. She never finished reading all my selections before her children interrupted. I tucked my father's gift under my mattress and snuffed out my candle.

Two days later, I wrapped my stained apron around my new book and stuffed the parcel in the bottom of my borsa. Clutching the bag under my arm, I climbed into the gondola for the journey to Modesta's home.

When I walked inside, my friend glanced first at me and then at her son, Pietro, who nestled against her on a lettuccio as she nursed baby Cecelia. "I'll finish the story later, Pietro. Maria will take you out to play now." He slid down from the couch and followed his nurse-maid to the inner courtyard.

I sat at one end of Modesta's couch and pulled out my prize. "Before we talk about our own poetry, let me show you a few poems that inspired me. Some even moved me to tears. This poet grew up in Ferrara and died before we were born, but she'll live on forever through her poems."

"A woman from our patria—what's her name?" Modesta snapped to attention.

"Olimpia Morata. Have you heard of her?"

She frowned. "The name sounds familiar."

I opened to a familiar page. "This poem is my favorite, because it reminds me so much of you, who left behind feminine things for poetry."

Modesta reached for the book and read the poem to herself, mouthing the words. She read it again, then flashed a smile. "Si, poetry is my glory and delight, just as this poet wrote. What a find, Lucia—such passion for poetry, and such eloquent verse! Could I read more?"

"Certainly. I've marked my favorite poems with ribbons."

She turned the pages from one ribbon to the next. Nodding and commenting after each poem, at last she flipped to the front to read the dedication.

She looked up. "Such an exciting life. I can't imagine lecturing at the Duke's court in Ferrara, especially at the age of sixteen!" Modesta looked off into the distance.

Our shared enthusiasm spurred me to tell more of Olimpia's story. "Sì, but then her father died, she left the Duke's court, and died young."

"What happened to her?" She frowned.

I flinched. I had said too much already. If I gave her a truthful answer—that Olimpia's allegiance to Martin Luther's ideas led the Duke of Ferrara to banish her from his court—she might report me to the Inquisition, yet I would undermine our friendship if I lied.

In the end, I recounted the rest of Olimpia's life story but didn't comment on her beliefs.

Modesta raised her brows and stared at me like a judge facing a criminal.

My throat tightened.

"Where did you get this book, Lucia?" I had never seen her posture so rigid.

I hesitated. "It was a gift."

Modesta spoke in a low voice. "Lucia, I'm still ashamed of how my uncle treated you and your father the first time we met. His behavior offended me, too, but he was trying to protect me from heresy. Today, you've exposed me to Luther's heresy through this poet. Are you trying to turn me into a heretic?"

"No." My shoulders sagged. "I worried you would think so and almost left this book at home for that very reason. I took the risk because I thought you would want to read her poems. That's the only reason." I leaned toward her and whispered. "I didn't plan to talk about Martin Luther, but you asked about Olimpia's life."

I looked her in the face. "Modesta, I don't want to endanger you—or myself—but since you mentioned Luther, I must tell you he doesn't deserve the label of heretic, even if the Roman Church calls him one. I've read his arguments." I inhaled. "The Church made a terrible mistake when it dismissed his ideas. Martin Luther helped me realize I don't have to wonder any longer if I've earned God's love. This freedom inspired me to write many poems."

She pursed her lips. "I see you believe this, Lucia, but is it worth the price you'll pay if the Inquisition finds out? Keep your opinions private to protect yourself. That's what I've done. If I spoke about the roles women should play in society, I would disgrace my family. Only the most discerning readers of my *Tredici Canti di Floridoro* might guess what I believe." She paused. "Do we understand each other?"

I nodded. "Sì, Modesta."

She squeezed my hand.

A moment later, we settled back into our places, and Modesta handed me a sheet of paper from the side table.

"Lucia, here's my new poem about Christ's resurrection. Tell me what you think." Then footsteps and a high voice announced the return of her son and his nurse and the end of our meeting. Pietro dashed into the room, and Maria followed him.

Modesta and I embraced, and I turned toward the door. Just before I left, Modesta's wooden platform shoes echoed through the portego.

"Lucia," She handed me the volume of Olimpia Morata's works. "You mustn't forget this."

"Grazie. I thought perhaps you intended to read more." I wrapped the book in my apron and buried it in my borsa.

"No. Arrivederci, Lucia." She turned back to her children.

When I stepped outside, Zuanne nodded from the gondola. I climbed down the steps, praying Modesta would keep my secret.

Out of the corner of my eye, I noticed Vincenzo watching me from the next pier. My heart beat all the way up to my throat. Could he know which book I carried with me?

I hesitated. If I threw Olimpia Morata's poems into the lagoon, I would be admitting my guilt. Vincenzo would likely retrieve the book with a fishing net, and I would have no defense before the Inquisition. I had no choice but to carry the heretical volume back to the palazzo. My life might depend on my nonchalance.

I lifted my foot toward the gondola and lost my balance. Only Zuanne's quick reach kept me from falling into the lagoon.

When the first light of morning brightened my windows, I rushed to the washbasin. Drying my face and hands, I donned the gown I had set out the night before and dashed to the kitchen to grab a piece of bread and an apple. I left the palazzo before my father emerged from his bedchamber. With Zuanne's help, I could find time for my errand before teaching my class.

Our gondola sped through the canals to Francesco Ziletti's bookshop. Zuanne reached his hand to steady me as I stepped out of the boat.

"Grazie, Zuanne, I won't be long. Enjoy these while you're waiting." I pulled the apple and bread from my borsa.

He smiled. "Grazie, Lucia. How thoughtful." His gray eyes crinkled.

I tucked my bag under my arm and hurried up the steps. When no one answered the door, I pounded harder. At last Signor Ziletti peeked out.

"Avanti, Signorina Locatelli." He beckoned me inside the dark shop. "I didn't expect anyone so early, but I've already lit the lamp in my office. Come with me."

I followed him, straining my eyes to avoid stray books in my pathway. Safe in his office, I handed him the package I had wrapped in cloth and tied with twine. "Here's my edition of Horace. Please let me know if you have any questions."

"Grazie, signorina. Your work is always neat, clear, and prompt, so I'm not worried." He smiled and untied the twine but stopped before taking out the manuscript.

"Before my workers arrive..." He closed his office door. "Signorina Locatelli, I consider myself a friend of your family, so I must tell you.

I've heard rumors from my bookseller friends that your father has been circulating books on the Church's Index of Prohibited Books."

My limbs stiffened and memories of Papa's arrest flooded my mind. "Are you sure?"

He nodded, grim-faced. "Once people could do such things here but not anymore. Recently Inquisition agents found prohibited books in several bookshops. They arrested the proprietors." His eyes met mine. "Signorina, I'm fond of your father. I would hate to see anything happen to him."

I thought at once of Alessandro and tried not to shudder. "Grazie. I'll warn my father and urge him to act with prudence." I picked up my borsa. "I have a class to teach this morning, so I must bid you farewell."

"Capito." He reached into a drawer and counted out coins. "Here's your payment, signorina. I'll send you a new assignment soon. Grazie." He led me out to the front door. As I walked out of his shop, he spoke in a low voice. "Be careful, signorina; that applies doubly to your father."

I nodded and walked down the steps to the wharf. At that moment, neither my tongue nor my brain served me, so I could only nod at Zuanne as he helped me into the gondola.

Giordano

"Papa, I must talk with you. It's urgent." Lucia clutched my hand as soon as I closed the door of our suite.

"Of course." Her flushed face had caught my eye during supper. Now I led her into my study and hoped the quiet, book-lined retreat would calm my daughter as it did me. I pulled a chair toward her and grabbed my medical bag. If Lucia needed my attention, my writing could wait. "Are you ill?"

She shook her head and remained standing. "No, Papa. I must be blunt. Rumor has it you've been dealing in forbidden books—books listed on the Church's Index. The Inquisition has certainly heard these reports, too. You're in danger, Papa."

Onion and garlic flavors from supper burned all the way up my throat. How could she know?

She gripped my hands. "I can't bear to lose you again, Papa. You must leave Venezia at once. Go into hiding, or go to Basel and stay with Uncle Cornelio." Her gaze lingered.

"Grazie. I appreciate your concern." I bit my lip. "Most rumors amount to idle gossip, so my situation may not be as grim as you think. I can't live my life in fear of a danger that may never materialize."

"Papa, believe me—it's true!" She pressed her lips together.

"Lucia, when I was your age, my friends warned me about the Inquisition, just as you did, so I fled from Venezia to the north. There I read Francesco Petrarco's letter, "To Italy," and realized how much I loved my homeland. When I returned, I vowed, like Petrarco, never to leave again."

"Then find a place to hide in Italy!" She squeezed my hands.

I straightened my shoulders. "I must stay in Venezia. I have patients to attend, research and writing to complete, and I can't neglect my call to spread Luther's message." I smiled at her. "I'm an old man, Lucia, too old to run away. I'm not afraid to die. In fact, I look forward to joining Caterina in paradise."

Her lip quavered. "Years ago you warned me to express my religious convictions only in private, with caution and prudence. You're ignoring your own advice, Papa."

A door creaked in the portego, and both of us flinched.

She leaned in. "You must understand. You're an easy target for the Inquisition. Please, Papa—leave Venezia! If they find any evidence against you, I'll never see you again."

My eyes moistened, and I glanced around my study to avoid her scrutiny. Soon I might be snatched away from my beloved daughter, facing damp prison walls or worse, instead of bookshelves filled with my treasured volumes.

The candle in my desk lamp flickered. I met her gaze. "That's what grieves me most, Lucia. And I worry about how you'll survive without me."

I yanked my desk drawer open and grabbed the key to my moneybox. "Take this. I pray my savings will hold you over until you can support yourself." I slipped it into her apron pocket.

"Little more than a decade ago, I despaired of surviving until I could see you and your mother again. During those dark days in prison, I vowed that if God allowed me to return to you, I would support and protect you and do anything in my power to avoid another separation—anything but ignore God's direction.

"Remember, Lucia, how Saint Peter denied the Lord three times but repented and became the rock upon which God built the Church?"

"Sì, Papa." Her voice dropped to a whisper.

"Peter remained faithful unto death, and I must do the same. Like Peter, I've denied my faith, but this time I'll hold it fast and face the consequences."

Lucia stared at me, her face now pale. "Such a costly faith we share." She shook her head. "Papa, I'm proud of you, but I fear the worst." Her voice broke. "May God protect you and reward your courage!" She threw her arms around me, and I held her in a long embrace.

Lucia
April, 1587

Like twisted threads of yarn, the day's conversations wound my thoughts into a ball of worry as I tried to sleep. The log in my fireplace broke apart, embers hissed, and soon Venezia's dampness chilled my fingers and toes. Papa's courageous words calmed me, but Francesco Ziletti's warning stole away my peace.

Maybe Papa was right, and the bookseller's message was only gossip. But what would happen to my father and to me if the Inquisition took him away? I whispered a prayer for God's protection and pulled my coverlet over my head, squeezing my eyes shut.

At first I thought the knock on my door was a dream.

"Prego, Lucia, wake up!" Zuanne's call finally roused me.

"Un momento." I pulled my cloak over my chemise, dragged myself to the door, and stared at Zuanne's shadowed face. "What is it?"

His stiff bow made my stomach churn. I knew what he was going to say.

"Signorina Lucia, I'm so sorry." The candle in his hand wavered. "They just took your father away. Two agents arrived, the one who's come before and a big man I hadn't seen."

The room swayed. The next thing I knew, Zuanne laid me on my bed.

He clasped my hand. "I hated to wake you, but I knew I must."

I nodded, blinking at the candle. "What can we do?"

He shook his head. "Your father—and Venezia—need a champion strong and brave enough to defeat the Inquisition, a David to kill this Goliath. We're not David, but we must make every effort. As soon as morning breaks, I'll come back, and we'll make a plan." He squeezed my hand and stepped back.

"Grazie, Zuanne."

"Try to rest, Lucia." He took his candle from the stand and closed the door.

Anger boiled up my throat. Papa should have listened to me and escaped Venezia, to protect himself and me. But after he refused to leave, I should have prepared for this outcome.

Papa's brave words couldn't change the inevitable. A voice inside told me I wouldn't see him again in this life. As Zuanne said, Papa had no David to face the Inquisition's Goliath.

In the darkness, I saw the mental image of a sailboat on a windless sea, unable to move or change course. At once I knew that stranded sailboat was me. Without Papa, I would have no place in Venezia—no home and no station in society. I sobbed into my coverlet.

Valeria taught my class the next day, and I wrote frantic letters to everyone who might possibly help. With no other way to help my father, I rushed to finish my latest editing project.

The following morning, Zuanne knocked on my door to announce Francesco Ziletti's arrival. I grabbed the busta of papers I had edited and stepped into the portego. The printer sat with his head bowed. I had never seen him still, let alone with slumped posture.

Dread filled me, and I ran toward him. "Signor Ziletti, you called for me?"

He scrambled to his feet and pointed to the lettuccio near his chair. "Signorina Locatelli, please sit down." When I had settled myself, he placed his hat over his heart. "As your family's friend, duty requires me to tell you—the Inquisition executed your father."

"What?" My heartbeat thundered in my ears.

"Because of his prior convictions, they expedited his case. Yesterday they tried him before their tribunal and condemned him to death as a relapsed heretic. Last night they carried out the sentence."

"What did they do to him?"

"I would spare you the details." He looked at the floor.

"I must know, Signor Ziletti—please!"

He clasped his hands. "My bookselling colleagues told me the executioners followed the Venetian custom, tying weights to his wrists and ankles, rowing him out to the lagoon, and throwing him overboard. May God rest his soul."

I couldn't allow my mind to picture this, and I stared at the bookseller. "Are you sure it's not another rumor?"

"Sì, signorina." He took my hand.

"Grazie, signor. Only a true friend would tell me this." I swallowed again. "However bitter the news, I needed to know."

He nodded. "I remain at your service. Send me a message when you need help, and I'll do everything I can."

"Grazie." Thank God, Signor Ziletti had the decency to tell me. I handed him my box of papers and watched him walk across the portego.

After the door closed behind him, I trudged back to my room. Opening the birdcage door, I stroked my canary's feathers. "Speranza, you're all the family I have left here."

Her chirp provided little solace. I pounded down the stone stairs, my heart first storming with anger at Papa for ignoring my warning, then swelling with pride at his heroism.

When I entered the kitchen, Valeria's mother, aunt, and cousin looked up from their tasks. I forced out the words: "My father is dead—the Inquisition drowned him last night in the lagoon."

"No, not that dear man!" Flora dropped her handful of carrots on the cutting board, rushed across the room, and threw her arms around me.

"I wanted to tell you before you heard rumors." Tears streamed down my face like a cloudburst. I turned away, but Flora clutched my hand and pulled me close. Her familiar lemon scent comforted me.

"Lucia, I'm so sorry." Glancing at her sister and niece, she continued. "You're another daughter to us, and we'll do everything we can to help you."

"You're too kind." I wiped my eyes. "Now I must write this news to my father's friends and family."

"As you like, Lucia. Remember, we're always here. Come down when you need help or comfort—anytime."

I nodded but realized neither she nor anyone else could provide what I most desired—changing my father's terrible fate from a reality back into a bad dream.

✤

With every step I took, the clack of my heels on the stone stairway jolted me out of my torpor. My first letter must go to the Capriolos, the next to my aunt and uncles, and the remainder to my father's scholarly correspondents.

Darkness greeted me as I opened my father's study door. Instead of the cheerful morning sunshine that usually blazed through the windows, light shone only through cracks in the curtains, like the glare of a night policeman's lantern.

As soon as I pulled open the curtains, evidence of the Inquisition's violation curdled my stomach. They hadn't pulled his books from the shelves or thrown his papers on the floor, but his quill lay in a pool of ink across a half-written parchment sheet. The inkwell next to it sat uncovered.

Papa always took great care with his scholarly tools. He must have been writing at his desk when the Inquisition's agents seized him.

I hammered my fists on the desk. My father deserved acclaim, not a criminal's death. I glanced at the sheet he had been writing and shook my head. Not only had the Inquisition taken away my father, they had deprived the world of a brilliant mind who could have saved many lives.

With trembling fingers, I set aside Papa's parchment and placed a fresh sheet of paper in front of me. Dipping his quill in the blue ink, I clenched my jaw each time I wrote about my father's death. Even so, writing kept my feelings in check, and I knew it would be the easiest of the tasks before me.

At last I shook out my right hand and pushed back Papa's chair. Stretching my legs, I paced the study. Papa's wolf-trimmed robe hung on a hook near the door. I stopped and pressed my face into the fur. When I closed my eyes and inhaled the scent, I almost believed Papa stood next to me.

Next I looked through his sketches and handwritten notes, the correspondence piled on a back corner of the desk, and the shelves crammed with his precious books. I wanted to believe that Papa had only stepped out for a walk. Closing my eyes again, I hoped against hope that when I opened them, Papa would smile at me from his desk chair.

A bleak emptiness greeted me instead. I swallowed, grabbed my stack of letters, and hurried out to the portego to find Zuanne.

Animated voices drew me down to the kitchen, where Zuanne sat finishing a bowl of turnip soup.

"Could you send these out for me, please, Zuanne? I must notify my father's family and friends." I held out the letters.

"Certainly, Lucia," He nodded, pushing his bowl away. "Anything I can do to help you." He seized my bundle, tucked it into his satchel, and headed up the stairs. Then he turned back. "Lucia, I'm so sorry about your father. He was a good man who deserved honor, not his sad fate."

"Grazie." I could scarcely nod. I started to follow him, but Valeria's mother took my arm.

"Lucia, you need to keep up your strength. Have a bowl of soup." She guided me toward the table.

"Grazie, but I'm not hungry."

"Mangia, Lucia, as a favor to me."

I pulled a bench up to the table and buried my head in my hands.

Chapter 27

UNCERTAIN FUTURE

Lucia

With each step away from the kitchen, my sense of warmth and comfort ebbed away. Back in my room, I knew I should plan for my future, but my mind refused to cooperate. I picked up a book and couldn't focus on the words. I tried to write a poem, but the paper remained blank.

As the sun dropped below the horizon, I stared out my window and recalled the sunsets Papa and I had shared. The evening shadows fell over the canal, and I wept for Papa and my life without him.

A knock sounded on my door. "Eccomi, Valeria. May I come in?"

"Sì." I hadn't the energy to stand, only sat watching her walk toward me.

She clasped my hands. "I'm so sorry about your father, Lucia. I had to come after I heard the news. How can I help you?"

"Sit with me." I pointed to a chair.

She embraced me. "Lucia, I'll teach your class as long as you wish—anything to help you. If only I could bring your father back."

My shoulders shook. I couldn't hold back sobs. Finally, I wiped my face and looked up at her. "Nightmares from my childhood haunt my sleep—as if it were yesterday, I see Inquisition agents bursting into our home in Verona, dragging my father away. I eat only because your mother insists. All I see before me is loneliness and grief."

She tightened her embrace. "Don't give up hope. Even in the depths of this tragedy, God hasn't forgotten you."

Her words shocked me. She must know my father was executed as a heretic, yet she, a loyal member of the very church that executed Papa, spoke with confidence about God's care for me.

"Grazie, but that's hard to believe now." Tears filled my eyes again. "After my father was arrested in Verona, I thought it must be my fault. When my mother died, I couldn't understand how God could allow such a thing. I try to keep believing God loves me."

I looked at the floor. "Now the worst has happened, and all of Venezia will shun me. No one will praise my father or allow me to honor him with a monument—he won't even have a grave." I wiped my nose with a kerchief.

"Lucia, anyone who endures so much might feel bitter toward God. But someday you'll be able to believe again." Valeria paused. "I know it's true. I felt God had abandoned my family, too, but His love drew me back."

She spoke softly. "A year and a half before you came to Venezia, the contagion killed my two older brothers. They had taken care of the boats and rowed the palazzo's residents. My father had to take on their duties. Mamma said I shouldn't burden you with our sorrow, so I didn't tell you." She pushed back her chair. "Come with me to the kitchen; cena should be ready now."

I dabbed my eyes. Arm in arm, we walked down the stone steps and joined her family around the table. When Valeria's mother handed me a chunk of bread, I forced down a bite to please her. By the end of the meal, I savored both the sweetness of an apple slice and the family's compassion.

Plodding back up the stairs to my bedchamber, I longed for a good book to distract me. When I scanned my bookshelf, the literary treasures I had considered dear friends had no appeal. They couldn't offer the warmth of human contact. I took off my shoes, slipped under my coverlet, and fell into an exhausted slumber.

I saw lights—the Inquisition's lanterns, searching for another heretic in the Locatelli family. Peering at my door, I waited for Vincenzo to burst into my room and haul me away, as he had my father. Finally, I rolled out of bed, cracked my door open and peered out. The palazzo lay silent and dark, but for the lamps that still burned in my room. I sighed—another nightmare. It had seemed so real.

Now anxiety settled over me like a cloud. Valeria's family offered me comfort, but the Soncinis might turn me out of the palazzo. In any case, my father's savings and mine wouldn't allow me to stay long in Venezia. Where else could I go, and what should I do?

My life stood still, like the ship I had pictured, until the day of my weekly meeting with Modesta. That afternoon, I mustered my energy and gathered my books and poems for my favorite and now only outing.

At last, standing outside Modesta's door, I lifted the black veil from my face and sounded the knocker. As I waited, I sensed eyes staring from the windows of neighboring palazzi. I nearly turned around to climb back into the gondola but instead pressed my boots into the cobblestones.

The maestro di casa opened the door, raised his eyebrows, and glanced over my shoulder. "Un momento, signorina." He closed the door and left me standing on the doorstep.

I tried to ignore his ungracious response, recalling how quickly the years had passed since I first called at this palazzo—from Modesta's days as a newlywed, to the birth of her first baby, Pietro, and now little Cecelia.

Modesta opened the door. "Lucia, I didn't expect you." She eyed my mourning clothes. "I'm sorry for your loss."

"Grazie, Modesta." I nodded.

She sighed. "Lucia, I've enjoyed our times together, but I can't meet you any longer." She looked directly at me. "My family's reputation must come first. I hope you understand my situation."

My throat constricted. I should have realized my father's execution would cost me Modesta's friendship.

The maid carried a squalling baby to Modesta. She turned to me. "I'm sorry, but I must take care of Cecelia."

I looked her full in the face, fixing her features in my memory. "Allora, Modesta. I will always remember your friendship and encouragement. Grazie."

Modesta nodded. "*Buona fortuna,* Lucia."

"Arrivederci, my friend." As the door closed behind me, a sob rose up in my throat, and I struggled to suppress it. Stepping down to the wharf, I felt someone watching me, and spotted Vincenzo sitting once again in a dinghy at the next wharf.

I stopped and pulled up my veil. "What more can you want, Vincenzo? Haven't you caused me enough grief?"

He climbed out of the boat and faced me from the wharf. "Lucia, I came to speak with you as an old friend. I beg you, take your father's example as a warning so I won't have to arrest you, too. His relapses into heresy left me with no choice."

His pleading tone evoked my sympathy, but only until I realized he had admitted responsibility for hounding my father to his death.

Vincenzo stretched his arms toward me, opening his palms. "Please, Lucia—stay away from heresy!"

We stared at each other. My stomach churned.

"Leave me alone, Vincenzo!" I pulled down my veil, reached for Zuanne's hand, and climbed into the gondola. We pulled away from the wharf. Breath by breath, I exhaled my pain at Modesta's rejection and my outrage at Vincenzo.

After our gondola left Vincenzo far behind, I turned to Zuanne. "I shouldn't have come." I wiped my eyes.

"I'm so sorry." He lowered his voice. "Lucia, I fear for your safety here. As much as I'll miss you, you need to find refuge away from Venezia."

I nodded and thought of my godparents in Verona. I didn't have time to send them a request for shelter and wait in Venezia until they responded.

Zuanne's rhythmic rowing calmed me, and by the time we arrived at the palazzo, I had made up my mind. Papa had been able to remain in Venezia to the end, but I hadn't the resources, even if I wanted to stay. I unlocked my father's money box and asked Zuanne to book my passage to Verona, praying the Capriolos would again take me in.

Pushing the chair away from my father's desk, I stretched my stiff legs. The sorting of Papa's belongings exhausted me physically but also tugged at my heart. Every item I discovered brought fresh sorrow as I realized Papa would never again use the book, cap, or cloak. Whispering "God help me," I snaked my way between the traveling chests I had filled with books and papers to gather the final pile of books from a dim corner of my father's study.

Near the top of the stack, an odd book caught my eye. Although its cloth cover had faded, I noticed the once-elegant brocade—not Papa's style—and opened the brittle volume with care. I recognized my mother's handwriting on its yellowed pages, and a lump clogged my throat. I read dates at the beginning of each entry, and realized I had found Mamma's diary.

At once, my heart surged with joy and pain. What fortune to find a memento of Mamma. She had left behind so few traces of her life. Yet my discovery reminded me of my double loss. I longed to read the diary on the spot, from cover to cover.

But my glance out the window showed the sunset dissolving into darkness, and I knew the diary must wait. Now I must finish packing Papa's keepsakes and gather my own belongings in preparation for a morning departure. Zuanne had agreed to take me and all my baggage across the lagoon to Fusina, where I would board a ship bound for Padova.

I placed the diary in my borsa. Moments later, I closed the final loaded cassone and walked down to the kitchen. By candlelight, I found a covered dish sitting on the worktable. Lifting the cloth, I found my meal: bread, a cup of ham and pea soup, and a pear. I thanked Flora silently for my supper and pulled up a stool.

As much as I wanted to read Mamma's diary, I forced myself to leave it in my borsa. The hour was late, the light dim, and I might soil the precious book with food. Instead I surveyed the warm kitchen as I ate. Even in the shadows, embers glowed in the hearth, and I recalled happy moments spent here with Valeria and her family.

These days, I could count on little more than the kindness of this family. Although the Soncinis hadn't evicted me from the palazzo yet, I knew they would welcome Roberto and his bride to our suite, rather than allowing me to stay without paying rent.

I placed my empty bowl in a basin of water. Heading up the stairs to my room, I could almost hear Mamma's voice reminding me to write a farewell note to my landlord.

Sì, *Mamma, I'll do it and be done with this exhausting day.*

My strained relationship with the Soncinis made this letter a challenge. I lumbered toward my desk, composing and correcting the wording in my mind with each weary step.

After another night of unsettled sleep, I awoke before dawn, eager to leave behind my painful memories of Venezia. When I opened the door to the portego, Zuanne's footsteps echoed up the stone stairs. To my surprise, he sat on a lettuccio with Valeria. After they greeted me, Zuanne took my cassoni out to the wharf.

Valeria smiled and beckoned me to join her. "My parents told me you were leaving today. I wanted to see you once more and say goodbye." Placing a tray of fruit, cheese, and bread in front of me, she held out a bowl of orange slices. "Take these; you'll need some nourishment." Dressed in a brown gown and cloak, she looked every bit the schoolmistress, but served me as if she were still a servant.

"Grazie, Valeria," I picked up a slice. "You're too kind—but won't you be late for your class?"

"It's still early, Lucia," She smiled. "Besides, school can't begin without the teacher." Her tone turned serious. "Lucia, you can't know how sorry I am to see you leave. You've been my tutor and my closest friend. You believed in me when I doubted myself. Without you I'd never have learned to read, let alone become a teacher." Her voice broke. "I'll miss you so much, Lucia, and I'll never forget you." She threw her arms around me. Tears rolled down our cheeks.

"Grazie, Valeria. "I won't forget you, either. You're a true friend."

Zuanne approached us from the canal door. "Pronto? The earlier we leave, the better chance of catching a ship to the mainland today."

Valeria stepped back. "When you're settled, write and let me know what you're doing," Her eyes twinkled. "Thanks to you, I'll be able to read your letter and answer it."

"Of course, Valeria." I sniffled. "Arrivederci, my friend."

"Arrivederci, Lucia." She wiped her eyes and walked away.

I swallowed and returned to my bedchamber. "Next time I see you, Speranza, we'll be on our way to a new home." After wrapping my canary's cage with a thick wool scarf, I balanced the cage in one hand and my mother's harp in the other.

Out in the portego, Flora stood near the canal door, wearing a heavy cloak. "Lucia, I'll go with you to Verona. You mustn't travel alone."

My heart warmed, and I hesitated for a moment. "Grazie, but the Soncinis need you to cook for them."

She touched my shoulder. "My nieces could do the cooking."

What a comfort her company would be, but I knew I shouldn't accept her offer. "No. You'd need to return by yourself, and that would be dangerous."

Flora wiped her eyes. "Then farewell, dear Lucia." She embraced me.

"Grazie, Flora. You've taken care of me, like a second mother. I can never repay you for your kindness."

She clasped my hands. "It's been my pleasure, and we can't thank you enough for all you've taught Valeria." She dabbed her eyes with her apron. "We'll miss you."

"I'll miss you, too. Arrivederci, Flora."

"Arrivederci, Lucia. May God protect you!"

I glanced around the portego for the last time and followed Zuanne out the door. As a dream fades upon awakening, now my life in this elegant palazzo would pass into memory. I lifted my skirt and walked down the steps to the wharf.

Out of the corner of my eye, I noticed Vincenzo watching me from a nearby wharf. My body tensed. I wanted to pour out my anger on him, but now he frightened me, so I restrained my tongue and prayed our paths would never cross again.

Zuanne maneuvered the gondola into the middle of the canal, and I blinked back tears until the palazzo blurred into a distant silhouette.

After seeing Vincenzo, I couldn't stop thinking about my father's execution in the very lagoon I now had to cross, where the tides would never leave his body in peace. Our boat was desecrating Papa's grave. Bile shot up my throat.

I had come to Venezia grief-stricken, and now I was leaving, sorrowful once more. This time, I had no family left to comfort me—only Speranza, my aged canary whose name reminded me of the hope I needed so desperately. I wiped my eyes and tried to console myself. God willing, the Capriolos would shelter me until I could support myself.

At last, the gondola pulled up to the wharf at Fusina. Zuanne helped me out and carried my luggage onto a ship bound for Padova. I followed him, carrying my birdcage and harp.

After he delivered my last cassone, Zuanne took off his cap and turned to me. "Godspeed, Lucia. You've been a second daughter to me." He bussed my cheeks.

My eyes moistened. "Grazie, Zuanne. I'll never forget your kindness."

He smiled and climbed back onto the wharf.

I watched Zuanne until he was only a silhouette on the lagoon. When he disappeared from view, I knew the Venetian chapter of my life had ended.

Shifting my gaze to the deck, I searched for a familiar face, but found none, and no other women among these strangers. I felt alone as never before and drew my cloak tighter.

Chapter 28

RETURN TO VERONA

Lucia

A weathered bench in the middle of the deck offered escape from the spray of wind chops. I tucked Speranza's cage under my cloak and placed my harp's cassone on the windiest side to block the salty breeze. With trembling fingers, I took my mother's diary from my borsa and turned to the first entry. Dated April 6, 1559, it began: "I, Caterina, must testify about my wonderful fiancé who gave me this book. God has answered my prayers and taken pity on me, a poor sister turned out of her convent, and given me this godly man, Giordano, to cherish as my husband. This book is his betrothal gift to me. I have no gift for him but my love. What a glorious surprise, after resigning myself to life as a bride of Christ, that now I will be Giordano's bride."

I wiped my eyes. I knew Mamma had been a cloistered nun and Papa a famous physician, but I hadn't thought about how late in life they had found each other—only after the pope dissolved her convent and expelled the nuns. Perhaps that explained why they had appreciated each other so much—why so often Papa had brought her flowers, why she had delighted in cooking his favorite foods. Their joy had overflowed to me.

A week after their wedding, Mamma wrote, "What a great and unexpected gift from God, this life of wedded bliss! When I told this to Giordano, he replied that God surprised him, too, and gave him a second life better than the first. He thought he would live out his years as a lonely bachelor. I told him how our marriage reminds me daily of God's mercy to people like me who have done nothing to earn it."

I sat up straight. Martin Luther might have written Mamma's last sentence, but she couldn't have sympathized with Luther's beliefs. She had modeled obedience to the Roman Church, teaching me to follow its rules.

Setting aside the diary, I stared at the dark water and searched my memory for clues that Mamma had accepted Luther's teachings. If my mother believed something different from what the Church taught, she had kept it a secret from me. Perhaps my parents had discussed Martin Luther's ideas in their bedchamber while I slumbered. Their congenial voices, muted through the wall between our rooms, had often soothed me as I drifted off to sleep, but I never made out their words.

I opened the diary again, this time where a faded purple ribbon marked the page. Not only a bookmark, the ribbon held a tarnished brass key. I puzzled for a moment. Mamma didn't own a jewelry box, so what did the key open?

Reading further, I found the entry following the date of my birth. My hands tingled. "We will name her Lucia and pray she will know the light of God's presence throughout her life. As much as Giordano and I thank God for our beautiful daughter, sadness tinges my joy, for I must instruct her in the doctrines of the Roman Church instead of the faith I hold so dear. If only I dared speak openly about my beliefs so she could learn the truth from her childhood. But someday she will mature enough to receive Luther's words and treasure them discreetly. Until then, I must sow the seeds of faith and nurture her tender heart."

My jaw slackened, and I reread this passage, written in her own hand. I couldn't doubt my mother's convictions any longer. Suddenly I realized the key in the diary must open my father's desk drawer, so Mamma must have known about Luther's book all along. Both of my parents had been heretics—little wonder I believed Luther's teachings.

From that moment, I saw them both as heroes—Mamma raised me in obedience to the Church's teaching to protect me, yet bore silent witness to the merciful God Luther wrote about, while Papa sacrificed his life for his religious beliefs. Their examples inspired me, but which of their paths should I follow? God help me decide!

"Padova!" The steward's voice rang out and the ship edged up to the pier. I gathered my cassoni, picked up my canary's cage, and turned toward the wharf.

"Signorina Locatelli?" When I nodded, the steward picked up my cassoni and waved to a driver standing next to a horse and carriage near the end of the wharf. "Ecco my cousin, Giovanni. He'll take you and your bags to the Leone Inn to spend the night. In the morning, you'll depart for Verona in his carriage."

"Grazie, signor." Thank God Zuanne had arranged the details of my journey to spare me the trouble. But as I approached the carriage, my steps slowed. Little more than a wagon, it paled before the elegance of Venetian gondolas. Sun, rain, and mud had weathered its canvas cover, and I could only hope the humble conveyance would hold together all the way to Verona and protect me from the elements.

After Giovanni loaded my possessions, I placed my canary's cage beside me on the well-worn wooden bench seat and pulled up the lower portion of the canvas cover next to me. Peeking out, I noticed a tall young man leaning on a cane. When he glanced my direction, my jaw clenched. I lowered the canvas and told myself Vincenzo's appearance could be only a coincidence.

"Avanti, *Bianco!*" Giovanni called to his horse, snapping his crop at the animal's flank. The wagon lurched forward.

Moments later, I stepped through the Leone's doorway, and a blazing hearth fire warmed me. Sailors at wooden tables devoured roasted cuttlefish and drank red wine. The fragrant aroma made my stomach growl, and I longed to stop and eat.

The men stared at me. Years before, my mother had taught me to ignore strange men, so I lowered my eyes. I had read enough to know the reputation of women who frequented inns and taverns, and I followed Giovanni through the dining room to my bedchamber.

After he filled the tiny room with my belongings, Giovanni brought me supper from the dining room: a cup of wine, a chunk of bread, grilled cuttlefish, and onion slices on a wooden slab.

"We'll start early tomorrow morning, signorina. If we don't meet rain or snow, the next day we'll arrive in Verona. Now I bid you buona notte."

"*Grazie* e buona notte." The door closed, and I placed my food on the bedside table next to Speranza's cage, slipping a wide plank across the doorway to secure the door.

I uncovered the canary's cage, and Speranza turned her head to view the room. Opening the cage door, I offered her a few crumbs from my *panino*. "Quite a change from our home in Venezia, eh, Speranza? God knows where we'll sleep tomorrow." Papa's gift of this canary had given me hope so long ago, and now she reminded me of my one remaining source of hope. I whispered, "God, strengthen me for whatever lies ahead."

When I finished supper, I covered the birdcage and pulled my mother's diary from my borsa. Stretching out on the bed, I pulled a thin blanket over myself and strained to read by the dim light of the single candle. When my eyelids grew heavy and the candle burned down, I set down the diary.

Rowdy chatter and full-throated drinking songs woke me more than once. With each awakening, my thoughts returned to Mamma's words about Martin Luther. If only I had known the truth about her beliefs, and both my parents had encouraged me in the faith of Luther. Instead of hiding Luther's commentary, they might have offered to let me read it. What discussions we might have enjoyed.

Images of Mamma and Papa alternated in my mind as I drifted in and out of sleep. With each change, my resolution shifted, leaving my life-and-death question—whether to declare my faith overtly or bear silent witness—unanswered.

Early the next morning, I climbed back onto the wind-chilled carriage seat and leaned against the wool scarf that now held hot stones around the outside of Speranza's cage. Giovanni guided his horse through Padova, showing skill and boldness as he dodged pedestrians, horses, and carts until we reached open countryside. Bianco's hooves pounded out an endless chorus, "You can't go back, you can't go back."

When I next opened my eyes, I pushed up the canvas and watched the sun's rays break through the overcast as we crossed a bridge and entered a town where two rivers came together.

We stopped to eat, feed Bianco, and stretch our stiff legs before resuming our journey. The oily, sweet residue of crisp pork and onions lingered in my mouth as our wagon passed houses, shops, and a large structure reminiscent of Verona's Roman Arena.

Snow-covered mountains soon appeared in the north. Despite their rugged beauty, the sight weighed down my spirits. Vincenzo's appearance in Padova had made me realize Verona might not be far enough to escape his scrutiny. If I followed God with the courage my parents had displayed, I might need to travel beyond the mountains to strange and colder lands.

After the sun sank below the horizon, Giovanni guided his horse to a small inn. The rustic sign above its door identified it as *l'Angelo*. The name revived my hope that God's angels would guide my path.

"We'll stop here tonight." He wiped his brow. "With good weather and an early start, we'll get to Verona before nightfall."

A wizened man welcomed us, and the inn's warmth and the aroma of stew made up for the humble surroundings. He led us to a well-used wooden table where his hunched wife fed us a supper of bread and a thin but comforting stew of ham, carrots, and rutabagas. After the meal, Giovanni stretched a blanket in front of the hearth, while our hostess ushered me into a small bedchamber.

I placed Speranza's cage next to the bed and eyed my room. The tidy bedchamber and the clean, if worn, coverlet put my mind at ease. I snuffed out my lamp, thanked God for safe travel, and prayed for a good night's rest.

The next thing I knew, I heard rapping at the door.

"What's wrong, signorina?"

I blinked and saw nothing in the darkness but recognized Giovanni's voice outside the door. "I must have had a nightmare. Sorry to wake you."

When I closed my eyes, my dream came back to me. The Inquisition's agents were pounding on the door of my family's home in Verona, just as they had when they arrested Papa—but this time they wanted me.

"Lucia Locatelli, come with us. You must answer the Inquisition's questions." They dragged me out of my bedchamber. I shivered in my thin chemise as they hauled me onto a ship bound for Venezia and a trial before my father's judges.

Opening my eyes, I realized where I was. I pulled the coverlet over me again but couldn't banish the images from my mind. I sensed the dream was God's warning that I shouldn't speak publicly about Luther's ideas.

Glancing at my canary's cage, I thought of a verse Mamma once taught me from Saint Matthew's gospel, "Be wise as serpents and innocent as doves." *God, may your wisdom and innocence guide me.*

"Buon giorno, signorina." Giovanni knocked on my door. "Bring your things out, and I'll load them."

Gray clouds hung low in the still-dark sky as we set out. The inn-keeper's wife had set out a generous chunk of bread for me, and I offered Speranza a few crumbs before placing the remainder in my borsa. Then I closed my eyes and listened to the beat of Bianco's hooves.

Our carriage's abrupt halt jolted me awake. While Giovanni climbed down to reassure his horse, I raised the canvas cover to look out. Across the meadow, red berries dotted the leafless branches of towering mulberry trees. Verona couldn't be far. Perhaps these same branches, at their leafy fullest, had sheltered my family from summer heat during my childhood as we walked along the banks of the Adige River on Sunday afternoons.

My joints ached from sleeping on the bench seat, and I cheered myself with the prospect of climbing out of the carriage, settling in at the Capriolos' house and stretching out on a soft bed. I prayed their surprise at my arrival would become a warm welcome.

I wondered if the Capriolos' daughters would remember me, if I would recognize them, and how their parents had aged. Just then I recalled that before he left Venezia, Stefano had mentioned his father's illness. How could I have forgotten? What a time to arrive unannounced seeking shelter!

At a turn in the road, the brick fortress and towers of Castelvecchio loomed ahead. At this first glimpse of my hometown after years away, my eyes moistened. When we passed the Roman amphitheater, I recalled stopping there during walks with my parents. We had watched boisterous *pallone* games, and I had laughed at the young men's antics as they yelled and tackled each other, ran with the ball, or threw it to a teammate. I cheered when either team carried the ball down the field. But those walks ended with my father's arrest, and that painful memory curtailed my nostalgia.

I mentally rehearsed my greeting to the Capriolo family and my request for refuge. They might refuse me because of Professor Capriolo's illness, especially if I spoke about Luther's message. Trembling, I imagined myself standing outside San Zeno in the cold, playing my mother's harp and pleading for alms as she did so long ago. Fingering the harp chords, I whispered, *"Dona nobis pacem."*

The carriage rounded the corner, and I caught sight of the Capriolo home. Weather-stained stucco and a patched roof tarnished the quaint bungalow I remembered from my childhood. The house reminded me of a decrepit old woman, her charm and beauty worn away by the years.

Giovanni reined his horse to a stop, climbed down, and tethered Bianco. He opened the carriage door, and I climbed out, stiff-legged.

Stefano opened the front door and walked toward the carriage, smiling. The knot in my gut eased. He clasped my hand. "Welcome, Lucia."

I nodded. "Grazie, Stefano."

His face turned serious. "We didn't expect you, but I'm always glad to see you." He lowered his voice. "We received your note about your father's death; you can't know how sorry I am." His eyes met mine.

"Even after you warned us, my father refused to leave. For a time, his stubbornness angered me." I shook my head. "I didn't expect to see you at your parents' home."

A shadow crossed his face, and I noticed gray in his temples and beard. "I've moved home again. After my own loss, my grief came back every time I walked inside the cottage Giulietta and I shared." He sighed. "I can help my family here. My father's health has declined, even since I saw you in Venezia. Mamma tries so hard, but he's getting worse every day."

His voice dropped to a whisper. "I can't talk about this with my mother or sisters, but I trust your discretion. My father's liver is failing. That's the price he pays for wasting his life on wine. You stayed with us, so you must remember how rarely we saw him. His drinking reduced my family to poverty. My mother has struggled to feed and clothe us all these years."

I nodded.

He inhaled. "My stories about my father shocked my wife. I thought all men behaved as he did until I married. After my wife died, I tried to discuss my father's drinking with my mother, but she couldn't bear it." His voice trailed off.

"I'm sorry, Stefano. I know your family's life hasn't been easy." I paused. "I'll do whatever I can to help."

"Grazie. Your presence will cheer my family." He walked toward Giovanni. "I'll show you where to bring the signorina's luggage." The two men strode into the house.

I hesitated. Not only was I intruding at a difficult time, but I doubted I could plan for the future in such an atmosphere. I sighed. The Capriolo home was my only refuge, so I walked through the doorway.

"Lucia, is that you?" Angelina called from a distant room.

Cristina added, "We're busy in the kitchen. Come join us."

I followed my nose toward the aroma of roasted onions and tripe, squaring my shoulders and summoning my social graces. Cristina stirred a steaming pot of meat and onions, while Angelina placed bowls and cups on the table.

"Buona sera, Lucia. What a fine lady you are." Cristina grinned at me.

"Cristina, Angelina—I only recognize you by your redhead and freckles, Cristina, and your dark curls, Angelina. You've grown up since I left Verona. Have you taken over the cooking?"

Angelina's lips tightened. "Mamma's resting. Since Papa got so sick, she does nothing but care for him. If we didn't cook for our family, no one would."

"My nose tells me you've mastered that skill." I smiled at her, but suddenly my eyelids drooped. "I'd like to help you, but could I lie down first? I'm exhausted from the long trip."

"Sure." Angelina nodded.

Cristina grinned. "You remember our room."

Passing Stefano's bedchamber, I recalled what he had told me about his father and wondered how many nights he had lain awake, wishing for his father's presence and affection. I continued to the twins' room and stretched out on a mattress.

The next thing I knew, a knock sounded at the door. "Pranzo is ready, Lucia." I recognized Cristina's voice.

"Go ahead; I'll be there soon." I smoothed my hair, slipped on my shoes, and walked to the kitchen.

Stefano, Angelina, and Cristina sat around the table. A stoop-shouldered, white-haired woman leaned her head on Stefano's shoulder. I puzzled for a moment before recognizing Signora Capriolo.

Recalling that my mother had once described her as a raven-haired beauty, I took her hand. "Piacere, signora. Thank you for opening your home to me again."

A hint of a smile lit up her pasty cheeks for an instant. "Welcome. My husband isn't well enough to talk with you. All these years, he's tried to be your faithful godfather."

Her greeting sounded sincere but weak, and I saw how caring for her husband had taken its toll.

Cristina offered me a steaming bowl of soup, and I dipped a chunk of bread in the broth. "Grazie, it's delicious."

Stefano turned to me. "My father's sleeping, so Mamma can join us at Mass. Will you come along?"

I glanced around the table. All eyes focused on me. If I tried to explain my reluctance to attend Mass, someone might report me to the Inquisition. I hoped that in due time, I could speak to these dear people individually. Finally, I choked out, "Of course," and turned back to my soup.

As we passed through the doorway into San Stefano church, a woman across the narthex startled, then smiled at me. She slid her arm away from a balding gentleman, stepping away from her children.

"Lucia, is that you?" Gray-streaked hair showed beneath a brown hat, and her once-slender build had turned matronly, but I couldn't mistake her voice and broad grin.

"Elisabetta!" When I embraced her, the fragrance of roses confirmed her identity. "What a pleasure to see you again." I gestured toward the man and children. "Your family?"

"Sì," she nodded, "My husband, Giuseppe Marini, our sons Pietro, Alberto, Leonardo, and Luigi, and our daughter, Annalisa. Have you moved back to Verona?"

"For now." I paused. "I'm not sure of my plans for the future."

"I've often wondered about your life in Venezia. But marriage and my children fill my days, and I never found time to write you a letter." She glanced at her husband. "Could you join us at home after Mass? I'd love to talk with you."

"If my hosts don't mind." I turned to Signora Capriolo, who nodded.

Throughout the service, my elation about the reunion with my old friend distracted me. At the end of the service, I said farewell to the Capriolos and waited outside for Elisabetta and her family. Her sons rushed out of the church, first a fresh-faced boy in short pants, then a plump, taller schoolboy, and finally two gangly adolescents. Following them came Elisabetta and her husband, each holding one of little Annalisa's hands.

A smile lit up Elisabetta's face. "You must tell me all about Venezia. For years, I've envied your life in that elegant city."

I smiled back. "And I've wondered what became of you since I last saw you."

"*Su, su.*" Elisabetta's little girl tugged her father's fingers until he picked her up.

After a brief stroll, we arrived at a two-story house down the street from where Elisabetta had grown up. The boys ran into the inner courtyard while their mother ushered me into a spacious sala. She excused herself to advise her daughter's nursemaid, and I circled the room, inspecting the many paintings on the walls.

When Elisabetta returned, a maid followed carrying a tray laden with two porcelain cups and a teapot. I asked my friend about the paintings and learned that her husband worked with her father in the art business.

"Giuseppe surprises me with a new painting every year." She beamed. "Nothing could please me more. I've loved art ever since your mother showed us the carvings and rose window at San Zeno, even before I understood my father's business. Giuseppe tells me that when we met, he couldn't believe I knew so much about art. That was the bond that drew us together, in spite of our age difference, and maybe that's why we've gotten along so well all these years. We married about a year after you left Verona." She took my hand. "Now tell me about your years in Venezia, and why you've returned to Verona."

I swallowed. "You haven't heard about my father's death."

"No, Lucia." She squeezed my hand. "I'm so sorry. That's why you left Venezia?"

"Sì. When Papa died, I couldn't afford to stay." I glanced around the room and lowered my voice. "The Inquisition executed him for heresy. Soon the whole city knew me as a heretic's daughter, so I couldn't continue to teach the daughters of Venezia's families."

Her face paled, and she looked toward the doorway. "Capito."

My throat clogged. "Maybe I should leave."

Her grip tightened. "No, please stay. I want to hear more."

"I returned to Verona hoping my godparents would offer me refuge. The Capriolos welcomed me into their home, but I'll stay only until I locate a new position as a teacher or editor."

I knew this might be my only private conversation with Elisabetta, and I longed to give her another opportunity to understand my faith. But could I trust my friend's loyalty in these dangerous times? In my mind's eye, I saw Luther's image of the baby chick safe under its mother's wings, and I surveyed the room again. "Above all, I want to live where I can express and practice my beliefs without fear of the Inquisition."

Her expression didn't change.

I continued. "Do you remember what I told you years ago about Martin Luther's ideas?"

She nodded. "*Si*, even though I tried to forget them."

"Luther convinced me then, and I still believe, that God loves us so much that if we believe in him, He gives forgiveness as a gift. Now I can't pretend I agree with the Roman Church that good works help us earn God's forgiveness. For years, my fear kept me silent, but I can't hide my beliefs any longer."

Elisabetta looked down.

In the silence that followed, I tried to keep my inner trembling from showing on the outside.

Finally, her eyes met mine. "Lucia, I admire your courage. May God protect you." She cleared her throat and asked me about my years in Venezia.

I followed my friend's polite cue and described my schooling with Messer Guadagnoli, my poetry studies with Modesta, my teaching and editing.

"Tell me about Venezia. I've heard it's the world's most beautiful city, and I've always wanted to visit." Her face brightened. "I hope Giuseppe will take me when the children grow up."

I described Piazza San Marco, the churches, canals, *palazzi*, and even the fish market. Elisabetta's many questions and comments made the afternoon pass quickly, and I enjoyed a supper of lamb and turnips with my friend and her family.

After cena, I put on my cloak and followed my hostess outside, where the family's carriage awaited me. I turned to her.

"Grazie, Elisabetta. Such a pleasure to renew our friendship." We embraced. "Arrivederci."

"Take care of yourself, my friend." She waved, and the carriage set off down the cobblestone street to the Capriolo home.

My knock on the door provoked a rush of footsteps. Cristina opened the door, her hands dripping.

"Buona sera, Lucia. Join us in the kitchen." She laced her fingers together and hurried away.

I followed her, tiptoeing past the bedchamber where Signora Capriolo placed blankets over her sleeping husband. From the kitchen doorway, I watched Angelina mopping the floor and Cristina washing the dishes.

Angelina cocked her head. "Ciao, Lucia. You must have enjoyed yourself to stay so long."

I smiled. "Sì. I hope I didn't worry you. I hadn't seen Elisabetta in many years, so we had much to discuss."

Cristina grinned and shook her head. "You hardly crossed my mind. We never get bored when Stefano's home. He stayed all afternoon, brought in wood and water for us, and helped Mamma turn Papa in his bed. After we finished *cena*, he went out for a stroll."

Before I closed my eyes that night, I thanked God for my refuge at the Capriolo home, for happening upon Elisabetta and her family at San Stefano, and my time with her that afternoon. Only one doubt nagged me. If Elisabetta didn't keep silent about my religious beliefs, she could place my life in danger.

Chapter 29

VALLEY OF THE SHADOW

Lucia

The next morning, Angelina ambled into the sala carrying a large straw basket.

I looked up at her. "Could I go to the market for you? I'd be happy to pick up whatever you need."

Her face brightened. "I won't object." She handed me the basket. "Here's my list." She gave me a scrap of paper from her pocket. "If you don't see what I want, buy whatever looks good."

I put on my cloak and strolled down the street, eager to rediscover my native Verona. A brisk wind spurred me to step up my pace until I reached Piazza delle Erbe. The market's offerings didn't compare with Venezia, but I filled my basket with asparagus, spring onions, bread, and sausage, and retraced my steps.

As soon as I walked through the Capriolos' doorway, Vincenzo and two strangers in black robes sprang toward me.

"Signorina Locatelli." Vincenzo's formal greeting gave me gooseflesh.

"Sì, eccomi. What do you want?" I recalled my father's arrest, remembered his courage, and gripped the basket so my hands wouldn't shake.

Vincenzo shook his head. "Stop pretending you don't know. The Holy Office must stamp out the poison of your heresy."

I set back my shoulders.

The gray-haired man turned to me. "Come with us. The Holy Office of the Inquisition has questions for you."

"Very well." I set the basket on the floor.

Each of Vincenzo's companions grabbed one of my arms.

Cristina watched, wide-eyed, from the kitchen doorway. Angelina ran toward us, her dark hair and skirt billowing behind her.

"Stop, don't take her! You've made a terrible mistake. We've known her all our lives, and our brother works for the Holy Office." She grabbed each man's shoulder. "Listen to me!"

The two strangers stared at her and then at Vincenzo.

"Take her away." Vincenzo motioned toward the door.

The gray-haired man frowned at Angelina. "Signorina, we must obey our orders." He opened the door, and they marched me out.

My captors said nothing as we walked to a part of Verona I didn't remember. They stopped in front of a dingy stucco building, perhaps an old monastery, and Vincenzo identified me to the guard at the gate. He nodded, opened the gate, and led me down a dark corridor into a tiny cell. He didn't say a word, only locked me inside and disappeared.

A high, narrow slat of a window provided just enough light to see a thin mattress on the stone floor, a moth-eaten blanket, and a filthy bucket in the corner. The odor of urine gagged me. I covered my nose and mouth with my kerchief and thought of my father. Now I knew the conditions he endured for so many months, perhaps in this very cell. *God, may I be as brave as Papa.* I sat on the mattress, closed my eyes and began to recite the psalm of David, the shepherd: "The Lord is my shepherd, I shall not want. He makes me lie down in green pastures; He leads me beside still waters. He restores my soul."

When I opened my eyes, questions streamed into my mind: What would they ask me? Why? Had I misjudged Elisabetta's welcome and sympathy? Had she denounced me to the Inquisition?

I looked around the cell again and wondered how long I must stay here, who had been in this cell before me, what had happened to them, and what would become of me. The dank silence allowed my imagination free rein.

Only the last glimmer of daylight remained when the jailer brought me a bowl of stew and a cup of wine. He said nothing. Even in the dim light, a glance at the watery stew took away my appetite. I set the bowl on the floor.

Darkness shrouded the cell, and a scene from my early childhood came to mind. On a foggy winter morning, my mother and I had returned from the market, our fingers and toes numbed by the cold wind. While I sat at the kitchen table, she dipped a spoon into the pot hanging over the fire, filled a cup, and set the fragrant soup in front of me. I stared but didn't pick up the cup, afraid I would burn my fingers or tongue.

Mamma placed the spoon in the cup, stirred, lifted out a spoonful, and blew across it. "Eat, Lucia, the stew will warm you." That cup of stew drove away my chill from the inside out.

As the memory faded, I groped for the bowl. A dark shadow flashed past. When I saw the long, thin tail, I gasped and realized a rat would gladly steal my supper. I gulped the stew, downed the wine, and my trembling ceased.

The night air wafted through the window. Huddled on the mattress, I pulled the blanket close. It scratched my neck and reeked of sweat and sickness, but I thanked God for its warmth. Throughout the night, one moment I thought I would never leave this bleak prison alive, and the next, hope and comfort sustained me.

Stefano

At the end of my workdays, I traded my job's tedium and unpleasantness for the ongoing family crisis of my father's illness. I tried to bring humor and encouragement into the household, but it had been a struggle since my wife and baby died.

That evening, I whistled as I walked home from work. In spite of her grief, Lucia brought life and energy into our family. She inspired my sisters and offered me a sympathetic ear.

As soon as I opened the door, Cristina's long face told me something had gone wrong.

"Is Papa all right?" I stared at her.

She shrugged. "He's no worse."

Angelina poked her head out from the kitchen. "Stefano, you must rescue Lucia."

"What?" I stared at my sisters.

Cristina frowned. "Surely you've heard what happened."

I shook my head. "No, tell me." My heart throbbed in my throat.

Angelina rushed toward me. "This morning, three men from the Inquisition came into our house and asked for Lucia. They waited and took her away as soon as she came back from the market."

My sister's words hit me like a punch in the gut. Images filled my mind, images of terrible things the Inquisition might be doing to Lucia at this moment. I struggled for breath and tried to block these mental pictures.

Both of my sisters stared back at me. I knew they expected me to take charge, to run out and retrieve Lucia. They didn't realize I couldn't give orders to anyone, certainly not to free Lucia.

I wanted to help her, but how? In my line of work, any sympathy I showed toward a heretic might cost me my job or even my life. My actions could hurt my family as well as me, since I supported them with my earnings.

I looked at the floor and wiped my sweaty brow. If I waited, maybe the Holy Office would realize they made a mistake, but I couldn't count on it.

The church bell sounded Compline, the final prayer time of the day. I sighed and looked up. I mustn't delay, or Lucia might suffer.

"I'll do all I can to help her." I grabbed my cloak.

Cristina handed me a chunk of bread, and I headed out the door.

⊕

Lucia

The jailer's keys rattled with his every step down the hallway, waking me from fitful sleep. When I pulled myself to a sitting position, my back and shoulders ached in protest. Could morning have come already? The noise grew louder, and my half-open eyes glimpsed the jailer placing a steaming bowl and cup in my cell. Frigid air assaulted me as I left the warmth of my bedding to grab the cup and bowl. This stew tasted no better than the last, but I devoured it all, drank the wine and pulled the blanket tight again.

When feeble rays of light finally peeked through the tiny window, I stretched my legs and paced the cell to warm my feet. As I walked the circle, I wondered if I would ever leave this desolate cell, except to die. I begged for God to rescue me. Then I recalled a scripture verse my mother once taught me: *I will never leave you or forsake you.*

Footsteps resounded in the corridor, and I whispered, "God help me!" The Inquisition might question me now as they had my father so many years ago. I remembered the scars on his wrists, and his hint at what he had endured. But I saw the silhouette of a taller man, not the jailer. As he approached, I recognized Stefano. Flush with energy I didn't know I possessed, I rushed to the cell door.

"Lucia?" He struggled to find me in the dimness.

"Sì, here I am." I rapped my fists on the bars.

He peered inside. "Did they hurt you?"

"No."

"Good. Have they questioned you?"

"Not yet."

He pressed his forehead against the bars. "You visited Elisabetta yesterday. What did you tell her?" He turned his ear toward me.

Stefano's employment with the Inquisition meant he might report anything I said, but on the other hand, he might help me. I vacillated about what to tell him, until the image of the baby chick under its mother's wings filled my mind.

I whispered. "I answered her questions, told her the type of work I enjoy, and that I want to live where the Inquisition isn't a threat, where the name of Martin Luther isn't anathema, where I can speak freely about God's love and forgiveness."

He sighed, gripping the bars separating us. "Did anyone else hear?"

"Not that I saw."

"Allora, I must speak to Elisabetta before it's too late." He reached his fingers between the bars and squeezed my hand. "Don't give up hope, Lucia." He turned away and vanished down the hallway.

I exhaled slowly and turned away from the barred door. Nothing had changed in my cell, but I saw it with different eyes. Who but God could have given such courage and clarity of mind to Stefano—the jocular classmate of my youth—and sent him into the Inquisition's dark recesses to bring me hope and comfort?

Stefano

Lucia's life depended on my reaching Elisabetta before the Inquisition did, so I wanted to run down the corridor. But I forced myself to walk, so I wouldn't arouse the guards' curiosity. They didn't question my visit since my work for the Holy Office occasionally brought me here.

Rushing toward Elisabetta's house, I kicked aside rocks and debris in my path. Lucia wasn't stupid. Why hadn't she seen the danger she faced? She would never survive if she didn't keep her mouth shut.

All these years, I had known she was headstrong but never realized she was a heretic like her father. I wondered how someone as outspoken as Lucia managed to conceal this and especially why she broke her silence after what happened to her father. How could such an intelligent woman do something so foolish?

Her behavior irked me, but I knew I must save her, because no one else could. Her beliefs held no attraction for me, but Lucia's vitality and strength of purpose awed and appealed to me. I couldn't let the Inquisition kill her.

Approaching the Marini home, I swallowed my anger and thought about what I would say to Elisabetta. Lucia's words might have scandalized Elisabetta as much as they did me. I hoped they hadn't destroyed her sympathy for Lucia. I must appeal to Elisabetta as Lucia's friend and would have to allude to Lucia's heretical comments.

A few minutes later, a servant ushered me into the Marinis' sala. Gold-trimmed couches lined the walls. I didn't want to soil them with grime or mud, so I sat in a wooden chair. I'd never given a speech, but now I rehearsed my words.

When Elisabetta entered the room, the jewels on her gown made me lose my nerve. Would she even remember me, a humble former classmate, let alone pay attention to me? I jumped to my feet.

"Buon giorno, Signora Marini." I kissed her hand.

"Piacere, Stefano—call me Elisabetta." She smiled. "What brings you here?"

"An urgent matter." I took another breath. "Are we alone?"

Her brows shot up. "Sì."

I spoke in a low tone. "The Inquisition suspects Lucia of heresy. They've taken her to prison and plan to put her on trial. But they need someone to testify against her. Because Lucia visited you, their agents will question you." I looked straight into her face. "If you tell them what she said about her religious beliefs, they may torture her, even execute her."

Her eyes opened wide. "God forbid! I would never do that to Lucia. What should I say?"

I thought for a minute. "The safest course is to tell them Lucia didn't speak with you about religion."

She nodded and spoke softly. "May God forgive me for lying to the Holy Office."

Worry shot through me. "You mustn't mention this in the confessional."

"Capito, Stefano. I won't tell anyone." Her face paled.

"Grazie, I appreciate your cooperation, as will Lucia." I threw my cloak over my shoulders and prepared to leave but glanced back at Elisabetta. "Did anyone else hear what Lucia told you—your husband, children, or servants?"

She cupped her hand to her mouth. "I don't think so, unless a servant was listening in a doorway. As far as I know, we were alone during that conversation."

"Grazie, Dio." I sighed. "I must speak with my family now. Arrivederci, Elisabetta."

She escorted me to the door. "God be with you, Stefano, and especially with Lucia."

I walked outside and exhaled, then hurried down the street to warn my own family.

By the time I got home, Angelina had set bowls of soup on the table for pranzo. Cristina took soup and bread into our parents' bedchamber, some for Mamma to eat and some to feed my father.

When Cristina returned, I sat down with my sisters at the table.

"Grazie, girls. The food looks good, but listen to me first—it's important! Lucia's in great danger. The Holy Office will ask you about her. Tell them only good things. Don't pass along any rumors or gossip, or they might kill her. Capito?"

"Sì, Stefano." They nodded, wide-eyed.

Angelina broke the silence. "But you work for the Holy Office. You should be asking questions, not warning us to watch what we say."

I shook my head. "That's not my job, Angelina. Even if it was, I must protect Lucia. After all, she's goddaughter to our parents." I pushed back my chair and walked into my parents' bedchamber to tell them the same message.

My father nodded but couldn't speak.

My mother sighed. "Poor Lucia. If only we could have hidden her. I have nothing but good to say about her. Years ago, I never realized how much she helped me with chores until she left."

Wiping my brow, I returned to the kitchen. My appetite had vanished, but I forced myself to eat.

Worries peppered my thoughts as I walked back to the Inquisitor's office. The Holy Office employed me, yet I was thwarting its work, trying to free a heretic. Lucia's arrest happened so suddenly, and I had thought only about rescuing her. But if Father Inquisitor learned what I had done, he might forget all my years of loyal service, dismiss me, or even try me for heresy. I prayed that neither my family nor I would suffer.

Lucia

The sun's rays brought the hope of a new day. I paced my cell to warm myself and thanked God that Stefano knew the ways of Verona's Holy Office. I still wondered why Inquisition agents brought me here and how Stefano could help me, but the scripture verse and Stefano's appearance calmed my fears.

Hours later, I heard footsteps and the jingle of keys. I expected soup and wine. Instead, the jailer unlocked my cell door and beckoned me to follow him down the corridor. We approached the main prison door, and I shaded my eyes from the brightness of the lamplight.

The guard opened the door. "You may go."

I gasped and burst through the doorway as if I were walking on air. Stefano stood outside, smiling. He took my arm.

I whispered, "Grazie, Stefano. I don't know how you got me out, but thank you."

A loud clicking sound interrupted me. Far down the street, Vincenzo lumbered toward us, stabbing his cane on the cobblestones. He shook his head and gestured toward me with his free hand. I froze, and Stefano tightened his grip on my arm.

The guard stepped outside the gate and glanced from Vincenzo to me, first shrugging, then waving us away. "I take my orders from Father Inquisitor, and he told me to release you, signorina."

We hurried down the street, silent until we rounded a corner. Then Stefano turned to me. "Vincenzo followed you to Verona. After years of spying on you and your father, he couldn't bear to let you slip away. The daughter of a renowned heretic would make another great prize for him. Imagine the boost to his reputation if the Holy Office convicted you of heresy, too." He paused. "But if you escaped, Vincenzo's reputation would suffer. That's why he questioned everyone you spoke with since you returned to Verona."

"Everyone?" God forbid that I had cast suspicion on my friends.

Stefano nodded.

"I'm sorry, Stefano. I hope I haven't ruined your family's good name or your career."

"You couldn't have known." He shrugged. "But I'm familiar with the Inquisition's trials, so I knew the court couldn't convict you of heresy unless witnesses denounced you in writing or spoke against you in person. I explained to Elisabetta's family and mine what would happen if they spoke against you. No one would testify, so the Inquisition had no case."

"No one denounced me, even when the Inquisition pressured them?"

Stefano shook his head and smiled.

My temples warmed, and I looked at the ground. First Stefano, and now Elisabetta, had proven themselves true friends. How could I have suspected that my old friend betrayed me?

I looked up at Stefano with new appreciation. He had risked everything for my father and now me. "Stefano, you saved my life. I can never thank you enough." My throat grew husky. "May God reward your courage and protect you from the Inquisition's retribution."

His face reddened. "I'm not worried about myself, but you're still in great danger. Lucia, you're too brave. Believe me, Vincenzo had one thing right. Anywhere you go in Italy, if you talk about heresy, he'll find out, and the Inquisition will arrest you again."

The image of Alessandro's face filled my mind, and I shuddered.

Stefano smiled at me. "Can't you talk about something else?"

Suddenly the baby chick protected by its mother's wings appeared in my mind's eye, crowding out the frightening image. "I must speak the truth as God reveals it to me. My life has no purpose otherwise."

He sighed. "Then don't waste any time. Go where you don't need to worry about what you say, where the Church can't arrest you."

I glanced back at the tall silhouette and clenched my fists. "Because of Vincenzo I must go to a strange land, leaving behind all my memories, my mother tongue, and everyone I love."

Stefano touched my elbow. "You've got plenty of reasons to blame Vincenzo, but the Inquisition and even the pope stand behind him. At the moment, he's their hero, and he couldn't find an easier target than you."

We walked in silence toward the Capriolo home. Regardless of Stefano's kind intent, his words sapped my strength. I dreaded the prospect of uprooting myself again, this time to a faraway place, alone.

Chapter 30

DECISION

Lucia
May, 1587

hile Angelina and Cristina prepared pranzo, I returned to their bedchamber and dug down to the bottom of my clothing cassone. Pulling away the chemise hiding my mother's Bible, I turned to Saint Paul's letter to the Galatian church and read: "It is for freedom that Christ has set us free. Stand firm, then, and do not let yourselves be burdened again by a yoke of slavery." The words jolted me.

I glanced at my canary's cage and suddenly I understood. "I've always kept you in a cage to protect you, Speranza. You've never known freedom." I began to weep. "Once I could talk about my thoughts and beliefs without fear. I didn't appreciate my freedom until I lost it after Papa's arrest. Ever since, I've been hiding what I believe."

Speranza lived in a cage made of wood; my cage was fear—fear of the Inquisition and fear of losing my family.

I opened the cage door and stroked my canary. "Speranza, I must cast off the yoke of slavery and choose the path of freedom, even if we must leave our homeland."

My father had told me stories about his sister, Annamaria, and his brother Cornelio. Both had settled north of the mountains in Basel. I must follow their example. God willing, someday I would meet them.

I wrapped a chemise around the Bible and pushed my clothes to the side of the chest so I could hide the Bible beneath them. Martin Luther's commentary lay exposed, and I leafed through the precious volume. The white rose and golden ring of Luther's printing symbol reminded me that I would find God's peace and joy in Luther's homeland or wherever I journeyed.

I tiptoed into Stefano's empty room and slipped Luther's book under Stefano's coverlet. Now he could read and understand what had inspired me.

Casting a final glance around the twins' bedchamber, I slung my borsa over my shoulder, picked up my cassoni and birdcage, and joined Stefano and his sisters in the kitchen.

I took a deep breath. "I'll miss you all."

The girls frowned and shook their heads, but Stefano nodded.

"Stefano, could you find me a carriage bound for Basel?" The quavering tone in my voice made my face warm.

"Of course, Lucia, but let's eat first." He patted my shoulder. "It's a long journey, and you'll need strength."

After a hurried meal, I expressed my thanks to this family that had sacrificed to shelter me. With tears and hugs, I bade them farewell.

Stefano, now laden with my cassoni and birdcage, escorted me out.

Before long, he set Speranza's cage next to me on the seat of a carriage. "I'll miss you, Lucia." He paused. "May God grant you a safe journey and the happiness you deserve."

A lump clogged my throat. "Grazie, Stefano. I'll remember your courage and kindness always."

"Andiamo." The driver barked his warning and picked up his reins.

Stefano kissed my hand and climbed down. As the carriage jerked forward, his wave and smile comforted me. When the driver turned a corner and headed across Ponte Catena, away from every person and place I knew, I brushed away tears.

I had chosen my own journey, a journey into freedom. Neither the Inquisition nor my fears would hold me back. Like a Venetian canary set free, I would fly out of my cage, spread my wings, and soar toward the sun.

THE END

AUTHOR'S NOTE

While researching in the Venetian State Archives, I read heresy trial records that brought to life a true story—the story of a medical doctor whose devotion to Martin Luther's ideas led to three trials and his execution by the Inquisition in Venice. Girolamo Donzellino, I hope I have honored your memory in my use of the bare bones of your life as the factual scaffolding for this work of historical fiction.

Fictionalized historical characters (especially Girolamo Donzellino) populate this novel. Historical records indicate that Doctor Donzellino had a child, and I took the liberty of naming her Lucia. The words I put into the mouth of Modesta da Pozzo (another historical figure) were my attempt to remain faithful to the sentiments she expressed in her poetry. Although I took pains to maintain historical accuracy whenever possible, I employed literary license and filled in gaps in historical records to craft this novel. Any errors are mine.

In addition to my family and my history mentors, I would like to thank the following people without whom this book would not have come to life: Barbara Booth Grunwald, who encouraged me to turn my thesis into a novel and critiqued an early version; Professor Antonio Rotondò, University of Florence, who encouraged me to study Girolamo Donzellino; writing mentors Ethel Herr, Gayle Roper, and Jane Kirkpatrick; agents Janet Kobobel Grant and Karen Ball; my fellow members of the Historical Novel Society Bay Area chapter and ACFW Golden Gate chapter; critique group members, especially Carol Park, Rosalie Nelson, Karen Ratzlaff, Janet Hallock, Vickey Kazarian, Carol Lee Hall, Bob and Gail Kaku; editors Peggie Venemon, Cindy Coloma, C.S. Lakin, and Gwen Leong; website designer Beth Phillips of CleanDesignNW; cover design artist and fount of practical wisdom Emily Cotton; costume consultant Jane Piller Wilson; beta-readers Lorrie Gemmell, Kathleen Card, Elaine Wilson, Jane Quist, Sarah Ngola, Pam Stewart, Jennifer Cilker, Patti Davis, Carole Grace, and Ingrid Lin; key supporters JoDee Raimondo, Carol Aust, Arpenny Hart, Ann McColloch, and Kathy Leong; photographer Ed Aust. Finally, I am grateful to the Sisters of Notre Dame at Villa Angelica House of Prayer in Carmel, California, for their warm welcome at multiple writing retreats. Their gracious hospitality, even as I wrote a novel focused on a dark period of Church history, reflects the healing of many of the rifts that erupted in the era of my novel.

GLOSSARY OF
ITALIAN WORDS

General note: Italian words frequently become plural by changing the final vowel (a, e, or o) to i (see below).

Italics use: When Italian words are used multiple times, they are italicized only the first time they appear; no italics for names or titles.

A domani—until tomorrow

Adige River—river curving through Verona

Agnus dei—lamb of God (Latin)

Allora—well then

Andiamo—let's go

Andron—simple bottom floor of a Venetian palazzo

Angelo—angel

Arrivederci—goodbye, until we meet again

Avanti—forward, get going

Ave Maria—Hail Mary, a Roman Catholic prayer invoking aid of
        Mary, mother of Jesus

Bambino/bambini—child/baby; children/babies

Basta—enough!

Bello, bella—beautiful

Bocca di leone—lion's mouth

Borsa—purse, handbag

Bravo, brava—exclamation meaning wonderful, great job

Buon giorno—good day

Buona sera—good evening or afternoon

Busta, buste—envelope(s)/folders(s)

Ca'—Venetian abbreviation for casa (house)

Calle—walkway/street (for pedestrians)

Campanile—bell tower

Campo—name for any town square in Venice, except for
 Piazza San Marco

Canal Grande—Grand Canal in Venice (the major waterway through
 the city)

Capito—understood

Cassone/cassoni—traveling chest(s)

Cena—supper, the evening meal

Ciao—informal greeting, hi

Compline—final daily prayer time for Catholic monks

Contessa—countess

Dio--God

Dona nobis pacem—give us peace (a Latin chorus from the Catholic
 mass)

Ecco—here is/are... (eccomi—it's me)

Finito—finished

Fratello—brother; mio fratello—my brother

Holy Office—short for Holy Office of the Inquisition, the arm of the
 Roman Church established in 1542 to root out the Protestant
 heresy

Grazie—thank you; tante grazie—thanks so much

Grazie a Dio—thanks be to God

Land door—door of a Venetian palazzo opening onto a walkway

Lazzaretto nuovo—new pestilence hospital (on a Venetian island)
 where people suspected of infection are quarantined for forty
 days

Lazzaretto vecchio—old Venetian pestilence hospital

Leone—lion (mascot of Venezia)

Lettuccio—daybed/sofa

Lido—beach, strip of land across lagoon from city, separated Venezia
 from Adriatic Sea

Loggia—open corridors supported by arches (outside prominent buildings)

Maestro di casa—Chief servant in charge of a household

Mangia, mangia—let's eat!

Mea massima culpa—my great fault/sin

Merceria—area near Piazza San Marco with shops selling clothing, household goods, and books

Mi chiamo—my name is...

Mi dispiace—I'm sorry

Minestra—soup

Momento—moment (un momento—one moment)

Napoli—Naples

Niente—nothing

Nones—noontime, when monasteries and churches rang bells

Nonna—grandmother

Padova—Padua, Italian town near Venice

Padre—father or priest

Palazzo—Venetian mansion

Palina—a single pole, sometimes striped, sunk in the water and used for mooring boats

Panino/panini—roll(s)

Pater noster—(Latin) our father; Roman Catholic name for the Lord's Prayer

Patria—homeland

Pazienza—patience

Per favore—please

Petrarco—Petrarch

Piacere—my pleasure, pleased to meet you

Portego—central room of large residence; long passageway where visitors were received

Pranzo—dinner, the midday meal

Prego—please, you're welcome, pardon me

Pronto—ready?

Ragazzo—boy

Ragazzi—boys or children

Ridotto, ridotti—Venetian literary gathering(s)

Risi e bisi—rice and peas

Riva—land bordering Venetian Grand Canal and Lagoon, ships and
   large boats moored there

Riva degli Schiavoni—originally the domain of Slavic fishermen, became a wide promenade along the Venetian waterfront,
   bordering Piazza San Marco and Palazzo Ducale, among other sights

Roma—Rome

Sala—living room

Salterio—primer including the alphabet, beginning reading, prayers

San Zeno—Saint Zeno, patron saint of Verona

San Zeno Maggiore—cathedral of St. Zeno, in Verona

Serata—evening party

Si—yes

Signor—mister

Signora—missus

Signorina—miss

Strappado—Torture device used by the Inquisition to extract information, in which ropes are tied around the victim's armpits
   and shoulders, attached to a hook in the ceiling, and he is
   hoisted up and then dropped, sometimes repeatedly

Su—up

Subito—immediately

Tante—many, much

Terrazzo—ceramic flooring imbedded with chips of colored stone

Venezia—Venice

Vengo—I'm coming

Venite—come! (plural imperative)

Zio—uncle

ABOUT THE AUTHOR

Renaissance history came to life for C.L.R. Peterson during a semester in Italy. Later the classic David-versus-Goliath battle of Luther and the Roman Church hooked her on the Reformation. She has pursued those passions ever since, earning a PhD in Early Modern European History at Stanford University and returning to Italy to research *Lucia's Renaissance*.

She belongs to two critique groups, as well as the Historical Novel Society's Northern California chapter and the ACFW Golden Gate chapter. She loves to tell the stories of little-known heroes of the Renaissance/Reformation era. *Lucia's Renaissance* is her debut novel.

I hope you've enjoyed this book.

Please share your thoughts in a review:

Amazon,com (Lucia's Renaissance; write a customer review)

GoodReads.com (Lucia's Renaissance; rate this book)

I'd also welcome your reviews on other social media platforms.

If you'd like book club discussion questions, to schedule a Skype book club discussion with me, or to sign up for news about my upcoming books, please visit:

www.clrpeterson.com

70001089R00181

Made in the USA
Lexington, KY
08 November 2017